STRIKE!

John Klawitter

STRIKE!

DEDICATION

For Lynnie & Rosie
Best friends forever

CHAPTER ONE

1922 - Hungry Hill, Chicago Heights, Illinois
Rosa Gambriotti was carrying a big platter of fresh cannolis and anamaretti fig cookies from the kitchen when young Ben Napoli backed into her, nearly knocking the still-warm bakery treats to the floor. Ben, who had been near to punching Jimmy Rosalini because Jimmy said all the White Sox baseball players were crooked, and this pissed off Ben so bad he didn't even notice the near disaster he'd caused. Lucky thing Dr. Lina Bright was at the table next to Rosa, reading one of her medical journals. Dr. Bright with her quick reflexes reached out and steadied her friend, saving the bakery treats.

"Hey," the feisty Rosa said, glaring at Ben, "What's-a matter with you?"

"See what you almost done," Louie Caproni said. "S'cuse me, comrades." He got up from the table where he'd been sitting with some of his fellow workers from the steel mill, and pushed Ben toward the door. "Get out-a here, you *stugatz*!" Nobody argued with Louie, who was a fiery little ball of energy, and even though Ben was ten years or so younger, he practically fell out the front door in his hurry to be gone, with Jimmy piling out into the street after him..

"What's wrong with them?" Rosa said. She set the plate of home-made sweets on the table in front of the men, who were still dressed in their Sunday finest from the Mass at San Rocco that they'd attended earlier in the day.

7

"Ahh, the war," Louie said, dismissing the subject with a wave of his hand.

"That's no excuse," Rosa said. "It doesn't automatically make men into brainless idiots."

""You're right, Rosa...but give the guy a break." Louie, usually the firebrand, in the unusual role of peacemaker. He wanted his sweet treats without interruption.

"Yeah, Ben served in the Eastern Front," Louie's pal Arturo said in that froggy voice of his. "In the mountains near Austria, I heard. It was real bad. He seen a guy get shot in the –" Arturo was Louie's best friend and he usually seconded whatever Louie said, but this time Louie nudged him a sharp one with his elbow to the stomach and he stopped short..

"I know it was bad," Rosa said, her lips pressed in a thin line. "That's where my Ralphie was." Her husband Ralphie, blown to bits in a trench somewhere in the Alps north of Italy.

"Ahh, sorry, Rosa," Louie said. "Arturo didn't mean to bring that up. Everything is upset these days, lots of problems at the mill."

She didn't have to ask. There was only one mill, The Inland Steel mill, and many families on Hungry Hill depended on it for their survival.

"What now?" she said. "Here, try a cannoli."

Arturo picked up a pastry roll and gave it a nibble before he answered. "Really good, Rosa, really tasty."

"The mill," she prompted.

"Dirty rotten no-good managers never learn. The stupid fools want to make everything run too fast again."

"But…I hear people say that's dangerous."

"Oh yeah," Arturo said. "But the big bosses at the top don't care. They don't have to wrestle hot steel."

"What can you do to stop them?" she said.

"Oh, we'll think of something," Louie said. "I promise you that, young lady."

Rosa was nobody's fool; she was bright and young and pretty (gorgeous, actually, in the classic *Italiano* way) and she had a knack for running her home grown business, the popular little Italian restaurant she called Rosa's Place or Rosa's Café, she hadn't decided which was classier. You didn't have to work at the mill to know how dangerous it was; they had attended the funerals at St. Roccos, heard the sad tributes, followed the horse drawn carriage to the cemetery.. To Rosa, this sounded like the same trouble all over again. Even shy of the fatal accidents, there had been plenty of burns and the loss of an arm or a leg or an eye or an ear here and there. The incidents and the general conditions and poor pay had led to lots of labor unrest over the years, so it was hard to say if this was anything new. Rosa went back to the kitchen to make sure her mom hadn't forgotten to watch the almond biscotti so they didn't burn in the oven.

It was the next weekend when Rosa and her good pal Lina Bright were talking girl talk in the front room of Rosa's old family home. They were sitting at a table in the formal living room space that had been widened by her *il bobbo* - her dad - and now served as the main dining room in her restaurant. Lina did her doctoring next door and rented a room over the café where she kept her few personal things and where she slept. This was in Rosa's wooden lunch pail house, on one of the main streets in Hungry Hill – the blueprint straight out of the Sears and Roebucks catalogue and originally hand-built by her dad back in his day. The house was a lonely survivor from an earlier generation; now in the roaring 1920s, it remained, stuck between a row of newer two story brick buildings that had business store fronts below and living quarters up on the second floor.

"Mama," Rosa yelled, impatient and yet with her boisterous good humor, "The doc's waiting for her eggs out here! She's got people dying over at her office next door and you're trying to figure out if it's one pinch of salt or two.."

Lina smiled and shook her head, "No, I don't...I could use a few more clients. Hopefully not dying, maybe just maybe a few sprains and a cough or two."

Rosa's mother's cheerful voice carried from the kitchen in back. "Dying can wait, Rosie-girl! People are dying all over the world, honey! You don't rush *eggs a la Gambriotti*."

Rosa playfully mussed up her friend's short strawberry blond hair, "See, I told you, Lina – there's no way to get a fast egg from my mom! Every plate is a masterpiece."

"Okay, Rosa. But you know nobody's dying over there. Nobody's even sick, a little bit. And that's because we've got no customers."

"Praise *Dio*, that is a very good thing for us here at my cafe, live people still have to eat!"

They watched out the big front window as two muscular young men in white t-shirts and Levis wrestled a wheelbarrow heavy with bags of cement on past Rosa's.

"Hey, that's one of the guys almost knocked you over last week."

"No, that was Ben Napoli. You sayin' all us wops look the same?"

"No, I am not saying that, you idiot."

"Which one you want?" Rosa grinned at her friend, raising one eyebrow.

"They're both too young for me."

"That one – the big one – that's Jimmy Rosalini. He's your age, maybe 28 now, but you can't have him."

"Why not?"

"He's already got four *bambino,* and a fifth on the way!"

"Wow! I see your point. Well, okay, Rosa – you get to take the other one, he's more your age."

"Yeah, he's twenty. Joey Zumbatti. He went to school with Pauli and me."

"Paulo, your best friend."

"Yeah, him. Fratello Paulo, these days, now that he gives himself to Jesu Christi. Just plain Pauli to me. But this Joey Zumbatti here, nobody lays their hands on Joey. You look even cross-eyed at him, his wife would kill you!"

"Not really?"

"She's big and fat enough, and she handles the heavy rolling pin good, too! No girl in her right mind wanna cross Mindy Zumbatti!" Rosa raised her voice again, "Mama, are you back there squeezing a hen or something?"

11

"Hey, Rosie Rosa, you mind your own business! People back here are cooking!"

Rosa shrugged and grinned, "She's good, but she is not very fast. So, how we gonna find you a good fella from Italy so you can settle down?"

"No, I don't think that is going to happen, girlfriend. Italian mamas are too protective of their sons."

"Is that your medical opinion, Doctor Bright?"

"No, Rosa. I think it's that I'm not ready to get serious."

"You better start! What, you're already the old lady."

"I am not! Twenty-eight is not old!"

"On Hungry Hill it is like *ancient times*. Here we say a girl over twenty is old as Moses. You know my family married me away, I was a teenage kid. I barely had my period."

"Noo...? That's not true, right?"

"I said *practically*, Doc."

"Maybe let's talk about something else than how old I'm getting," Lina said. "Tell me, how come they call this Hungry Hill? I don't see a hill anywhere around."

Everybody in the South Chicago suburbs knew Hungry Hill was the local Italian community in this part of Chicago Heights, the place where the folks from Napoli or Genoa or Rome who were new off the boat settled to find comfort in the bustling American Midwest of the 1920s. Hungry Hill was a colony of already established immigrants who were mostly Italians and Sicilians. But there were a hundred different ideas how it got its name. But one thing was sure; it attracted the majority of folks fresh off the boat from Italy. The newcomers felt more comfortable starting their new lives on *the Hill*, getting things going with people from *the Old Country* to help them make their way in the land of promise and opportunity.

"That's a funny thing, I have to agree," Rosa said. "Nobody knows how come, why it got that name, Hungry Hill. Makes no sense, but it's not gonna change."

"Everything changes."

"Some things do. Since my parent's time, Twenty Second Street changed from family homes to business, that's a change. This house, my grandpa and Pop built together for my mom and Pop's family. We change it now, put my café in front, rent you a room upstairs. Mom and Pop live in grandpa's old house. That's change. But when the people come from the Old Country, they still come to this part of town and they still call it Hungry Hill."

The Gambriottis had converted the space where Rosa and Lina were sitting into a warm and welcoming dining room featuring a mixed collection of second-hand tables. On one wall they had pinned an old green-white-and-red tricolor Kingdom of Italy flag. And there was a black and white sketch of the ruins of Pompeii with a dormant Mount Vesuvius looming in the background.

"Sometimes remembering all that stuff makes me feel sad," Rosa said.

"What stuff?" Lina said, hoping to help Rosa skip away from the subject she knew was coming.

"You know. Ralphie stuff."

"Hard to avoid it. He was your man."

"Yeah, he was. And there were some good times. Ralphie was a good singer, you know. He'd sing love songs from Italian opera, and he'd come in here and dance around the room."

"I never met him, but he sounds nice."

"He was okay. But he was an impulsive guy. Once he got his crazy notion to join the Italian army, nobody could talk sense to him. I certainly couldn't. Like he was going to save the nation of Italy, or something. I guess I can understand it, in a way. After all, he grew up over there."

"I bet they were delighted to have him back."

"Yeah, they were. Greeted him with open arms. But, honest to *Dio*, Lina – for me, it all happened so fast…you know, way too fast, I think. First papa drops the surprise on me that they found my perfect husband for me. It's one evening around the dinner table on a Friday and we're having special *meatballs a la Napoli* in the fresh home-made spaghetti and he says 'Hey, let's not even talk about it, it's all arranged, you're getting married!' So that was that."

"Just like that?"

"Yeah. That was that, exactly *just like that*, subject over. A few weeks later, the guy gets off the boat, we meet, six weeks for the courtship and then papa buys me the white dress with the lace veil and Ralphie and I show up in front of the altar at San Roccos and *bam!* the priest seals the deal."

"I'll bet you looked beautiful."

"Mama has my wedding photograph somewhere – I'll show you – but then, see, barely two months later Ralphie gets his big idea and dances back across the ocean to Italy to fight the

Austrian *bastardos.* And before you know it six months go by and I get the telegram, *We are sorry to inform you,* and just like that I'm the young widow that everybody whispers about at Sunday Mass."

Lina was still trying for a happier subject, "After you got married, did you have a honeymoon?"

That seemed to work. At least Rosa smiled as she remembered, "Sort of. Ralphie took me fishing in Wisconsin."

"Hey, wait a minute – here this guy's just off the boat, how did he know there were fish in Wisconsin?"

"Papa paid for the trip."

"Oh, it was Papa's idea. Of course! I bet he went along, too."

"Yeah, he did. Him and mamma. He said it was the honeymoon he never gave her, back when they got married."

"I was just kidding."

"That's alright, Lina. It was okay. We had our own rooms and they gave us plenty of space. And the Dells of Wisconsin are very beautiful."

"You catch any fish?"

"Not me! I don't wanna touch those things! Ralphie and papa did. There really are lots of fish in Wisconsin."

Rosa sighed and looked down at her clenched fists, and then she gave Lina a determined smile. "He came, we got married, and he went. I'm not gonna let any of that drag me down. I wear widow's black to the Mass, but, no way, I will not sit with those bent over old ladies in their own sad little section at the back of San Rocco's."

"That's the way to go," Lina said. "You have your whole life to live, yet."

Lina admired her friend's spunk. Rosa was her best friend (actually, pretty much her only friend) and Lina would do anything to support her.. Rosa ran her little café with a fierce Italian spirit, a dark sense of humor (if this be hell, there's always heaven to look forward to) and plenty of her own blend of a spicy tomato sauce (not too much sage, that's where the Sicilians go wrong). She did about half of the cooking herself; mornings and in the busy times her mom and dad – aging but not slowing down so much, and now, living in her grandpa's house a few blocks away – were happy to help out, seating guests, handling the cash, cooking when Rosa had to go out for groceries or to handle the finances, or like now when she was having a moment with her pal Lina.

"How come we became friends, anyway?" Rosa asked. "You're this big time doctor and I'm just the kid next door."

"What are you talking, *big time*? Look at me; I'm a doctor without any clients of my own. I'm lucky grouchy old Doc Whitber lets me take temperatures and sweep the floors."

"What does he know? You have your own Doctor of Medicine degree. I see it on the wall. And you did the impossible thing for a girl, you actually were in the Great War, like Ralphie."

"Yeah, I did do that."

"Blinky Old Doc Whitber's lucky he's got you. His eyesight's so bad I bet he can't even see the big letter E on the chart on the wall. And with those shaky hands! I wouldn't let him take my temperature, he'd probably poke my eye out!"

"Well, there's several good reasons we're friends: I work right next door, I rent a room upstairs here, and you really know how to cook!"

"Love me, love my cannoli."

"Exactly."

CHAPTER TWO

The area was off to one side at the end of the furnace run at the Inland Steel mill. It was the end of the day shift, and that was when Anthony Anselmo had his first look at Louie Caproni: What he saw was a grimy little steel mill guy. A midget, *for Christ's Sake*, not even five foot tall and round as a big bowling ball. Louie had just finished his shift, and he was grinning from ear to ear, white teeth and white eyes shining out of a face sooty black from eight hours up on the hot beds. Louie had a roll of dirty black overalls stuck under one arm, he was wearing a faded red wool shirt with sleeves rolled up to his elbows, the shirt sweat-stained under the arms, and old khaki pants probably discarded by some fat army sergeant, the pants cut off at the knees, snug around the ball of his waist, held up with wide tan suspenders. And he was wearing a bright red workman's bandanna around his cannon ball shaped head. There was a stained cloth lunch bag under his other arm. He was being patient, but not too patient, clearly wanting to get out of there, eager to go home, wherever that was, probably the Italian ghetto over on Hungry Hill.

This was all new to Anselmo. They were standing next to the smoking hot beds at the end of the line of repeaters that bent and shaped hot metal at the steel mill in Chicago Heights. It was a place where they reheated old railroad tracks (of which there was a seemingly endless supply, shipped in by rail from all over the country), and turned them into

18

steel fence posts and concrete reinforcing rebar. The blasts of heat were nearly unbearable, and the noise made it impossible to be understood without yelling.

Anselmo was not a steel worker by trade, and he did not need the money – a paycheck that was, when you thought about it, next to nothing. He'd come into town from half way around the world and he was trying to fit into the community. He'd taken the job because this opening had come up in a conversation after Mass at San Rocco, and although he had his assignment from his grandfather and his reason for being in Chicago Heights, he was drifting through this time in his life looking for some meaning and he couldn't think of any believable way to say no and so he'd agreed to take the job. That was a couple of weeks ago and now it was the end of a work day at Inland Steel and here was this short little guy saying he was Anselmo's new partner, *'cause the boss says so*, and they were gonna be together up there with the sparking white hot steel where people got hurt really bad or even died in ways too horrible to be imagined.

Anselmo found himself looking at the fellow and thinking this couldn't be right; he was new to working in factories so he couldn't be sure of anything, but any fool could see the mill was a dangerous place and this Louie looked totally out of place. He looked like somebody who belonged in the traveling circus, the juggling midget or maybe the world's tiniest strong man, the guy in the poster wearing the Tarzan suit who could bounce cannon balls off his big stomach.

"How long you work here?" Anselmo shouted. You had to shout, even to the man standing right next to you, to be heard over the oven roar and the metal clank of the cutters.

"Oh, God-almighty, going on now, near to twenty years!" Louie said. "I hear you the man new from the boot." *The boot.* The Old Country. Italy.

"Yes, I am. My name is Anthony Anselmo. Tony. Just plain Anselmo." He held out his hand and Louie crushed it in his own. "Some grip you got there," Anselmo said, giving him a closer look.

The short little round man squinted back at his new partner, getting that first impression that meant everything. "You are how old now? Thirty?"

"Thirty two. Born 1890. You?"

"1891," Louie said.

"You in the war?" Anselmo asking about the War to End All Wars, wanting to know if Louie had been in it. Anselmo knew some stories about that; some patriotic Americans of Italian descent – some even two or three generations in the U.S.! – had signed up and gone over there, *Dio help their souls.* Anselmo had traveled here from Italy to resolve issues remaining with the surviving widow of one of those unfortunate men.

"No, I missed that one," Louie said. "My wife wouldn't let me go. You?"

"Me? Not so lucky," Anselmo said, his smile fading. "You got kids?"

"Two son, two daughter – watch out here, now!" Surprisingly light on his feet, Louie carefully pushed Anselmo back out of the way as a heavy hand cart loaded with steaming rebar rumbled past, the awkwardly long and heavy metal cart manhandled front and back by two men in a hurry. "You have-a the kid?"

"No. Not so lucky about that, either. No wife, no *bambino*."

Anthony Anselmo had a far different history from Louie's: his grandfather, Giacomo Anselmo (Giacomo I) – now over eighty years of age – still supervised the family vineyards, and the hazelnut and olive orchards in Northern Italy. Anthony's father, Giacomo II, ran his own corporation, Futura Industries, in Rome.

Before World War 1 began, Giacomo II had had tried to persuade his young son to join his corporation in the capital, but that hadn't gone so well.

"Give me one reason why not," Gio II had growled at Anselmo from behind his big marble topped desk.

"There's one right there," Anselmo said, pointing a finger directly at his father.

"What are you talking about?" Gio II snarled and sniffed and ran a hand through his thick head of hair. He was dark Italian like Gio I; Anselmo was light haired and blue-eyed, like his mother. Anselmo instinctively knew, the way sons always did, his father resented this in him.

"He's talking about you, Dear," Anselmo's mother said. She was ailing, sitting in a wheelchair to one side of her husband's desk, pale and weak and not long for the world. But her voice had a determined bite to it, and they heard her well enough. "You've never gotten along," she added.

"And why do you think that is, *dear*?"

21

Well, Giacomo, you're rude and abrasive. You don't respect his ideas –"

"He's just a kid, all that money for private school, and not even

a degree yet!"

"And see, you put him down, just like that! That's your way. No. Better he continue his education in Switzerland."

"I won't pay for that."

"Grandpapa will. It's all settled. Nothing for you to worry about."

"You've done this behind my back!"

"Oh, you've done so much behind my back, haven't you, dear?" As she spoke, Anselmo's mother gave a passing glance at his secretary, one of the ripe young tomatoes with pouty lips he hired as his personal assistants. She was sitting nearby, and, with nothing else to do, was looking out the window. Gio II had no answer for his wife's conversation.

So Anselmo left his angry father in Rome and went back to study in Switzerland and then on to college in England where – instead of the business courses his father demanded – he studied philosophy and literature and joined the college choral club, the debating club and the fencing team.

But then the war had come and Anselmo abruptly left all that to join the Italian army. Not that he was feeling patriotic; back then his blind raging purpose had been to fight against the hated Austrian *bastardos* he believed had killed his beloved older brother, Giacomo III. Unknown assailants had somehow shot Gio III dead under circumstances that were never made clear. Was it an enemy raid behind the lines? Was it just a mistake, a careless misfiring at a rifle range, a wild bullet out of nowhere? Nobody knew. Or, if they did, they wouldn't say. And the mystery only deepened when Anselmo, sent to retrieve his brother's body, realized he had been shot in the back, and from a distance of only a few paces. Anselmo had enlisted in a blind rage, and his tour of duty had been a disaster, but he saw no reason to talk about any of that with Louie in a clanking steel mill that was half way around the globe from his home in Turin.

CHAPTER THREE

Lina watched as Mary Franconi brought her son Billy in to the doctor's office with his pants down around his knees. "The dumb stupido has a BB still stuck in his behind," Mary said. She had the BB gun rifle strapped around her shoulder as if to prove it. She wheeled him in, the sobbing boy standing backwards on a hand cart, and she slapped him in the head every time he wailed. "I gave him some of Dr. Whitber's magic tonic," Mary said. "Hasn't quieted him down at all."

"How much did you give him," Lina said.

"Half a bottle. Why, that too much?"

"Enough to kill a horse."

"Jesu Christi, I didn't mean to kill him! Whadda we do now?"

"Nothing we can do. It's just opium and licorice extract. If he isn't dead already, he'll probably be okay. Wheel him into the surgery room. I'll get the BB out. Unless you'd rather wait to see if he dies or not."

"Mighty dio, no! How do you get that BB out?"

"Medical pinchers will probably work. Or a workman's needle-nose pliers." Lina was only half-kidding. For her young years, she had more practical experience with wounds and broken bodies than anybody she knew.

She had Mary help her son lie sideways on the operating table. It took five minutes of probing with Billy howling like a wet cat and his mom slapping him every time he tried to get up, but Lina finally extracted the little grey ball. The wound was small, even with the surgical cut she had to make to get her pinchers deep into his buttocks. Four stitches stopped most of the bleeding. "He'll probably be okay," she said. "All that bleeding is good to stop any possible infection."

"I don't have any money," Mary said. "I'm going to give you Billy's perfectly good BB gun. It's a repeater, the expensive pump model his no-good dad got him."

"Noooo, Mom!" Billy howled.

"How did he get shot?" Lina said.

"Claims he shot himself."

"That's impossible."

"Well, he's a liar. Probably playing war with the kids in the neighborhood. Anyway, thanks for what you done." She slapped Billy on the head for good measure and they headed for the door.

"Here. Souvineer," Lina said, holding out a bloody napkin with the BB in it.

"Yeah. Good reminder of his stupidity," Mary said, taking the bloody napkin. "I'll frame it on the wall in his room next to the picture of Abraham Lincoln."

She took her son by the neck with her left hand, and the hand cart with her right and had Lina hold the door open as she made her way out into the busy street. Lina stared after them, wondering what she was going to do with a pump action BB gun that looked nearly brand new.

Anselmo was running at a slow pace down Dixie Highway, about a mile from his hotel room in

Chicago Heights. There were times when he ran until he was exhausted and this sometimes helped him forget the images burned in his mind from his time in the Tyrolian Alps. He was remembering a bright blue sky morning in December when he was high in the mountains, directing a small recon unit northeast through a mountain pass toward southern Austria. It was the second week December, 1916, and the snow lay in heavy white blankets all around them on a steep slope angling up from the pass, and also on the down slope side that cut sharply away toward the valley below. His group of six riders gingerly rode single file, their hopeful mission to find a path that several divisions of the Italian army might use to get them to the front. Their horses were breathing deep in the thin air, steam from their nostrils, the air frigid in spite of the clear day and the bright blue sky overhead. Anselmo, aware of the high altitude and wary of the deep snow, was moving his mounted horsemen along at a slow pace.

Too slow for his commandante, eight hundred yards to the rear, who was impatiently waiting with the rest of a Tuscan cavalry company of mounted troopers. "What is he afraid of? Get him to move!" the commandante shouted to his bugle boy.

"What shall I do, sir?"

"*Digli di mouvi il culo!*" the commandante said, "*Blat him to move his ass!*"

The bugle boy winced, but he put the brass horn to his lips and gave the sharp three notes that signaled "Advance!"

High above them on the narrow trail through the mountain pass, Anselmo's horse Juno perked up its ears at the bugle notes. Anselmo was two dozen yards in the lead. He looked back at his small squad. "Men! Stop!" Anselmo shouted. *The commandante was sounding his bugle!* It was stupid to make any noise with the unstable snow thick and heavy all around them and on the steep slopes both above and below their path. "Retreat!" Anselmo shouted. "Back the way we came!"

His men, new recruits all, looked at him like he was crazy. "Men! Go! Now!" They looked confused, their horses shuffling about and bumping into each other as they started to turn around on the narrow trail.

But it was too late. There was a ground shaking roar from above and by then a huge wave of snow was rushing down on them. .Anselmo, separated from his men, spurred Juno and outran the heavy avalanche. The rest of his recon unit was not so lucky.

Now, over six years later and a half a world away, Anselmo's recollections of the inquiry that followed were bitter. The bugle boy had somehow vanished and was unavailable for testimony. The commandante, a portly man in his mid-forties with a fiery temper, had no recollection of ordering a bugle call, though he remembered Anselmo as being reluctant to go on his recon mission to the point of near-mutiny. The only other witnesses who might have testified in his favor were Anselmo's men and their horses, still silent in the snowy grave they shared far away in the high Alps. Their remains were never found, even when the Spring melt came in 1917.

The outcome of the inquiry was a disaster for Anselmo. He was stripped of his officer's rank and ordered to return to the front as a common foot soldier. He left immediately in a small horse drawn carriage, a coach that had been rented for him by his grandfather. But his exit wasn't fast enough; five miles out of Turin, on the dusty highway headed north, his team of horses was overtaken by a small contingent of armed horsemen. The newcomers were clothed in nondescript greys, in uniforms that could have come from the Baltics or even Russia. They stopped the carriage, surrounding it and hammering at it with wooden staves and clubs, demanding the cowardly Anselmo present himself. Their leader was the comandante himself. He brandished his sword, waving it in the light of a setting sun. *"Fallo bastardo!* Your silly accusations have tarnished my honor and dragged my name in the mud!"

Anselmo had given up his officer's uniform, but his sabre was a gift from his mother, and he drew it as he stooped through the doorway of the coach. The commandante did not dismount; instead, he forced his horse close and took a vicious swing intended to decapitate Anselmo. Squinting as he was in the bright light from the sun to the west the commandante's sword missed Anselmo's head by inches; it banged against the curved wood framing the roof of the carriage and then slashed across Anselmo's chest, leaving a bloody gash.

Reacting on instinct, Anselmo's counter thrust ran cleanly through the commandante's torso, just below his ribs. The man's eyes widened with the shock.

"You've killed him!" one of the commandante's men said.

"Maybe," Anselmo said. "You'd better get him to a medical man."

The commandante did live, and he became a business and political enemy to Anselmo's family in the years after the war.

This wasn't the end of Anselmo's war story: Once he went back to the front as a foot soldier, there were other actions he'd taken, other things he'd done and the things he'd been forced to do. It had become more than a matter of family honor; with Aselmo it had become personal. Shock and horror piled on top of shock and horror, and yet he stayed until the bitter end. Germany formally surrendered in November of 1918, but the treaty of Versailles wasn't signed until the following summer, and Anselmo didn't leave the mountains until autumn, trying without success to find any trace of his men lost in the avalanche.

Years after the war, a few months before he left for Chicago Heights, Anselmo had walked slowly through the hazel nut orchard on his grandfather's estate with old Gio I. His grandfather's physician had fashioned a wooden hip brace that Gio I strapped on. and so he was able to stand fairly straight, though he walked along beside his grandson with a cane and a cautious limp.

"I'm going to be well, Anselmo," the old man responded, as always, to his grandson's concerns. "My father lived to be ninety four. By my counting, that gives me 14 more years, at least." He grinned, "It's a contest, you know. Can I outlive that tough old *scoreggia*?"

Anselmo smiled, "You call him an old fart."

"You can call the people you love anything you want. The ghosts understand."

"And he was a good man?"

"He was a strong man...and good, in his own way. As are you, Anselmo. Tough as a nut." He gestured at the row of bushy hazel nut trees on either side of their path. It was late autumn, and though the nuts had been harvested, Gio I found one remaining on a branch. He plucked it and threw it to his grandson. "Your lucky hazelnut," he said. "You'll need it."

"Why so, *Grand-pere*?"

"I know remembering the war is very hard for you, Antonio, and were I younger, or had I anyone else I trusted so much as you, I would not ask...but our family has yet one more broken pot to glue back together, my dear grandson. The government has sent me the paperwork, and I will pass it on to you."

"Why is this one more difficult than the others?"

"This one is half way around the world."

Anselmo knew it would be, yet again, a matter of family honor. The family had recruited and funded their fighting company in the Italian army. They had fought in the Alps even after their cavalry company was whittled to a few remaining horses, and the battles had not gone well. This was not rare or uncommon; Italy had lost over a half million men to a stupid and foolish war. Anselmo's grandfather, against his will, had participated, and now, even though the conflict was already over for a half dozen years, Gio I still felt obligated to compensate the wives and families of those in the company he had funded.

The old man had already bound Anselmo to more than one mission to pay this debt of honor, and now was sending him across the Atlantic and to the middle of far-away America, to an industrial town thirty miles south of Lake Michigan, to make a payment he saw as a necessary debt of honor. "Your mission, is to make apology and present financial reparations to a young widow named Rosa Gambriotti"

Anselmo's face went white. "Gambriotti...?"

"Yes, Private Ralph Gambriotti. I think I recall once you spoke of him."

"I knew them all. This one – I was there when he died."

Anselmo was badly shaken. He would never – could never – reveal his actions to his grandfather or anybody else, but the raw and naked truth was, he had helped Ralphie Gambriotti die, and as a born and baptized Catholic, he still felt the heavy weight of what he'd done. It was an action that a man went to hell for, no exceptions.

Gio I seemed not to notice his grandson's distress; or, if he did, he went on detailing the arrangements, the date of Anselmo's departure, the tickets, the manservant would help carriage his heavy travel trunk to the ocean going steamer and so on. But all that was just words to Anselmo, who was nodding his head without really listening. Ralphie Gambriotti, Rosa Gambriotti's soldier-boy husband, would never be coming back home to hug his wife and fold her in his warm embrace. She

31

already knew that; Anselmo's assignment would be to try to explain to her why, as Ralphie's officer, he had been personally unable to prevent her great loss, and to provide her with the allotted sum of financial compensation.

"Yes, *Grand-pere*," Anselmo said. *Yes to everything.*

Back then, in late autumn of 1921, walking in his beloved grandfather's hickorynut orchard, Anthony Anselmo had agreed to take charge of the widow's dole, the money to be presented to her. But now, a half year later, in early Spring of the new year, he was in Chicago Heights, Illinois – and he didn't know how to conduct his official duty to this young (not-yet-even-twenty years of age) Rosa Gambriotti without telling the rest of the unpleasant truth, without having to tell her exactly what had happened, and without revealing his own shocking role in Ralphie's terrible end.

He should have spilled the story the first day he got to Chicago Heights, should have confronted Rosa Gambriotti and told her the small necessary part of it – the official military lies – and then hopped on a train back to New York City. But the widow was just a young girl and Anselmo's courage (or his ability to tell falsehoods, he wasn't sure which) had failed him and now he couldn't decide on the best way to do what was needed. He was renting a small room on the third floor rear of the Victoria Hotel in downtown Chicago Heights. Corporal Ralph Gambriotti's widow's payment was safely deposited at the nearby Citizens National Bank of Chicago Heights. *But what to do next?*

Money wasn't a real problem for him, or even a temptation. Anselmo had his own money – a substantial amount set aside by Gio I, who was still in charge of the family finances, still living in the big house in Northern Italy – and Anselmo had reserved a return ticket on an ocean liner that would be taking him back to Europe. There was the pressure from his father, Giacomo II, who had aligned himself with the rising political might of Benito Mousseline, and was furiously charging ahead with his business in Rome. The father was once again making noises that he needed Anselmo to take over some responsibility. Futura Industries needed him, Gia II said, as they converted their factories from making military uniforms to civilian clothing... or, *per l'amor di Dio*, at least could he take over from doddering old *grand-pere* and manage the vineyards in Turin? But Anselmo didn't see Gio I as doddering and he wasn't going to work for his father in Rome. There were a lot of reasons for that. The biggest one – he despised the man. Maybe as much as for any other reason, Anselmo had watched as Gio II took up with the latest of his nubile young secretaries while his wife was on her deathbed.

Then too, his father had chosen to believe the Italian army's version of his son's tragic war experience over Anselmo's own sworn testimony. Reasons enough. Anselmo was never going to work for his father. *Mai!*

Now that he was in the energetic and bustling Midwest of America, Anselmo didn't know if he wanted to go back to Italy at all. He was finding out something about himself: he very much liked the

United States. Everything seemed fresh and new to him here. The Americans had a bustling, energetic way about them; he was constantly being uplifted by the little things, he remembered a popular song he'd heard while walking down a Manhattan street, the music drifting from an apartment window on a pleasant Spring morning, *Toot Toot Tootsie, goodbye! Toot Toot Tootsie, don't cry!* It amused him to think of his father as 'Tootsie'. He imagined himself greeting Giacomo II, "Hi there, Tootsie – and goodbye!", and the hyper man having a heart attack right there in the foyer of his extravagantly furnished offices in the business section of town south of Rome's city center.

When Anselmo was on the train heading west to Illinois, he read an ad in the newspaper: GO WEST, YOUNG MAN!

"What do you think about that," the salesman in the light tan suit sitting next to him had said.

"Anselmo had been reading a story on the opposite page about some rich old lady who'd married a young fellow who may or may not have pushed her off a look-out bluff to her death in the Hudson River. "I think he did it," he said. "But how can they prove it?"

"No," the guy said. "Not the murder. Of course the bounder did it. He married her for her money. I mean about going west."

"Well, we're doing that right now."

"No, you day-dreamer! Our train's going to Chicago. I mean the real west!" He pointed to the big headline, Go West! "Oklahoma. Wyoming. Even California."

"Well, I don't know about that," Anselmo said. " I'd hate to get stuck with an arrow in my behind. What do you think?"

The man sniffed and pushed his glasses on his nose with one finger. He looked to be in his middle forties, a little chubby, and he tipped his hat back to scratch his thinning hair. "Hey, I'd be tempted, but I've got bad eyesight. And there's that other thing – I have the house and a pack of kids in Chi-town. But I tell you, if I was a little younger, maybe…"

"Well, I do know how to ride a horse," Anselmo said.

"Hey, it's not all like that, anymore. It's got civilized."

"How so?"

"Well, I hear San Francisco has over a half million people! You don't need a horse, you can take a dim box – you know, a taxi!"

Anselmo didn't say any more, but as the train wheels clicked endlessly over the tracks he found himself thinking about it. What if he bought a train ticket to Oklahoma or Wyoming or even California and said goodbye to Italy for good? Maybe that was the best way; just leave a note for Rosa Gambriotti and tell her about her money deposited with the bank manager in Chicago Heights and get the hell out of there. But he knew in his heart of hearts he wasn't going to do that. He'd promised his grandfather more than that, sworn a vow on his family name to tell a story to clear the *commandante* and the *commandante's* brother's name. He had to do that, even if it was a partial truth, a fabrication to cover the harsh reality of what had happened.

And then Anselmo wasn't on the train headed west or in his grandpa's orchard or in the war in the mountains. He was back in the mill. He heard the roar of the furnaces, the hiss of the glowing steel being squeezed thinner and thinner into fence posts and concrete reinforcement rebar. He was standing next to the repeaters at the Inland Steel mill in Chicago Heights, and this tough little cannonball of a steel worker he'd just met was smiling at him.

"I hear we work together." Louie said, the little fellow looking up at him with an inquiring glance, eyes wide and white against his skin stained black with mill grit.

Anselmo nodded. "That shift boss fellow says so. You okay with that?"

"Sure, plenty okay, fine with me." Louie wiggled the thick fingers of his left hand in front of Anselmo. "I teach you to be careful, not lose any fingers. But I gotta go now. I cannot be late for dinner. Anna, my good wife will kill me and worse, my kids will eat up all the food." Louie's quick grin widened. He reached up, clapped Anselmo on the back and moved away from him, heading toward the nearby grey metal door, on his way to the men's locker room they called *the shitter*, looking forward to a quick cold shower to rinse the soot off, and then to duck past the paymaster's window and head out the factory main gate.

Anselmo was still thinking this had to be some mistake, this stubby little guy couldn't be his new partner, even a raw novice (like he was) knew the white hot steel was deadly dangerous, people got killed up here on the line, it happened all the time.

Then he had his moment of awareness as he realized what it meant that he was the new guy; he, Anselmo was only a few weeks off the boat and a few days at Inland Steel. They'd been working different shifts; Louie didn't know him, but he was probably thinking the same in reverse, thinking he had to be careful – chances were, this new guy from Mother Italy was the weak partner, the dangerous proposition in their new team.

CHAPTER FOUR

Lina and Rosa heard the flutter of Brother Paulo's bicycle when it was still a few doors down the street from Rosa's restaurant. *Fratello* Paulo Ricci, Rosa's best friend since they were little kids.

"Here comes your pal, crazy man boy-priest," Lina grinned, "And I'm still sitting here waiting for the eggs and biscuits your mom's supposedly cooking for us."

"Don't worry, the eggs are coming. Mama's cooking and she's also rolling out the fresh pasta. Two things at once, she's good at that. About my friend Paulo, you know he's not exactly the priest yet. Just a brother, a *fratello.*"

"What's that mean? I mean, what's that mean for him?" Lina, a not-too-serious Protestant, found the Catholic rituals full of riddles and mysteries.

Rosa frowned, "He's gotta take his final vows and then we give him up, lost to *Dio* forever. But not yet. They won't let him do the ceremony."

"Who won't?"

"The bishop in Joliet, mostly. He let Paulo drive him in his bishop-mobile."

"What's a bishop-mobile?"

"Just a Stanley Steamer with a bishop in it. Only Paulo got a little enthusiastic – I mean, it was winter, ice on the streets, too bad the patrol wagon was parked right there in front of them."

"Paulo ran the bishop's car into the police car?"

"Yeah, with the bishop in it."

"Was he wearing that big, tall hat?"

"No, only popes wear that. But the Stanley Steamer got a dented fender and poor Paulo was put on *la lista di merda*. The bishop's assistant told Paulo he's gotta be more mature. I think it's just an excuse on their part. They know he's not ever gonna grow up."

"Well, he does pretend his bicycle has a motor."

"Yeah. Kids do that, not the grown men."

"You know how they do it? They put an empty matchbook in the spokes of the bike."

"Well, it sounds like a farting cow."

They were laughing as Paulo came in through the front door, a sporty brown leather English traveler's hat pulled low on his head, his black robe tucked in his pants so it wouldn't catch in the bike chain.

His face was flushed bright red from the bike ride from San Rocco's church. "Hey, what's so funny?" he said.

"Cows breaking wind," Rosa grinned at him.

"Not if you're standing in the wrong direction." He returned her happy smile. Lina saw yet again how the two of them seemed to light up when they were together.

Rosa handed him a paper bag and he started for the door. "Hey, hey, hey you, Mister! Why such a rush? You don't get away so fast! Pauli, I got a question for you."

He turned and gave her his impish grin, "*Fratello* Paulo, to you."

"*Fratello* Pauli, then. Just look at what a mess you are – that funny racing hat all crooked on backwards and your hair all mussed up like that!

Curious people here want to know – how come you always ride your bike so fast? I mean, where's a guy like you supposed to be going?"

"I dunno, Rosa, I just like it, to go speeding around like that. I tell you, sweet girl, I wish I had an automobile. I want that more than anything! I would take off the fenders and the hood, race it at the track like Sonny Talamonti."

"Who's that?" Lina said.

"Sonny Talamonti, he's our own racing hero here in town. He raced at the brick works at Indianapolis. He calls his car *The Spirit of Chicago Heights*."

"I thought Jesus was your hero, Pauli," Rosa said.

The expression on Paulo's face clouded for a moment, but then he thought of something and his smile returned. "I bet *Gesu* would have been a great racer. Miracle finishes. Think of it, Rosa; he could turn water into gasoline when he was running out!"

Rosa poked him in the ribs. "I don't know, Pauli. That sounds like cheating to me, and you know *il figlio di Dio* wouldn't do a sin just to win the gold cup."

"Aww, I'm just kidding, Rosie Rosa. But the idea of it, the feeling, the wind in your face, the world rushing past! Come on, you gotta like that!"

Rosa shook her head, "Maybe that's what you like, but not me. You take the fenders off your Papa's old Model T, and he'll kill you!"

"No, I wouldn't do it to Pop's car. I want the big time! My wish is to drive a Sunbeam Gran Prix car in the Indy 500!"

Rosa gave him a playful shove, "Come on, Pauli, you're almost the priest now. You should act your age. What, you are even wearing the black robe! Take your breakfast and get out of here!"

He made a frowny face at her. "Okay, okay, I am going."

A minute later and they heard his bike making its fake engine brap-brap-brap sound as he headed back toward the San Rocco rectory.

Rosa smiled, "He's just a kid at heart."

"You fix him breakfast every morning?"

"Most mornings. He says the cook at the priest house don't know an egg from a green bean. I do for him egg and grated parmesan on a toasted bun, with some tomato sauce with the touch of rosemary sprinkled in, just like he say his grandma used to."

"I don't know that much about it, but I thought when a man takes on the black robe, he is supposed to be poor like church mice. Where's he getting the money to pay you?"

Rosa pointed to a lumpy burlap sack Paulo had left behind. "Those are tomatoes. He pays me with vegetables he snitches from the priest garden. They have a big garden out back and he takes care of it."

"Stolen holy tomatoes! I guess that's not a sin, huh?"

"We're really just borrowing them to eat. And Pauli says they have too many; anyhow. The sin would be to let them rot."

" How does he get tomatoes in the springtime?'

"The priests have a glass house in their garden in back of the priest-house. They call it a *casa calda*, a hot house. And their other secret is chicken poop. They have a chicken coop, and nothing goes to waste. Pauli told me; they give him that smelly job, too. Clean out the poop. But it works: They have good tomatoes most of the year, many more than they can use."

"Huh. Pretty fancy. But let me tell you what I think, my friend: I think this whole tomato trading deal with you, it's just an excuse for him to come over here to see you."

"What? No, Lina...I don't think so."

"Oh, come on *Rosie Rosa*! I see the way he looks at you, a little temperature going on there! You have to see there's something in the air."

"Well... too bad on that one, he is reserved for *Dio* now."

"Yeah, that is a big waste!" Lina agreed. "What's God gonna do with a sparkly fresh young man like that?"

"Now, Lina, we gotta not think about that; I'm-a the widow, you know, the used goods."

"That's not the way I see it, Rosa. You're just a kid, yourself. Maybe *Gesu Christi* could loan your friend Pauli over to you for a while. I mean, after all, *Dio* is *Dio*, he's the one got forever to do whatever he likes. Us poor mortals here on earth, *we got to get hoppin'*, as the saying goes."

"You talk nonsense, you silly girlfriend." But Lina saw her friend's face redden, and then take on a wistful look, as she headed back to the kitchen. "I'll be right back; I'll go stir up Mama and bring you those breakfast eggs *a la Gambriotti,* less than five minutes."

"Maybe with a slice of fresh holy stolen tomato on the side?"

Rosa's bright spirits returned, "You got it for sure!"

CHAPTER FIVE

But a few minutes later, at the same time when Rosa came back from the kitchen with the plate of steaming hot scrambled eggs and the promised fresh tomato sliced up around the rim, the front door opened and two blood-spattered farmers banged their way in, half-dragging a limp teenage boy with his left hand wrapped in a bloody burlap sack.

Because the doctor's office where Lina worked was right next door; Rosa's family was used to emergencies of one sort or other trooping on in at any time of the night or day, but a moment like this never failed to turn the young widow's stomach. "Hey, this is a diner! Why you come in here like this?"

"Where's Doc Whitber?" the eldest of the farmers said, staring around the room like the doctor might be hiding somewhere. "We need the doc right now!" The old man looked to be over seventy, bald-headed but with a big grey beard that was untrimmed and almost a foot long.

Rosa's face blanched when she saw the blood dripping on her clean wooden floor. "Oh, no…" Blood was everywhere, red blood dripping on her clean tablecloths, blood spattering her white napkins.

Lina jumped to her feet, "Okay. Lie him down. Put that bleeding hand of his up on this chair seat. If we keep it higher than his heart, that will slow the blood from coming out."

"We was at the doctor's office!" the second farmer said. He was middle-aged, looked to be in his fifties. Once he started talking, it seemed he couldn't stop. "Nobody's over there! My name is Willy Weiss. We are three generations, present right here. This is my papa. And now my dopy kid here is gonna lose his hand." Willie seemed a little slow, as if he had to give excuses, to come up with reasons why they were messing up Rosa's Café.

"Never mind! I can clean up the mess! Just do what Doctor Lina here says," Rosa said. "She works with Doctor Whitber!"

"But –" The farmer started to protest.

"No time to argue," Lina said. "Rosa, I have to stop this bleeding." Lina had clamped one strong hand over the farm boy's wrist and was looking around for anything that might help while she talked to the slow-witted farmer. "Doctor Whitber is on vacation. He's at his sister's farm outside Saint Louis. Thank your lucky stars it's not an artery." She shook her head, her short strawberry blond hair like a halo around her head, her voice curt, pointing to the nearest of the farmers. "Your belt. I need a belt."

"I don't got no belt," the man said, looking confused. "You see we just got on these farmer overalls." He pointed to his son on the floor; the kid looked like he was barely a teenager. "Damn fool boy. We stopped for a bit with our plowing to rest the horses. My boy, fool Peetie here, was sharpening the plow shears, and he spots an arrowhead in the dirt, that there field used to be a Sauk Indian camp right on that spot before God's people come to farm the land. So the boy-fool here

45

takes his mind off the job just for that long, them plow shears come down, now he's gonna lose a hand, and all for this dang thing right here." Willie was fingering a small light grey object, the offending Indian arrowhead.

"Maybe not," Lina was examining the wound, "Maybe he won't lose it. We'll do our best so that doesn't happen. Rosa. We need string…Butcher's string, maybe."

Rosa ran to the kitchen and returned with a ball of used string the size of a small pumpkin. She watched while her friend chewed off a foot long length and snugged it around the boy's bloody forearm.

"He doesn't look so good, Lina. Anything else I can do?" Rosa said. The boy's eyes were not focused and his skin was white as chalk.

"No, I don't think so, not for the moment. How long ago did this happen?" Lina said.

"We're from Richton Park. We're Weiss's. From the Weiss farm. We come by tractor, the Sauk Trail across McCoy bridge and through the woods."

"So 15 minutes?"

"Half hour, maybe," the bearded old farmer said. "We didn't stop or nothing. No, sir! We come right away, soon as we could, fast as our old McCormick could go.."

Willie Weiss, the slow one, had been watching Lina in open mouthed amazement, but when he spotted Lina's breakfast sitting deserted on a nearby table he sat down, picked up her fork and began shoveling in the eggs.

"You're lucky," Rosa said. "Hey, Lina – this guy's eating your food."

Willie started like he'd been bitten. "I ain't had no breakfast yet!"

"Well, those are not your eggs. This is a restaurant. You gotta pay for what you eat here."

"We ain't got no money."

Lina shook her head, "Let it go, Rosa."

Willie took the arrowhead and placed it solemnly in Rosa's hand. "This should pay for what I 'et. It be a very rare arrowhead," he said.

Old Man Weiss pawed a hand through his wild tangle of long grey beard like he might be shaking out bugs or straw. "You say we are lucky. But from what I can see a thing like this is looking real bad: How so could it be that we is lucky?"

Rosa took the plate of eggs to a nearby table with the simple-minded farmer after her like a barnyard chicken following a trail of bait. "You are lucky because Doc Whitber's old as dirt and his eyesight is not very good. With Lina here, there's a chance she can save your boy's hand.."

"Come on, now, this woman is no doctor," the oldest farmer looked skeptically at Lina. "She be just a young woman."

"She is a real doctor! And she's ten times the doctor that old bum Doctor Whitber ever will be. She served at the front in France. She's saved lives. Many, many lives!"

"I did not know anything about that. We heard about her at St. Ann's church. We heard she was just an ambulance driver."

"That is not true! The stupid generals wouldn't let her do her true calling. Said a woman couldn't

47

do a man's work. She did it anyway! The way it is, generals don't get much up to the front lines, so they never knew."

"Still…" The old farmer looked dubious.

Rosa heated up in defense of her friend. "You shut your mouth! You don't know nothing! It's \ this lady doctor right here gonna save this idiot-boy's hand," Rosa said.

"And I'm not that young," Lina added.

The teen's eyes fluttered and he shook his head. "Nobody is gonna take my hand," he said.

"No," she agreed. She spoke in a low voice to reassure him. "We are going to make sure of that. You will have lots of two handed planting and shucking left in your future on the farm."

Lina borrowed a red-and-white checkered table cloth and had the injured hand tightly bandaged by the time Frankie DeAngelo came in through the front door, waving his night stick like a baseball bat. "Alright, alright, where's the guilty criminal? Who parked a gul-danged tractor towing a farm wagon in the middle of the street?"

Willie raised his right arm like a wide-eyed second grader. "I done did that. Had to. We was in a hurry."

"This poor fellow cut his hand on a plow blade," Lina said.

Rosa sidled up to the young patrolman. "Frankie, sweetie, could you pretty please emergency drive this poor boy over to St. James Hospital in your paddy wagon?"

"I'm a cop, not a taxi man," Frankie said.

Rosa changed tactics. "Now Frankie," she said. "You want this man *to die*? What would your mama say?" She gave him *the look* and just like that he changed his mind and agreed to do it.

Lina smiled. Her pal was a force of nature; whatever it took, one way or the other, men never said no to Rosa Gambriotti.

A few hours later, Lina was manning the front reception desk in the doctor's office when Rosa came in with a steaming plate of *Eggs a la Gambriotti*.' Rosa, who was wearing a worn and frowsy housewife's dress and her waitress apron, set down the blue rimmed ironware plate in front of her friend. She took off the tin cover with a proud flourish. "Ta-daa! Late is better than never! See, we've got the delivery service! It's my new invention!"

"Oh, Rosa, you're always inventing something. I'm glad you showed up. I say praise *Dio* for the interruption! I've been going through Doc Whitber's mail. Mighty bor-r-ring!"

"He gets a pile of mail most every day," Rosa said. "We see the mailman drop it off from next door."

Lina shrugged and shook her head. "Well, there isn't anything at all important if you don't count the Doc's medicine business, and that comes in regular enough: See here, it looks like from the last few days we've got five new orders for Whitber's Original Cold & Aches Remedy and four envelopes with cash money for bottles he's already mailed out to steady customers."

"Well, it's a sure-fire remedy for what ails a body."

"He's a medicine man, for sure. Sometimes I wonder if there will be any actual doctoring to take over when he finally does kick the bucket."

"Don't count on him going to his reward any time soon," Rosa said. "The man's tough as an old oak tree."

"I shouldn't have said that," Lina said, "about him kicking the bucket. Lord forgive me." She crossed herself with the sign of the cross.

"I didn't know you Lutherans did the sign of the cross."

"I'm Protestant, sort of…one of those denominations, not sure which…my father kept switching us around. But even that, I've never been much for praying. The thing is, you see what happens in war, you'll try anything. Sign of the cross. Charm bracelets. Voodoo magic. Chants."

"Spit in your eye, hope to die?"

"Yeah, anything. Pray to the devil, even." She saw the way Rosa was eyeing her. "Well, maybe not that. You know, Rosa, I feel guilty the way I talk about old Doc Whitber, but sometimes the business of a woman trying to do medicine in a man's world gets to me. It's simply not fair. Not that I wasn't warned often enough."

"Who warned you?"

"Well, the first one was my father. Dear fusty, crusty dad – *the erudite old Doctor Bright.* My dad hated the idea of me going into medicine."

That started Lina thinking back to the earliest times she could remember, back when she was five; her mother had left her father without any warning (it was three days before he realized she was actually gone and three weeks before he would

50

admit it and three years when Lina showed him the Christmas card Mom had sent her postmarked from Kansas City).

"So then I can figure pretty safe she's probably not coming back to me?" he had said to his daughter, his comment really more a belated realization than a question.

"I don't think she is, Papa," she told him. Young Lina came to realize the bare truth was, after his wife left, the noble-looking but brittle Dr. Charles C. Bright, Professor and Head Surgeon at Columbia U in New York City, didn't have the slightest idea what to do with his young daughter.

With no other choice that he could think of, the somewhat bewildered intellectual in his expensive but outdated woolen vested suits hired a part time housecleaner lady and set Lina up in the back of his classroom with coloring books and a tin lunch box of assorted crayons. He also dragged her along to sit in a corner of his operating room, *You be quiet – you don't make a sound or you'll get a whupping on your fanny you'll never forget*! As the years went by, Lina learned to be increasingly grateful – single dads usually dropped their young children off at the nearest orphanage. In her case, she blossomed under her strange upbringing. Her young mind was a sponge, her lit curiosity burned to know more, she absorbed everything and forgot very little. And she had a knack for doctoring.

Their biggest argument came when she started leaving his class to sit in on other lectures. He yelled and made a big scene.

"You have to allow it," she said, a stubborn edge to her quavering voice. "You have to, or they will take me away."

"Who will?"

"The authorities. I have to go to school, it is a law."

She refused to give in, and they resolved the problem with a compromise; whenever she left, she had to sign where she was going, leaving a small note in the lower left hand corner of the blackboard, the corner nearest the door, something like "Lina, Rm 233, Latin" or Lina, Rm 317, Arith." Many of the courses were advanced, and once the rumor spread about the little Bright girl who wouldn't hear the word "no", the teachers would bring in beginners text books to get her started. She had strawberry blond hair cut short by some amateur, probably her dad, and she peered over the desk, looking at whoever her next teacher might be with a deceptively calm appraisal. Incredibly, in a week or two, she would be raising her hand and asking questions. Good questions, the right questions, the ones that showed she had absorbed the basics and knew what was going on.

Looking back, she had to give her father some credit for not simply deserting her, for not just dumping her off on a street corner somewhere, but at the same time, as a parent he didn't have a clue what a child's needs were. He was a brisk and busy guy; early on, he didn't pay attention when her crayons got used up and she asked for pencils (he did get her the pencils, but without any questions as to why she wanted them), and he shrugged when, later on, she started taking the tests with the rest of his students, never bothered to look at how she was doing. After all, she wasn't even ten years old. And he accepted the help when, after some years, she got up from her quiet corner in his operating room at the school hospital and started handing him the surgical instruments he asked for.

When she went to the Dean and demanded to take her finals (she was in her mid-teens), they had to let her be tested and when she aced everything – and actually did a few simple operations with her father hovering nearby – they had to grant her an M.D., even though, of course (they said to each other), she would know all the answers, she'd been in all their medical classes for a decade or more. Something of a joke, they said to each other, but some of them who had been there since she started were secretly proud: there she was, a product of their teaching skills. In the end, they had to graduate her and give her that precious M.D. There was a precedent for it at the university; all teachers' kids got free educations.

CHAPTER SIX

"Rosa, we need a little holiday," Lina said. "You and I need a break from our ordinary hum and drum, something to lift our spirits a little bit. I say we go on a frolic."

It was a lazy Saturday afternoon, Rosa's mom and dad were taking care of the café. The breakfast dishes were washed and a spicy white-meat chicken breast soup with early season carrots was bubbling for the evening offering. Rosa was easy to persuade, and as they left, Lina tacked a phone number to the front door of the doctor's office. It was the number for a local hair salon. *Call only in case of emergencies!*, she added under the number.

"We'll only be over on Dixie Highway," she told Rosa. "In case crooks steal all the spaghetti and meat balls and you have to make more."

"Chicken soup," Rosa said. "It's chicken noodle soup for dinner." Rosa shook her full head of curly black hair. "I don't know about this Trixie's Salon. I hear they try to persuade you to do the bob cuts, and that's plenty too short for me."

"Don't be an old lady, *Rosie Rosa*. Bobs are all the rage. Serious now: dear friend, you have to try it, Rosa. I can see you with short hair. You will look great."

"I don't know. How would I keep it in control?"

"Hey, lots easier than now. With your long hair, I'm always worried you're going to catch fire on the stove. You have beautiful curls – you cut them just a *skinch* shorter, then you control everything with a band. And you tie on a different ribbon for every mood. Come on, take the shot! We'll get you *the Bohemian Bob!*"

"Huh…that might be nice…I guess."

"It's gonna be great!"

"Here comes the dimbox." It was Rosa's birthday, and Lina had called a taxi to help celebrate the occasion. "Oh, oh, I forgot my doctor bag." She ran back into the office and picked up her emergency bag. On the way out, she passed a tall blond man who looked to be in his early thirties. He was dressed in the knickerbocker fashion, maybe a little too fashionable for the Hill, but (she told herself) it was a Saturday. She smiled at him as she rushed past, and he tipped his striped band wheat straw hat. In no time at all, she and Rosa were in the back of a battered old black Ford sedan with the word TAXI painted on the side in official looking letters. As they drove off, the well-dressed man gave them a tentative wave. Lina smiled and waved back.

"Who was that?" Rosa said.

"We've seen him around. It's that new guy from the boot. You should know better than me, you know everybody on the Hill."

"No, I don't think I've seen him."

"Old Doc says there is something odd about him. Weekends he dresses fine like he's loaded for money, but he works at the steel mill."

"Yeah, well maybe…I think I have seen some guy like him walk by sometimes or two. He never comes in to the café."

"Well, maybe someday he will."

55

Lina told the taxi driver where to take them, and they settled back for the ride, a real luxury as they didn't have many opportunities to get around town in an automobile, much less to be driven by their own driver.

"Talking about old Doc Whitber," Rosa grinned, "between us girls, how did you ever meet that old fartster?"

"After the war. On an ocean steamer. My father had died and I was on my way back to the States."

"Did he try to take you to bed?"

"Oh, sure. Yes, he did try. He was something of a joke in our circle."

"Your circle?"

"There was a group of us doctors and nurses, coming back to America on the same boat. That's the way the army did it, they tried to dump everybody together, buy a whole steamer, get a cheap price that way. We were pretty close in our circle, and everybody knew Whitber was a horny old man. He was a joke. We all said, *Old Whit never met a woman he didn't want to examine more closely.*"

"Was he ever married?"

"Mighty *Dio*, I don't think so."

"How come he never did?"

"Men are a puzzle. Anyway, who would have him?"

"You got that one right."

Talking with her pal Rosa about her return trip to the States set Lina thinking back to that unsettled time in her life after the armistice. She had bumped into Dr. Whitber late one evening about half way on their trip across the Atlantic. He was drunk and she was still in her Red Cross uniform and he pawed at her a little before offering her a job as his 'assistant doctor' in the town of Chicago Heights, which he said was bustling with new industry and manufacturing plants. While that was true enough, the reality of the job he offered her set in too late; she was in town, set up a few days in his office as his assistant when she realized her real responsibility was to keep his schedule, to help with his booming mail order medical syrup business, and to hand him instruments when he fumbled through his minor operations. Since he wouldn't let her attempt anything even slightly challenging, she tried her best to persuade him to send his difficult cases to Saint James Hospital located a short way north across Chicago Heights near Lincoln Highway.

Lina shook her head, looking at her friend. "You know, Rosa, the way I see it, Old Doc Whitber is just another one of the doubters. He was hoping he would get into my pants, and he never thought I would turn out to be much help in his office beyond keeping his schedule. I took him up on his offer and he was stuck with me. But now – with his tremors getting worse every month – he's getting called on less and less to handle anything more than looking down sore throats and prescribing salve for insect bites and poison ivy. Problem is,. I don't know how long my job here is going to last. He should have turned in his stethoscope years ago. Really, the only thing he has going is his mail order dope medicine trade."

"Everybody likes a good slug of Doc Whitber's Magic Medicine."

"Yeah. Right. Opium magic. And I keep telling myself *Better days are coming.* But, you know, in the back of my mind I can still hear my dad laughing at me, saying things like, *I told you, my little wanna-be doctor, you would have made a good housewife.*"

"That is a really mean thing to say! What was wrong with him?"

"Rosa, I'm sure he blamed me for mom leaving him. And for me not being born a boy."

"Well, *shinola crapola*, blame the kid! Like any of that's your fault?"

"Right. But that's the way some men see it. Think about it, Rosa. How was I supposed to tell him that? There are times I doubted I was even his kid. Even today I still wonder: was it some smooth talking vacuum cleaner salesman from New Jersey – some fellow with the oil-slick hair – who swept Mom off her feet?"

"You think so?"

"Oh, Rosa, I don't really know. I was too young. Maybe, more like, it was some literature professor who got Mom to drop her pants for the sweet language of love."

Lina's dad had made clear his disappointment, had told her exactly how she'd failed him, barked at her so many times over the years, and he repeated his feelings one final time in a brief note to her, mailed a few days before he was fatally struck by a double decker bus in downtown London. *Lina*, he wrote, *Your sole assignment in life is to furnish me a grandson who will grow to become a great surgeon and carry on my legacy. So far, you have failed. Old age has got me now – too late for me, but there's still time for you. Get going! Don't let me down! Get me that grandson to carry on my legacy! Love, your loving Dad.*

Lina told herself she had to put those old, sad thoughts out of her mind. It was Rosa's birthday and LinLinaa's plan was to talk her friend into trying the new short-hair flapper look that was all the rage. Time to go forward, to get on with life!

CHAPTER SEVEN

Francesco Monafusti knew he didn't have a soul. His papa angrily gave him the bad news – shouted it at him in a furious rage – when Monafusti was just a kid, and of course, being who he was, Francesco told himself he didn't really give *un'oncia di merda* one way or the other.

"You are not a normal human being," the dad said.

"And you are not my real dad," Monafusti said. "You adopted me because you had weak loins."

"You are right," the dad agreed, his attitude stiffening at the insult. "But that was after you had been returned to the orphanage three times. Your cursed mother was too soft-hearted. If we'd had a brain in our heads between us, we would have sent you back, too."

This was after Monafusti had disemboweled the family dog, Gnarli, who had been pestering him for a walk through the streets of Naples late one afternoon when it was cold and raining. And also before the lad was expelled from the Nunziatella Military Academy of Naples, a difficult feat to accomplish because his father was headmaster of the place. You can imagine what it had taken to bring the dad to finally have to inflict that punishment, a disgrace to himself and the entire family as well.

"You have no soul," the older man said. "You have glass eyes – do you know what that means? You don't care about life, about living creatures.

No actual human person kills their own dog for no reason."

Monafusti gave his dad a piercing look. "For me, reason enough that he annoyed me. He was only a dog. End of story, papa."

The pet dog slaying was in 1890. Francesco was ten years old at the time. He had wiped his blade clean and tossed out the bloody bedsheet, but his damnable brother caught him dragging Gnarli's corpse out the back door to bury it in the neighbor's small orchard. Francesco had the sword in the first place because sabre training was a course at school, and he'd permanently borrowed his personal weapon and brought it home, hiding it behind a loose board in the floor of his clothes closet. It took some years, but of course he made the damnable brother pay. The clumsy fellow fell off a second story roof, crippled for life. Terrible accident. *Too bad.* The brother, justly afraid for his life, said nothing. His dad, not totally convinced of Francesco's innocence, signed him up with the French Foreign Legion. That lasted a few years, long enough for Monafusti to gain the dubious nickname *The Ice Pick Killer* before he was thrown out of the service for his inability to obey orders. He came home, but only a few months later the dad suffered an unfortunate fatal accident, somehow falling in front of an electric train.

On his own, Francesco migrated from Naples to Rome in 1911, where in his early thirties he taught fencing lessons and hand-to-hand combat to wealthy men's sons, and picked up freelance *soldier of fortune* assignments when they became available. It was early June and fencing school was out for the summer and so, otherwise unemployed, Monafusti was hanging out at the Café Greco, and offering the graces of a beautiful raven haired young teenager named Sarafina Janika to unwitting gentleman travelers seeking comfort in a bustling urban environment far away from their homes. He and Sarafina had met a few days before and already knew all the necessary details about each other. At least, Francesco had decided that was the way it was going to be. It would be a few more days before she changed his mind.

"So, Monafusti is not your real name?" she said.

"So what? Janika is not yours."

That ended the conversation. Truth was, he had made up his name some time ago because it pleased him, in his mind's eye, *Mona* meaning 'the one' and *fusti* meaning 'powerful fist'. Something like that. But he wasn't going to reveal that to a teenage know-nothing street slut. Or to anybody else, for that matter. The silence between them might have gone on for a while, but two young hunkers from Hungary or Slovenia (someplace like that) came trolling by and they gave her the eye and in no time at all Francesco had her gainfully employed for the evening.

It turned out he had underestimated her. She left the two tourists in their hotel room, sexually sated and lying on the same bed where they'd taken their pleasure, stirring about in a drunken and drugged semi-stupor. She hired a carriage and returned to the café for Monafusti, bidding him to get at it – for God's sake, if he was half the man he claimed to be – to do the rough-up job so they could pick the *foreign hicks* clean. And that led to an off-and-on relationship that had benefitted them both over the next decade.

CHAPTER EIGHT

Before dawn on a Sunday morning Anselmo woke with a start. The steam heat had gone off in the Victoria Hotel after midnight with a few last clanks from the radiator, and, Spring weather being what it was in Northern Illinois, his room was chilly. Grey dawn light was showing through the curtains in the single window that looked out on the back alley. He felt feverish and lonely. He sat on the edge of his bed, knowing he would not be able to go back to sleep. He got up and did his daily dozen, the military exercises he had learned in the Italian army.

He put on some loose exercise clothes and went for a run through the quiet streets of Chicago Heights, running up the street to the new Lincoln Moving Pictures Theater. A poster said they were featuring The Sheik, starring Rudolph Valentino. Anselmo shrugged mentally, wondering what women could possibly see in a soft-eyed desert man who lived in a tent and probably had fleas and ticks all over his body. He dismissed the motion picture as silly, if not impractical, and moved on down the street. While he jogged, he began thinking back to the all-important meeting he'd had with his grandfather a few months before he was to travel to America. It had been a pleasant day, a late afternoon in autumn. The vineyard workers were busy with the harvest in the lower acres, the sound of their singing and laughter drifting up the Hill, "*O sole, o sole mio, Sta 'nfronte a te!*". At the turn of the century, Anselmo's grandfather, Giacomo I, had been a successful financial advisor in Rome. He had retired at the right moment before World War I and, fearing the foolishness of the Italian government and worried about the perilous political times in Europe, had stowed the bulk of his fortune in Swiss banks and bought a winery and a hazelnut orchard in Northern Italy near the town of Alba (close to the larger town of Turin at the foot of the southern Alps). He still lived in a dank (but much loved) medieval house that came with the property. Now in his early eighties, his favorite pastime was walking Bacio, his prized Italian water dog, to hunt the precious white truffles the fields around Alba were known for. But the reason he had called for his grandson was – once again – a matter of preservation of the family honor.

As they walked between two straight lines of trees with branches now free of their harvest of hazelnuts, the brown, curly haired Bacio snuffled around the tree trunks and the old man complained bitterly about Anselmo's father. "I know it is unfair and certainly not the truth, but the *commandante* continues to speak negatively to your father of you, and your father has had the bad judgment to believe him.."

"I did no cowardly act."

"They say you disobeyed a direct order."

"That is not true. I was moving forward slowly to protect my men. But there was nothing I could do to save them. Commandante Fresnogari denies to this day he sounded a horn that caused an avalanche that killed my men.

"You are blamed for everything."

"I deny it. But I am here as you request."

The old man held him by the shoulders with both hands and looked into his eyes. "Antonio, I believe you. But the *commandante,* through his lies, continues to darken our family name."

"I know, *Nonno*...you explain it every time."

"Just this one last time, Antonio. For me; for our family name. Just this one last time."

"I will do as you wish, and with no reservations. War is not just. We do what we can to make amends." Anselmo loved his grandfather, and in truth would say yes, no matter how many times he was asked. "But you have your contacts with the military. Do they say anything more about my brother's death? Have you found out anything more? We both know, had he not died, none of this would have happened."

"We don't know that, not for sure."

"Well, I am convinced of it. I know it in my heart. My brother was a natural military man. He was a leader. Had he lived, had it been him up there on the mountain instead of me, I'm sure he would have saved all of our troopers."

At the heart of their involvement in the war, Anselmo's father, Giacomo II, had been a hawkish war lover, eager to see Italy victorious and prosperous. At the start of the conflict, he had ordered Giacomo III, Anselmo's older brother, to join the Italian army. But shortly after Giocomo III left for the front, in the days prior to actual combat, he had somehow been killed with a bullet to the heart. And even a half dozen years after the war's end, just how that had happened remained a mystery.

"No. They tell me nothing," the grandfather said. "To this day we do not know anything more than I have told you."

"You know I left the university after he was killed," Anselmo said. "I did it willingly. The military wasn't my calling, but it was my duty and to this day I do not regret my decision. But it grieves my heart that we have no explanations for my brother's death."

"I know you did your best as a soldier. But it is so troubling. Your brother, killed with a bullet to the heart! That family tragedy will always be on your father's conscience – not yours! The deepest truth is, I believe it was entirely your father's fault. Your brother was undecided about the war, and he never did agree to go on his own, and I was against it. Your father volunteered his son – pushed him into volunteering, and, in so doing that, gambled the future of this entire family – sacrificed his life to a fool's war. He encouraged your brother to go – no, he *commanded* him to go! I had no granddaughters, only you two grandsons, and I was very reluctant to let him go. But your father went behind my back and forced him to enlist while I was out of the country. And I was right – look what happened! We lost one of my grandsons to the war! We also gave a small fortune to finance our cavalry company. For what? For nothing."

"I thought it was you who sponsored our army unit."

"*Si.* At the time, fool that I was, I believed it was the way to keep *Numero III* safe from harm."

Anselmo asked again the question he'd asked over a dozen times without a satisfactory answer.

"*Nonno*…what do you personally think happened to my brother? Please, what do you know? Surely, at some point, you must have heard something from the military. How did he actually die?"

Yet still, this time, the answer from his grandfather was no different: There were tears in the old man's eyes, but no comfort in his words. "Antonio, I hold nothing from you. No one knows for sure. At least, no one is saying anything to me. Maybe we will never know. One moment he is wearing his splendid uniform and rushing off to war – the very next week we get notice, and then his body in a box for burial in the family cemetery."

"But what do you think?"

"You will think me crazy, but my suspicion is it has nothing to do with the war."

"What? How can that be?"

"We are a wealthy family…you get old like me, you suspect everybody."

Anselmo himself felt suspicious of the circumstances surrounding his brother's death.

He had been the one sent to transport the body back from the war. "I do know he was twenty kilometers behind the lines when he was killed," he said. "And there was no enemy engagement. I have no explanation for it."

"None was ever given to us," the grandfather said, now openly weeping.

One thing Anthony Anselmo knew that he had never told anyone, and particularly not his beloved grandfather. He had opened the casket, had examined his brother's dead body. And he knew something that no one else in his family did: His brother had been shot in the back, and from the burn marks on his uniform around the wound area, he was shot at close range. His brother had been murdered. Knowing that, Anselmo also felt the eyes of the world were on him – and so he had left the scholarly life and signed up to fill his brother's empty boots.

And then the war had gone on and on, and once it was finally over, his father, Giacomo II, the one the old man called *Numero Due*, used what he could squeeze of the family wealth from Anselmo's grandfather and went on to make a name for himself building a garment company in Rome. At least on the surface he seemed to do well, though was obvious he was trying to be even more of a success than the old man. The father openly and publicly mourned the loss of his own eldest – and favorite – son, but he didn't care about family honor the way Anselmo's grandfather did. Anselmo's father was all about profits, and if he'd had his way he would by now have gained total control and be running everything in the family finances. But to a large extent, in spite of everything he had tried in his behind the scenes efforts to take over, the clever old grandfather still controlled the orchards and the vineyards – and had control of the money tucked away in Swiss banks that was the bulk of the family fortune.

Anselmo had hoped to dissuade his grandfather from giving him this last assignment, hoping they could agree to declare the War to End All Wars was finally behind them both for good. "Can't we agree that the war is over, *Nonno*? Our commitment is in the past, a part of history. Our army unit is disbanded and disgraced. Our troopers are retired or dead, every one. It was a terrible venture in a bad war; our campaigns were poorly thought out by incompetent generals and they were conducted by an inexperienced *commandante*. We were unlucky and out-gunned and out-maneuvered over and again, but none of that was our family disgrace – as some people who were not there have claimed. I was there. I know. And it is all in the past now."

"Almost," Giacomo I said. "But please, Antonio. Yet this one more act remains. You must help me."

At the beginning of World War I, filled with equal amounts of national pride and fear of the Germans to the northeast, the grandfather, pushed by Giacomo II, had (in spite of his own misgivings) funded his own army unit, The Golden Cavalry Company, one third of a battalion in the Italian military. This venture – men and horses – had gone to fight in the mountains to the north, and their expedition had ended in disaster. In his own heart, Anselmo still believed that the family should have hesitated, should have considered more carefully the dread things that might happen before recruiting their own company of young men to be soldiers. They should have read the signs, should have been warned off when his older brother was shot dead at the very outset, but – filled with angry pride – they went forward. Maybe it was, as an old priest friend of the family had declared, the fate of the Anselmo clan. Or maybe it was just the arbitrary fortunes of war, but – no matter what the reasons were – it ended in a series of terrible blunders and many Italian soldiers had died.

The old man took hold of Anselmo's arm and looked to the north, staring with his ancient eyes at the distant Alps, beautiful with their cover of snow. He was thinking back to the disasters that had befallen their family in the so-called Great War. "I made a vow then and I keep that vow now; to make right as I can for every man who served in our unit."

"And you kept that vow. I have been to many places at your request, consoling so many widows and their children in our name."

"Yes, you have – and no, we are not yet made whole. Almost finished, but no. There is this one more wrong to be righted, and then maybe I can rest my guilty soul. And you must help me. Please, for me, Antonio."

Anselmo listened with a sinking heart. Since the war, when not supervising the tending to their vineyards and orchards with his grandfather, he had traveled throughout Italy, stopping in many towns and villages to make small payments to ease the guilt of this beloved grandfather of his. And now he was being asked to give up his own attempt at a quiet life of forgetting, to go abroad to smooth over one remaining scar, this time to travel to the heartlands of far-away America. One last time, to relive again the horror of his own battle experiences and correct this one last wrong, and this the one death that cut closest to his own heart. His grandfather assured him everything had been arranged; the funding, the tickets for his passage through the Mediterranean and across the Atlantic, money for expenses, a little set aside for extravagances, follies along the way. Anselmo sighed and listened, and then nodded and agreed he would go.

CHAPTER NINE

What happened next, as Anselmo set about to journey through the Mediterranean and across the Atlantic, seemed a little disorganized or maybe even odd. It certainly was out of the ordinary and unexpected. A few months after the Christmas Holidays, as he was preparing to leave for America, a man on a bicycle stopped off at his grandfather's villa with a telegraph message from his father's office, MEET ME ROME BEFORE YOU GO USA. This was in mid-March and Anselmo had already nearly finished packing his steamer trunk and was preparing to carriage west to board an ocean going ship that would be leaving from the Ponte de Mille in Genoa. He'd already sent his trunk on ahead to Chicago, on its way to the far-away heart of the United States; but, instead of walking up the gangplank, Anselmo changed his plans and caught a train south to meet his father.

However, when he showed up at the Futura offices in Rome, there had been some sort of mix up and his father wasn't there. In fact, he wasn't even in Italy. His executive assistant, Sarafina Janika, seemed flustered and unaware of what was happening. This was odd for her, as she was close to his father and seemed to know everything that was going on. She apologized. "Your father is attending a conference in Berlin. Totally unexpected, but very important to the future of the company. I'm sorry for the misunderstanding, but I can make it right for you. Don't worry, I can fix everything." In a flurry of activity she arranged upper class tickets and passage on an ocean liner leaving from Napoli the very next day. "If you hurry," she assured him, "you can just make it." He thanked her and politely said he accepted her kindness.

That plan changed that evening when, over coffee in the Café Greco in Rome, he heard that Jules Massenet's opera Amadis de Gaula was opening in Monaco. Massenet had been a favorite of his mother's, who had dragged him to over thirty of his operas. Massenet had passed to his reward nearly a decade before, but Amadis de Gaula was being presented for the first time, at the Opera De Monte-Carlo at the casino.

And then he was met with a smallish but odd coincidence (and, since the war, he didn't believe in coincidences): When Anselmo went to the travel agency to turn in his ocean liner tickets, he noticed a man he'd seen before at Futura Industries. The fellow was sitting in the lounge area, apparently waiting for someone or something. He was in his mid-forties, in good physical shape with the distinguishing facial features of a big handlebar moustache, and a small, neat (even undersized in comparison with his huge *mustachios*) Van Dyke beard. The man was wearing a Monsignor's robe, black with red trim, but Anselmo recognized it was the same man he'd seen talking with his father's executive secretary. Then, the man had been wearing a fine Italian suit, but Anselmo was sure it was the same fellow. For feelings that had no logical explanation, Anselmo turned around and quietly left without turning in his ticket.

He went to Monaco without incident, and the performance of Amadis de Gaula turned out to be typical Massenet, a romance featuring a Spanish knight and the usual boom, fluff and bother of romantic operas. After an evening of reflecting with old school fellows, instead of boarding a later passage out of Napoli, Anselmo took a train from Monaco to Genoa and, following his original travel plan, booked a steamer out of Ponte de Mille. His father was a wealthy man and shouldn't even notice his finances had been nicked with an upper class sailing ship ticket that was never used.

Now, chugging his way back to the Victoria Hotel in Chicago Heights, a half a world away from his home in Northern Italy, Anselmo recognized an irony in his situation, and also the justice being doled out to him by the Almighty *Dio*: In his younger days he had enjoyed an easy life; he had been educated at the finest schools in Switzerland and England. He had studied literature and art, had trained in fencing and boxing and equestrian sports, had even learned to drive an automobile and several times flown in a double-winged airplane, himself at the controls (even though the actual pilot was carefully monitoring from his own cockpit behind him).

There lingered in Anselmo's mind and heart what he recognized as an overriding guilt, not only for his deeds in the war (he had killed more than one soldier), but, in the final analysis, he was – *per grazia di Dio* – alive, while his beloved brother had been taken down with what everyone said could only have been an unlucky shot to the heart, and as a result was now in his grave.

Anselmo returned to his room, gathered his shaving gear, left his hotel room and walked down the hallway to bathe and get a clean shave. The Victoria Hotel had its own small café; they would be serving Midwestern style American breakfast, probably thick beef steaks and fried chicken eggs on a big blue rimmed ironware plate, and he was hungry.

While he shaved, he thought over the assignment his beloved *nonno*, his grandfather, had given him, and some unbidden images from his war times once again churned up in his memory. Once again he was back in the Italian Alps, and it was on a dark and stormy pre-dawn morning in the Spring.

Horses gone in the avalanche, his company in tatters, over the next weeks, Anselmo and what was left of his unit joined forces with other Italian troopers and dug positions in the ice cold stony ground. What he remembered most vividly of this new phase was the freezing cold, the lingering faint smell of mustard gas, the clinging rotten smell of dead bodies, and the bone jarring blast of artillery shells going off nearby.

And Anselmo remembered the day when there came that one mortar attack that changed everything; he recalled every detail, the horror of the screaming wounded and the pitiful wails of the dying. And he remembered his young American friend Ralphie, the one they called *quello stupido Americano,* remembered Ralphie maimed and already doomed to his cruel fate, with nothing but the stumps of bloody bones left to him below his waist. Poor shattered Ralphie, stunned but aware, looking into Anselmo's eyes, into his very soul, and begging him for death.

Anselmo rubbed his hands over his face, felt the stubble of a three days old beard. He was trying to hang on to his sanity, to realize *he was here and not there*. He knew they did not care down at the steel mill if you shaved or not. But Anselmo didn't like anything about letting himself go – he would not allow himself to become an unweeded garden. This man he saw in the mirror wasn't the person he wanted to be.

Sunday, he thought, and he felt his heart beat slow down as he moved his mind away from those bitter war images. It was Sunday. He was in Illinois, in the United States of America. No mortars. No chlorine or mustard gas. No unlucky rifle shots to the heart. He was safe here. He returned to his room with a freshly shaven face and only a few nicks on one cheek. He retrieved his worn cavalry boots from his steamer trunk, then decided to go casual. He replaced the boots with a two tone pair of loafers that had been a rage a year before in Turin. He chose light brown knee length socks and tan knickerbockers, a long sleeve tan shirt, and he decided he would go with a light wool sleeveless sweater over that. The clothes were wrinkled from the trip across the Atlantic and smelled faintly of moth balls. He shook them out and smoothed them on the bed as best he could. They would have to do.

He found a checkered maroon and tan tie his mother had given him at a long-ago Christmas in that time before the war when he was a young student, home from the academy in Switzerland for the holidays. He fingered the silvery, small caliber revolver his mother had also given him, decided to leave it behind. Don't be silly, he told himself, this was no upcoming battle, he was only going to the Victoria Café for breakfast, and then maybe on to Mass at San Rocco over on Hungry Hill, the church where the Italian community worshipped. He carefully double-locked his heavy trunk, made of tin metal and wood slats to travel anywhere in the world. He topped himself off with a soft light brown tweed race car driver cap. Then he locked the door to his small third floor room and took the back steps two at a time to the side street. He decided to skip breakfast at the café. He would walk out to the front of the hotel to catch a trolley ride. And luck was with him; the trolley car the locals called the Dinky, the one headed for Hungry Hill, was just pulling up when he got there.

CHAPTER TEN

At San Rocco's, the eight o'clock Mass was already out, Italian families walking back home, kids frisking about, parents in their Sunday go-to-church clothes calling to each other, friendly chatter and lots of kidding around. A giggling bunch of dark-haired girls bubbled on past Anselmo, giving him the once-over, full of playful *ou la las* and saucy I-dare-you looks as they passed in their own carefree little group. A happy day ahead for them: Sunday Mass was over, no school, an afternoon to look forward to. Anselmo wondered if he had gotten himself up a little too fancy for the occasion, but there were several other men dressed as he was, perhaps without silk ties and with suit coats rather than his wool sweater, but still, maybe about the same look. He wondered if the checkered pattern on his tie conflicted with the squares on his sweater, but then he gave up on that sort of thinking. He didn't pay much attention to his own fashion statement, never bothered to consider he even had one.

Anselmo liked being outside; the fresh air off Lake Michigan and the people on the busy street reminded him of the citizens of Turin, out for a walk on a Sunday morning, and the cool Spring breeze was like the one off the Mediterranean. This Chicago Heights was a half a world away from Northern Italy, a late April morning in Northern Illinois, but he could see why the Italians who settled here liked it. He gazed at the puffy white clouds with their light grey bottoms that were making their way south thirty miles from the tip end of Lake Michigan; one of the locals had pointed out clouds like that, told him they held the promise of showers in the early afternoon. *So much like Turin!* If the winters were only a little warmer, if only they grew grapes here, if only he could forget the war!

The Italians of Hungry Hill seemed mostly friendly, accepting Anselmo as one of their own. He made his way past a half dozen pleasant *Buongiornos* and *Bella giornatas* toward the crowd still lingering around the church steps. He could see his European outfit was a touch formal. He needed a more casual look. It was the best he had of the clothes he'd brought with him on the boat and so it would have to be okay until he could do a little shopping. As he passed Rosa's restaurant there had been a sign hung on the front door, *Back After 8:00 Mass*. Another block and a half walk and he was mingling with the after Mass crowd at the base of the steps of the church.

Young Brother Paulo shifted his weight impatiently from left foot to right and back again. He stood at the top of the stairs outside the open front door of San Rocco, feeling impatient that he had to be there saying polite replies to the compliments on the altar decorations – one of his many jobs was furnishing flowers for the big side baskets next to the main altar – when all he wanted to be doing at that moment was talking with Rosa. Standing solid as a rock next to him, a newly assigned priest, the cold and somewhat mysterious Monsignor Monafusti. The Monsignor was looking trim in his red trimmed black robe, and, as usual, saying nothing to anybody, particularly not to the parishioners, who he seemed to feel were beneath his stature. Of the small squad of San Rocco priests – mostly Irish – the Monsignor was the newcomer who gave Brother Paulo a bad taste in his mouth. Paulo wasn't sure why. On the one hand, it made no sense to have Irish priests at a church with an Italian flock, and yet they seemed to fit in. But for some reason – and Paulo for the life of him couldn't figure any sane reason – the Monsignor was far more alienated from the flock than the Irish – and yet in physical appearance he looked like he could be Italian, though it was hard to be sure about anything with him. The man clearly looked down on Italians as inferior – *you could see it in the expression on his face* – and yet he himself had something of an Italian name. And with the olive cast to his skin and that hook nose, he looked *Italiano*…or maybe *dal Portogallo* or *dalla Spagna*. You couldn't tell from his speech. Another odd thing – he never said Mass. He did confessions, but Paolo knew priests were supposed to conduct the Mass, and their new Monsignor never did. What a puzzle he was!

When Monsignor Monafusti said anything to anybody, to the locals he sounded like a foreigner, no matter what language he spoke. A few weeks before, the ever-curious young Paulo had casually asked him about that and was rewarded with a bleak and suspicious stare, "My father was a Vatican ambassador. I grew up many places, and I never had a home I could call my own."

This didn't sound right to Paulo. "I didn't know the Vatican had ambassadors."

"And there is so much in the real world that you do not know," the Monsignor said.

That ended the conversation, with Brother Paulo knowing as little as anyone else about the stiff mannered and secretive new priest. And one other thing; the man wasn't as old as he pretended. Paulo had seen him practicing gymnastic movements with his cane. He was agile, quick like a spider, and he didn't move at all like an old man.

Anselmo, of course, had spotted the man in the Monsignor's black robe with the red trim. And the first things that swarmed into his mind were *The man is no Monsignor. The man is a fake!* And then the realization blossomed in his mind, *This Monsignor was only here because he, Antonio Anselmo, was here.* Anselmo didn't know exactly what was happening or why, but that was the only explanation that made any sense. *There were no coincidences.* Had his father sent mustachio man to keep track of him? If so, why would he do that? Or was it entirely something else?

Paulo saw Rosa right away. He could read her like an open book. She was his old pal from as far back as he could remember, and to him she was looking sad and vulnerable in widow's black. He caught the gleam of the silver cross around her neck, a simple gift he'd given her mostly as a joke when they'd graduated from eighth grade. He was struck yet again by how young she was, how young they both were, how life moved on too fast and – the tragedy of it! – already he'd missed his chance to have a life with her. If only her parents hadn't been so eager to get her out of the house! If only he and Rosa had followed their crazy dreams and run away together. If only, if only, if only! But no, she'd given in to the family pressure and married this Ralphie *testa del pene*, a guy no older than Paulo that they had imported from Rome! And then the *bastardo* got here, got married to Rosa and turned around and ran back to Italy to defend the motherland! So that was the way of it, the way it had been for them. It made him angry: Little girls married men their parents dictated, sometimes they were rich old men and sometimes boys who had great promise of inheritance. (Ralphie had not been rich, but they didn't know that until later) And, as it happened to Rosa and Ralphie, sometimes these stupid, idealistic boys who were not yet men ran away to fight wars, and sometimes they were unlucky and died before they got to live out the story of their lives. Not that Paulo felt sorry for Ralphie, the stupid *idioto*. If anything, Paulo thought with more than a little bitterness, he was feeling sorry for himself. Monsignor Monafusti frowned and nudged him with his elbow, his rude gesture saying *Get out there, boy, mingle with the sheep.*

Anselmo stood a few steps apart from the crowd, wondering how to approach Rosa Gambriotti. He wanted to talk to her alone, but Rosa seemed never to be alone. Right next to her, linked arm in arm, was her friend Lina Bright, Lina taller by a few inches, standing out from the crowd with her level blue eyed gaze, her face framed by her short, strawberry blond hair, newly cut in the flapper look that was all the current rage.

Anselmo found himself watching Lina, who was maybe five years older than Rosa, half way between Rosa and his own age. *What a lovely girl!* Woman, really. He found he was more than a little enamored, unconsciously attracted to the graceful way about her, her confident composure. He'd heard she'd been in the Red Cross in Europe during the war. Maybe a nurse or a doctor, though the latter seemed doubtful. From the little he knew, there was no room for women doctors in that horror of seared lungs and blasted flesh, and the years didn't work out, she'd have been too young, something like a child doctor. He'd met no women doctors at all at his front in the Alps. But, he reminded himself, he could be wrong. Women had powers all their own, and intellect, and grace under pressure. He'd loved his mother, had always seen her as the power behind his father's throne, while she was alive the force that kept his dad from falling off the trolley tracks. His mother had been a woman of social graces, charm, wit, and intellectual resource. Many women, he knew, had unexpected strengths. Maybe Lina had them, too. Maybe, if he was lucky, he might find out.

The clouds drifted apart for a moment, and bright morning sunlight struck the two young women, one with raven dark hair and olive skin, the other all gold and pink, both beautiful, each in her own way. Whether Rosa was alone or not, Anselmo decided it was time to make his introductions and get on with his assignment, but then he saw young Brother Paulo was frowning down at him from the church steps, and he wondered how much the parish priests had been informed about him. That might be something to consider; back in Italy, there were whispers and harsh opinions about what he had done during his time in the mountains on the border between Northern Italy and in *the land of the Huns*, lies told and judgments formed by both military men and by men of God who had not been there, chubby middle-aged *uomini militari* and *uomini di Dio* who had been comfortable in their own bases and rectories far from the terrible unpredictability of the wind driven poison gasses, hundreds of miles from the bone jarring shock of the exploding shells and the cutting wails of raw youth dying before their time. Someone from the Old Country, maybe some enemy of his father or grandfather, could well have sent some damning comments across the ocean to Chicago Heights. Maybe it was the mustachioed Monsignor who kept showing up in unexpected places. Anselmo could feel the possibilities in his bones; the holy men of San Rocco were watching him.

And yet he knew that above all he had to talk to Rosa Gambriotti; he had been commissioned by his grandfather, and had traveled half way around the world to see her and to pay the family debt. Still, it wasn't Anselmo's way to make easy accord with strangers, particularly not since the war. He'd seen much of the casual evil that men could do to men with innuendo and false conclusions. He was finding the Italians of Hungry Hill, though friendly, were a tight community and he had no idea exactly how to approach Rosa Gambriotti and discharge his responsibility. No, closer to the truth, he admitted to himself that he was actually afraid, fearful to look back into that time in his life and open that old can of *serpenti* for the world to see and to yet again pass damning judgment on him. He felt he truly was an outcast, expelled from the Catholic church for sure, and probably from the good graces and the approval of mankind as well.

Looking down at his parishioners from the top step outside the big church door, Brother Paulo was having his own problems. He found he was yet again struggling against what he had come to think of as his *sins of the flesh*. The truth he couldn't admit to himself was, he was losing the battle to fight off his strong attraction to his old pal, now the Widow Rosa. He lived with a bitter awareness that his feelings for her were unhealthy for his vows of celibacy, his commitment to *Gesu Christi. It was unfair!* When he and Rosa were growing up, he figured they were close pals – nothing more – but once she was lost to him, he could see there had been so much more. Now, too late, he knew in his soul that she had been fated to be his life-companion, and he was starving to take what little he could get of her, even if it was only on the fringes of his life. Simply put, he really was in love with her. Love all the way, true love, real love, eternal love. If she would only come to church service without that ever-present girlfriend of hers, maybe he could talk more with her about this or that, nothing serious, just to stay friends like the old days. And, boy, was he glad he hadn't taken those final vows tying himself forever to *Gesu*!

Paulo wondered what Rosa and Lina had thought of today's sermon, the typical Irish priestly warning against short skirts, short hair and the evil temptations and loose morality of the jazz music of Louis Armstrong and his kind. Lina was more worldly than Rosa and he worried about her influence on his friend. Paulo was thinking to make his way down the steps and to wander over in their direction when he became aware of the tall stranger from Italy with his lean aristocratic face and light hair – the man had been looking in Rosa's direction and now was looking directly at him! The rectory had received a brief and puzzling telegram from a high ranking Italian army officer warning them to keep a watchful eye on this man, and yet here he was with his fancy knickerbockers and expensive sweater, his obvious attention on the young widow Gambriotti and for sure the man was up to no good! Paulo felt he had every reason in the world to be suspicious. An inquiry of his own through a pal of his at the diocese headquarters had revealed this *man from the boot* was reported to be a renegade Catholic, a drop-out from the church who had joined the Italian cavalry as an officer in charge of his own company. And his unit had been wiped out, practically to the last man. Yet he, himself, had somehow survived. *Was that not a sign of cowardly behavior?!* There was even some foul business beyond that, something they said Anselmo's rich patriarch of a grandfather was able to cover up. *Something, but what?*

Brother Paulo had hoped to bar the man from attending services at San Rocco, but he'd talked the matter over with the Monsignor, and the man had given him a sharp glance and directed him to be cautious, though he wouldn't say exactly why. Something to the notion that Anthony Anselmo was from a family of such great influence that Rome – far away as the Vatican was – still was having a say in this matter, whatever it was.

"What would you have us do?" the Monsignor had said to Paulo. "He does not enter the confessional. He does not come to the altar for communion. He asks for nothing; so what can we refuse him?"

Brother Paulo kept his eye on *the menace from the boot*, and what he saw agitated him even more. Anselmo had shifted his attention back to the widow Rosa and that friend of hers, Doc Whitber's girl Friday, Doctor Lina Bright. *Sangre sacro*, what was going on?

The Monsignor nudged Paulo again, the man of many secrets, more aware and possibly knowing more than Paulo would have thought. "He is probably a murderer," the Monsignor said. "No, do not look at me that way; it is very possible. A vile and evil man exiled to this course-mannered, remote colony in the United States for his unforgivable sins. *Un assassin. Dio il Padre* damns him to hell forever."

And yet, in spite of the damning things the Monsignor was saying, Paulo had the feeling that the mysterious man with the red-trimmed robe wanted to keep himself hidden in the background. He had the impression Monsignor Monafusti did not want Anthony Anselmo to see him or to know that he was being watched.

CHAPTER ELEVEN

Five o'clock Monday morning at the Inland Steel mill: Anselmo met Louie exactly on time for their first day partnering together on the day shift. Louie was wearing the same red wool shirt, washed clean without last week's stains under the arms, and his old army uniform tan colored pants, bought from some thrift shop, again held up with the faded yellow suspenders.

"There's a trouble on station one," Louie said. "Come on, I'll show you what to do. Same like always, the fat evil rail, she's-a sticking in the rollers!"

At the front end of the mill the roar of the furnace was deafening. A huge black man shouted something at Louie and pointed to the white hot-rail, now split in three parts, the top third stuck in a repeater, shuddering but not moving, as the furnace roared and the rollers relentlessly squealed and churned.

Louie yelled at Anselmo even as he moved closer to the black man, "Anselmo, meet Ollie Pickens!"

The black man waved at Anselmo, but kept his eyes on the steel bar. He shook his fist, pointing to the problem. "Crazy bastard been sticking like that on and off since last night."

"I fix it, Ollie," Louie said. He picked up a heavy mallet that was placed nearby on the floor. "We use the smack-it method!"

Louie made sure Anselmo was watching while he banged at the white hot bar with the mallet and jumped back as it released and shot forward. *"Christos!* That evil *bastardo* want to cut me in half!"

"Then you'd be really short, Louie!" Ollie Pickins grinned, showing a big smile with a golden front tooth.

Louie grinned back but he didn't take his attention off the rollers. The bar was running through, but not as smoothly as he would have liked.

"Is okay now, Ollie, maybe. But you be plenty careful of that one."

Ollie rubbed sweat from his bald head, waved his thanks and stepped in to grab the end of the thick bar with a tongs and wrestle it in a 180 degree curve to jam it in another set of rollers.

"No way to turn them off?" Anselmo shouted.

"What? Shut it all down? Boss man hate that," Louie yelled back. "Stop the mill, blame the worker, and dock the pay."

"Well, that doesn't seem fair."

"Fair!" Louie eyed his new partner. "Where is this fair place you come from? Nothing fair in life! Life is hard, and then you die!"

"If you're lucky..." Anselmo said, his mind unhappily shifting back to another place and time.

"You and me, shift boss has us on hot beds today," Louie said, giving him a little shove to make sure he was listening. He led Anselmo past sets of repeaters, each in a row designed to squeeze the bars smaller and smaller, until they came to the hot beds. At this end of the mill the roar of the furnace was somewhat less, the long bars of steel now thinner, still glowing a dull red hot, but now squeezed down into seven eighths inch wide ropes of cherry red rebar.

Young Freddy Warberton waved his set of four-foot long metal tongs at a big wall clock and yelled at them, "Hey, you *stugatzes*, you're late! I'm supposed to be off five minutes ago!" *Stugatz.* Street slang for *stupid dicks.* Freddy's dad was an old schoolboy chum of Elmond Ridgeway, the man who ran the Chicago Heights branch of Inland Steel. Freddy himself should have been in high school but he told his father he hated school and it was this or he would leave town and ride the rails with the hobos.

As Freddy yelled at Louie and Anselmo, there was a loud clank and a giant mechanical scissors clipped the still moving rebar into a glowing fifty foot length. Freddy grabbed his end with a tongs and his partner, a middle-aged Polish guy named Parowski, snagged the far end with another tongs. With a graceful, synchronized motion the two of them whipped the bar to one side as the next glowing red rope was already making its way down the channel.

Freddy did a little bow in Anselmo's direction, "See, New Guy – that's the way you do it!"

Louie yelled at Freddy, "You stupid *idiota* – pay attention! Quit you fooling around!" He turned to Anselmo, "You see how he do that?"

"I think so, yeah."

"Get a pair of grabber-tongs from over there." Louie took one and gestured how to grip them. "They catch one more and then we be ready, you on this end, and me over there." Louie showed the way it was going to go: he would be the catcher, a job that took a more experience, and Anselmo would snag the slowed down length of bar on the far end, and then they both would work together to whip it off the rolling line to rest on a steaming pile of bars cooling on the stacking side.

Louie went through the motion for Anselmo, but before they could take their positions, the next bar was coming down. Freddy was in a mild adolescent fit because Louie had yelled at him; he saw Louie as just another grown-up idiot telling him what to do. So he was distracted, and missed catching the bar on his end. Parowski yelled "Hey!" and jumped back, showing how nimble he could be in spite of his big beer belly. But management had the men running the mill fast, and that meant the rebar was coming out red and hot and so when the front end of the length Freddy had missed hit a metal stopper plate it bounced back and snaked around and caught Parowski in the fatty backside of his thigh.

The chubby middle-aged man gave out a high-pitched scream and fell to the steel floor of the hot bed, flailing around like a speared fish.

Anselmo didn't know what to do, but Louie was already in motion. He yelled "Shut down! Shut down! Shut down!" And, quick as a cat, he ran over to the writhing man and smacked him unconscious with one brutal punch to the side of his head.

The shift boss looked up from a paper he was reading and yelled, "No! Louie, are you crazy – you know we're running behind – " Then he saw the red hot metal smoking in the back of Parowski's shuddering thigh. "Oh, Holy Christ!" He cranked a telephone sitting on a small metal desk in front of him and yelled into the horn-tube speaker.

In the same moment, Louie grabbed a rubber water hose and sprayed the rebar stuck through Parowski's leg, and yelled, "Torch man! Torch man!"

"Should I try to pull the bar out?" Anselmo yelled.

"No! That way make him bleed to death! And you get burn yourself!"

Somewhere an alarm blatted and the line ground to a halt, but still nobody else moved. It was as if everybody but Louie was frozen in time, staring in horror at the man with the smoking rebar punched through his leg who lay shuddering on the hot bed.

"Mangia il mio cazzo!" Louie swore at no one and everyone, running to one side of the large room and getting the cutter's torch himself, not bothering with the welder's mask, popping the flame on with a spark starter, squinting but still risking a shower of metal bits to his eyes as he cut off the rebar six inches from each side of Parowski's thigh.

"Right. No blood," Anselmo said, seeing the wisdom of what Louie was doing.

Louie pointed, "Come on, now, Mo! We maybe save his leg! You help me; we get him out of here!"

As they half carried and half dragged Parowski away from the hot bed, Louie yelled over his shoulder, "You – you, the line boss! You get the kids to clean up. Give a ten minute warning. Rollers start up. Ten minutes! No more or they gonna take it from our pay!"

The older man stood up from a chair in one corner, shaking himself as if he'd been dreaming. "Okay, Louie. Right, right, right." He honked a small air horn and the last thing Anselmo saw as he and Louie carried Parowski out the door, two grimy kids who looked like they should still be in grade school came running from the other end of the mill with brooms and dust pans.

Outside the mill, Louie grumbled as a dented and dusty old black Ford chugged up close and they piled Parowski into a space where the back seats had long ago been pulled out. "*Stupido* wise ass show-off Freddy, and now look what happen! I could kill him! This Polack here, he got the wife and family. Who's gonna feed their mouths?" Louie pulled himself up into the passenger seat. "Hang on the side, Mo. Watch, make sure he don't fall out."

"You want we should take him to St. James?" the driver said. He was a squat little man who usually worked as one of the breaker in the yard, his regular job to line up the old railroad rails before they were winched onto rollers for their journey into the fire.

"No time," Louie said. "We go to Hungry Hill."

"That won't work; Doc Whitber's on vacation."

"His assistant lady is there," Louie said. "She is much better for us, anyway. Old doc, he is blind like the bat."

"She ain't no doctor." The driver spat a brown wad of chewing tobacco out the window. "She can't handle something like this. I say we go direct to St. James Hospital."

"You shut your mouth or I hit you with my fist here! She is twice the doctor more than Old Medicine Man Whitber! You make your ass in gear right now. Go!" Louie took a closer look at the bar in Parowski's thigh, and in the middle of the grim situation he had a thought that amused him. His face lit up like a happy Halloween pumpkin. "Hey, Mo – It's not gonna be like a real operation, you think?"

Anselmo grinned back at his partner. "More like an extraction."

"Yeah," Louie said, riding along with the humor. "Dumb Parowski got a steel tooth stuck in his leg. Could only happen to a Polack."

"The man does not know his head from his back end," Anselmo said.

Lina and Rosa were playing two handed pinochle at the old wooden desk in the reception room outside Doc Whitber's inner office when the Model T skidded to a halt on the street near the front door, and, moments later, Louie and Anselmo awkwardly pushed their way in, clumsy because they were carrying a semi-conscious man with a short piece of metal stuck in his thigh.

"Open the door to the operating room," Louie said.

"It's locked," Lina said. "Doc's not here. He locks it when he's out of town. Nobody knows why."

Without hesitating, Louie shrugged and gave it a bump with his hip and it popped open. They carefully laid Parowski on his back on the examination table. The man groaned, "Where am I?"

Louie put a comforting hand on his shoulder. "You no worry, Comrade. Lady Doctor Bright is here – she will have you fix up in no time."

"*Sheista gevault,*" Lina said, unconsciously muttering a curse she'd learned from a German soldier just before she cut off his shattered leg. "*Shit on everything.* I've never seen one like this before. I don't think we've got a big enough knife."

"I got a butcher knife," Rosa said.

"Better run and get it. And that long thin one I've seen you use to peel potatoes."

Anselmo gave Louie a skeptical look. "No, no, no," Louie said. "You wait and see – this is gonna work out just fine!"

CHAPTER TWELVE

Sarafina Janika relaxed on a tufted lounge chair stuffed with horse hair that she'd had the maid set back from her apartment window so she could look out over the classic view of Rome's ancient hills without passersby on the street below seeing her *nel nudo*. Rollie, her hair dresser, was petting her naked breasts with one hand as he nipped at the short ends of her fashionable helmet cut hair style. His actions were not overtly sexual – Rollie was, after all, gay as a holiday fruitcake – it was companionable and pleasant, his actions something more like stroking a favorite lap dog. The casual stroking was innocent enough and Sarafina allowed it – looked forward to it, actually – Rollie's one hand carefully snipping away at her dark curls, the other wandering inside the open folds of her see-through pale blue silk gown to caress her, first the left breast and then the right, often reaching to a side table to apply light oil to his fingers.

"I am too damn regular," she said.

"What's that, lovie?"

"My period. It is too predictable."

"Oh, yes," he said. "The woman's curse."

"Well, no, Rollie. The curse is not my problem, not exactly. Well, yes, it is, I guess, same as all women. But what I'm telling you, my *particular* problem is that Giacomo insists we will not have a baby. I want a baby. I *need* a baby with Gio. And he absolutely will not sex me if the time is wrong."

"So the dirty dog knows your schedule. That is a very suspicious male of the human species."

"Oh, yes. The *bastardo* even has a marked calendar with my name on it. I have seen it."

She gave a little gasp as Rollie reached into an open jar, dabbed more oil on his fingers and then unexpectedly traced a soft circle around her left nipple. "Well, darling, you have to find a way around that. You know men don't keep accurate records when they've had a bit too much wine."

"Gia is too damnable self-controlled for that. Believe me, I've tried."

"Well, perhaps he needs a love potion. Perhaps something one might put in the Chianti to loosen his calculating a little bit."

"Oh, dear sweet Rollie, I knew you had some knowledge of these things. I don't really have the contacts – I mean, I would, but I don't know anybody, do you think you could find me such a helpful tincture?"

Her legs were spread, relaxed on the lounge chair. He set down his scissors and moved to kneel in front of her. He smiled up at her, their gaze locking over the curve of her belly and the swell of her breasts. "You know you can count on me for anything," he said.

CHAPTER THIRTEEN

Louie's fingers were too pudgy to be a nurse's helper, and Rosa was feeling a little faint headed at the sight of so much blood, so Anselmo stepped in as Lina's assistant for the procedure, the intent to take a piece of metal rebar out of a man's thigh. That was Anselmo's way. He didn't think twice about it; he just saw the need and did it.

Parowski was restless so Lina gave him several tablespoons of Doctor Whitber's calming medication.

"What is it? Is that medicine what I think?" Anselmo frowned; he'd been to war, he didn't know why he asked – he already knew the answer.

"Yes, of course. The soldier's friend. It is mostly cherry flavor opium," she gave him a sympathetic nod. "Don't worry, I'm careful. He gets just enough to knock him out."

"I know. If it helps save his leg," Anselmo said. "I am all for it."

"You speak English like an Englishman."

"I am from Italy. From Turin in Northern Italy, actually, but I went to boarding school in Switzerland. And then Oxford."

"My dad taught at Oxford. Maybe we were there at the same time."

"That could well be, Doctor Bright. The world is a funny place."

"Call me Lina. And you are?"

"Anthony Anselmo. Tony."

"Okay, so tell me, Tony: How did this poor fellow get a piece of steel in his leg? Seems to me like a lot of accidents happen over there at the Inland Steel mill."

"I'm not the expert, but I can tell you we work in teams and my mill partner, Louie – who is right here with us – he swears they make everything run too fast. *Dollar signs on the brain*, he says."

"I've heard that."

"There was a young fellow at one end who was supposed to slow the bar coming down the line, supposed to grab it with a big pair of tongs designed to do that – but he wasn't paying attention and he missed. The bar hit a stopper plate, but it whipped around like a wet noodle and caught Mister Parowski in the leg. That part was a freak accident, actually, but some carelessness, too, that made it possible in the first place. Bottom line, the young fellow on the catching end should have caught the bar."

They worked in silence for a while, Anselmo handing her knives and cutters and flesh saws while she probed to find entry around the bar while doing the least damage to his thigh. There was more blood, but only seeping and not gushing. Lina selected one of Doctor Whitber's operating knives that had a serrated edge and started to saw through the burned flesh as close as she could to the still-warm section of rebar. It took a half hour but she finally was able to pull the 16 inch metal piece from Parowski's leg without cutting a major vein or artery. "If he's lucky, he'll just limp a little."

"What could go wrong?"

"The worst thing would be infection."

"How do we prevent that?"

"I don't know what they do at St. James. If it was me, I'd use leeches."

"Yes, leeches can work to clean a wound. I've seen it."

Lina give her patient another tablespoon of Doctor Whitber's special formulation and that kept him quiet while they waited for an ambulance to take him to the hospital.

Rosa went next door to fix lunch for two elderly women who had taken the Dinky back to the Hill after a half day of shopping *for lady's things* in downtown Chicago Heights.

Lina left the door to the operating room open and sat at the reception desk in the front room. Louie excused himself and left to report back to the mill. Anselmo promised he'd follow as soon as Parowski was on his way. Lina went to the kitchen and returned with two cups of hot tea.

"He is a very lucky man," she said. "Not one in a hundred."

Anselmo eyed her, curiosity plain on his expression. "Yes, I think so. And, I think, very lucky you were here, Lina. And lucky that Louie knew what to do. Oh, you should have seen it! He was a wonder! He didn't have to stop to think what to do. With him it was automatic. Spray the bar with cold water. Get the bar cutter. But really, it took the two of you! I saw what you did here. I think you're a wonder, too!" He paused, eyeing her, wondering if he should say more. "Surgeons only learn those tricks in war. Up at the front. How to stop the blood, cut away the dead flesh. And yet you are so young…"

"Delighted you think so," she said. "Most people here think I'm *over the hill*."

"Certainly not. A maiden in full flower," he said with a gallant half bow.

"Thank you, sir. To your question, I was forced into the role of a child prodigy. My mother left my father, who was a teacher and a brilliant surgeon, and he cared for me in his classroom."

"And you became a doctor at a very young age…"

"Yes. And I found a way to help the wounded. I was near the trenches in France, and Belgium. We would drive up from behind the lines."

"We both know women were not supposed to be there."

"A few of us found a way around the rules."

"So you have seen it," Anselmo said.

"Yes. Things you never forget." Lina gave him a second look. Working together to get the piece of metal out of the Polish man's leg, Anselmo had shown her a calmness and assurance that had added to her own confidence that she could, indeed, have a decent chance at a successful outcome in this unusual surgery. Anselmo was a head taller than her, maybe a few years older, in his early thirties. Lean, with an erect posture and a casual, self-confident air about him. It was automatic; she just liked him. "You are not afraid of blood," she said.

Anselmo nodded, and his smile was sad as he thought back to his times in the Tirolean Alps. "I have seen some things, as well. The things we never forget. Truthfully, you're more optimistic about me than my own self-appraisal. There are times, I don't think I'm totally whole, not the way I was before."

"After war, maybe nobody ever is."

"For me, my war time adventures – if you want to call them that – were in Northern Italy. The Northern Front. In the mountains, in the winter. So cold, toes went black and frozen, and they fell off or had to be removed. Over a half million of my countrymen died in that war."

She saw his expression, the look of sad remembering, youth and innocence gone, stolen by the war. He reminded her of some of her father's friends; as a little girl she'd overheard them talking with her dad about places like Vicksburg and Gettysburg. She was a good listener and she had learned a lot, what to expect when her time came on the battlefield. "And?" she said.

"I'm sure for me, the same as for you. People I fought beside went up in bits, chewed apart, torn to bits by the mortars, punctured by the stray fragments, strangled by the gas, even killed by the weather. We've seen it, you and I. We know what happens in war."

"And now we have to figure out how put that behind us."

"Yes, you and me. For me, right now I work at the steel mill. I stay busy. I do my best to keep my mind on the present."

She nodded, thinking about it, careful what she said next. "But people say that's not why you came here."

"Ahh. So Hungry Hill talks about me. They say what else, Lina?"

"You are the big secret. Nobody knows why you came here…though there is a new priest at San

Rocco who doesn't like you. At least that's what I've heard."

He looked at her, liked what he saw and made up his mind to confide in her. *Solo Dio lo sa,* he needed a friend or two. "Well, I am not that big-a secret. I will tell you right now. It is simple: I made a vow to my grandfather. I agreed to take a boat from Rome through the Mediterranean Sea and across the wide Atlantic Ocean and then a railroad train from New York City to Chicago, and then the electric south to Chicago Heights and then the little trolley car they call the Dinky, all that to talk with the widow Gambriotti, your friend who lives next door to right here."

"What? Rosa? No...why?"

He saw it was the time; she would call her friend over, he would have his talk and reveal everything, and Rosa Gambriotti would curse him to hell forever and at last he would be free – if not of his guilt, at least free of his promise to his grandfather. But that was when they were interrupted by the blat of an air horn from the street outside. The ambulance wagon had showed up and was blocking the street in front of Doctor Whitber's office, impatient to take their patient to St. James Hospital for his doubtful recovery, doubtful because very few people injured in the mill survived. By the time they and the ambulance driver had worked together to get the Polish man loaded up and on his way, Rosa was busy preparing for the evening offerings at her restaurant, and Anselmo's time had run out. He had to get back to the mill.

He saluted Lina, and yet he lingered at the doorway. "I have been honored to serve as assistant in your brilliant surgery operation, Doctor Bright. I hope I'll see you again."

"I'd like that…but you wanted to talk to Rosa…"

"Another time. I need to talk with her. I wish I could now, but I must get back to the mill. If I'm not there to work with Louie, he'll find a way to go on without me.

"And that's bad?"

"Very bad. Dangerous, even."

"Until we meet again, then." She returned his salute, smiling as she did so.

"Yes, Lina Bright, *doctor extraordinaire*. Until then."

Anselmo left, thinking what a wonderful smile she had. Everything about her seemed to lift his spirits. He passed a young brother coming from the church as he was heading the other way. The brother was coasting to a fast stop on a two wheeler bicycle.

"No need of your services," Anselmo said by way of a friendly greeting. "Looks like the patient might live."

The young brother didn't think that was funny. He pursed his lips, saying nothing as he leaned his bike against the fence in front of Rosa's house. With an unfriendly look in Anselmo's direction he gathered his black robe around him and hurried into the café.

"Rosa. What was that foreigner doing hanging around here?"

Rosa smiled, "That was Anthony Anselmo. There was an accident at the mill. He was helping

Lina next door. He's not a stranger, he's from Northern Italy."

"You sure that's all there was to it?"

"What do you mean, Pauli?"

"I don't like that man being here. You don't trust him, Rosa! Not even one bit. I don't like this at all."

"Oh, poor Paulo, my dear old friend. Are you suffering a tiny bite of the jealous bug?"

"You are being the silly one, Rosa. I tell you, I heard some things about him. Bad rumors."

"Like what, Pauli?"

"He is a fall-away Catholic. He left his responsibilities to fight the war."

"What responsibilities, Pauli?"

He gave her a frustrated look, "I don't know, Rosa. I just know he is an evil man!"

Rosa didn't know why, but she found herself defending *the man from the boot*, who – from the little she knew – hadn't seemed at all untrustworthy. "If that is true...maybe there is a reason for what they say he has done. Maybe *Gesu* forgives him."

"Now you're the one talking silly, Rosa."

"No, Pauli. The nuns taught us *Jesus forgives everybody.*"

Back at the mill, Anselmo joined Louie and they headed for the hot beds. As they walked by, Ollie was hammering away at another reluctant wedge of white hot metal with the heavy mallet.

"You be careful, Ollie," Louie warned.

"I got this, Comrade." The big black man grinned and jumped out of the way as the steel shot forward.

"How's your kid doing with the fut-a-ball?"

"FOOT-ball, Louie," Ollie corrected him. And he's doing great. Gonna play for the Chicago Bears, some day."

"That will be the day when the pigs-a fly."

Louie and Anselmo moved on toward their station at the hot beds.

"Why is that, Louie? Why can't his kid play fut-a-ball for the Bears?"

"Black man only gets to play on the black man's team."

"Why? They are not good enough?"

"*Shoooz,* naw, Mo. They are plenty good enough. But the owners, they don't think white people want to see black men play the American fut-a-ball."

"Huh, interesting." Anselmo was thinking how different it was with soccer in Europe. Over there, they didn't care if your skin was black or white or green, so long as you could kick that ball through the net. Then he thought of something else. "Louie – he called you *Comrade*."

"Sure-a. Ollie and me, we join the party, a few month ago. All my pals join. The newspapers call us the bad guys, the Commie Reds! We don't care. They are wrong. We are not Russians. We are good Americans, and we are also full and true and proud members of the C and the P of the USA."

"Communist Party... But that is the Russians."

"No, not Russians, Mo. CPUSA. Americans. There is a big difference. We are for the red, the white and the blue. They are only for the red, for the bloody sickle."

"But... I thought we already have our union."

"Oh sure, yes we do – that wobbly bunch of chicken foots."

"But the socialists are helping us, right?"

"Not so much. Namby-pamby weak sisters. What do the wobblies or the socialists or the unions do for us? You take a look; they only are out for themselves."

"So we have three friendly allies and they do nothing for us?"

"Four, if you count-a the priest."

"But Louie, you look around and you see – at least, I see – they all hate each other!"

"*Shoooze,* yes, Mo. You are right with that. But don't worry. It's our job: we will get them to work together."

"How do we do that?"

"My friend, I make 18 cents an hour. You, too. And that is before the boss take away for this and for that, a penny here, and a penny there. Every time the mill stop, they blame us. Nobody put clothes on my kid's back and food on my table for 18 cents an hour. You wait until you have the *bambino*. You will see."

They shrugged into their grimy overalls, picked up tongs and then they stood ready for their turn in the rotation. The shift boss, who was unhappily catching bars with young Freddy, spotted them and yelled in their direction, "Hey, where you lazy bums been?"

"Do not give us that crap!" Louie yelled over the roar of the furnace. "You know where we were: you were the one, you, yourself – you told us *Take the Polack to the Doc!*"

"Well, you took way too long. You know I gotta dock you *slumbolas* for that."

"Aw, come on, Artie."

"Sorry, Louie – Can't help it. Big boss says so."

Louie nodded and gave Anselmo a look of grim determination.. "Next worker meeting will be at the church hall. Everybody will be there. You come with me."

"At San Rocco?"

"No. In Steger, just south of here. Meeting hall in the basement under St. Liborius School."

Anselmo nodded yes, "Okay, I'll do it. Why not? I can get a car, drive us there."

"Hell, it's only three miles, Mo. We're not city sissies."

"What if it's raining."

"Well, there is that thing."

"Yeah, it's called *getting wet*."

Up on the line, Freddy whipped one more bar and stepped aside for Anselmo. "How's the Polack doing?"

"That lady doctor did great! She somehow was able to dig the bar out. He might lose a leg, he might not. It is too soon to tell."

Freddy snorted, "Dumb Polack don't know his ass from a hole in the ground." He was laying blame for the accident on Parowski. Anselmo had been there, he'd seen what had happened. But he also knew it would not do any good to get in a shouting match with an immature teenager who – if Louie was right – could cause everybody a lot of trouble.

Later at their next break, Anselmo talked it over with Louie.

"*Shurrra,*" Louie said, "Of course Freddy-boy make blame like that on the Polack: Freddy, he's a bad worker, but nobody lay him off. I tell you before: he's gotta connections with the bosses."

"What do you mean?"

"Freddy Warberton is a stoolie pigeon to the management. He is the one helps them keep an eye on us. One of the ones."

"So that's how it works."

"You getting the idea, Big Mo."

Two grimy kids rushed up and handed them towels and glass quart milk bottles full of water. Louie took a bottle and poured half of it on Anselmo's head. "Two more spells, we take the shower, we go home, and we forget for a few hours that we work in hell." He gave Anselmo a curious look. "Why you do this, Mo? You are a man of education. You do not have to do this."

"It's just temporary, Louie. I guess I have to do something. Maybe...you know, to keep my mind busy. Maybe to forget..."

"Ahh, the war."

"Yes, there is that."

"You know there is a war going on still."

"What do you mean?"

That got Louie started: "Right here. A real war, too. We, the working man, against those bad guys, the owners. They have everything, we have nothing. They live in their big mansion; we sleep five or six people, whole family, in one room. They drive in the fancy Stanley Steamer and the big

Douzie, we walk the streets in our old shoes with holes in the bottom. They have the big gold coin money and the cigar in the mouth, and we have the small nickel coin and smoke the cheap stogies and chew the two-penny tobacco plugs and our kids wear rags and the worn-out old clothes. They eat the steak, we suck the fat out of the bones of the pickled pig's feet. When you come to our CPUSA meeting we will talk more about this, Mo. About *what to do* about this."

"I don't know about these socialists..."

"Faah! I told you, Mo! – the socialists are weak babies! The communists, Comrade! We are the American Communists of the CPUSA, marching together as one! We are the only ones who care for the working man. You come, you will see."

Anselmo had already said he would, but Louie was looking for affirmation. Anselmo nodded, he'd already made up his mind. "Sure. Why not? But like I said, if it's raining, I drive."

"Oh, now you are a rich man, you got the car and everything?"

"I'll borrow something."

Before Louie could say any more a horn blatted, signaling the 15 minutes rest period was up. They picked up their tongs and stepped back up on the hot beds.

After work that evening, after cleanup, Anselmo was walking out the main gate with Louie. "You gotta meet my wife," Louie said, taking his new partner's arm and ushering him over to where a small group of women was waiting on a wooden platform by the side of the road. "Anna, *il mio nuovo partner* – Anselmo!"

Anna's plain housewife's outfit and her seamstress apron couldn't hide her classic Italian beauty. She smiled but indicated she couldn't shake hands because she was carrying an arm full of shirts. "*Ciao*, Anselmo," she said.

Louie pointed to a mahogany skinned lady approaching them. "Anna sews the clothing for that lady with the wagon heading for here. That's Anita. Anita is Ollie's wife." Anita was pulling a children's red wagon stacked with neatly folded clothing. She grinned as she heard Louie introducing her. "Hello, I'm Anita. Anna here does the sewing and I do the laundry. We got the fair trade going." She shook Anselmo's hand, and then inspected her husband as he approached. "Hey, Ollie – Honey-bun, what, you got that burn on your arm again!"

"Ahh, it's nothin', baby! Nothin' a manly man wants to complain about!" She started to protest but he wrapped her in his big arms and gave her a kiss on the top of her head. "Come on now, baby – what you got cookin' up for dinner?"

That night Anselmo dined alone in the Victoria Café, in the same building but around the corner from the front entrance at the hotel where he was staying. He had a few oysters as an appetizer, and he probably should not have done that. They tasted a little of iodine, like maybe they were left-overs from lunch (or maybe dinner the evening before). Later on, his stomach was upset and he was restless in his sleep. In his dream, the one that he'd had

112

more than once, he was reliving his worst moment in the war. He was back in the Tyrolian mountains. He knew the time and place: It was in 1917, a freezing February night, sometime after midnight. The hated *bosche* soldiers had been lobbing mortar shells in their direction, one every half hour or so, just so nobody got any foolish ideas to climb out of their trenches and start some grappling death scene that nobody wanted. Anselmo and five of his troopers (including the crazy American) were huddled together under wet and icy blankets. There they were, side by side, Ralphie the mad fool who had come back to the mother country from the safety of far-away Illinois to fight for his vague and outlandish patriotic craziness, and Tony Anselmo, the just-as-crazy fellow who had signed up for the horrors of war to avenge his brother's death from a random bullet through the heart.

"I'm getting this icy rain in the face," Ralphie said.

Anselmo gave him a friendly poke in the ribs. "I thought you Americans were all tough cowboys."

"No, seriously, Mo. I'm freezing here. Is there any space on the other side of you?"

Anselmo said there was, and that gesture of kindness was what saved his own life. He helped Ralphie step over him to huddle next to the rest of their squad.

Ralphie settled in, head down and feet pointing away from Anselmo on a stack of used wooden racks, and soon he was snoring away. And then there was a blinding flash, the noise that deafened, the shock that shook the bones and stunned the brain, and then panic everywhere. The shell had landed not far away, had exploded in the trench about twenty yards down the line. On Ralphie's side.

Italian soldiers came running; they stared; they threw up, emptying their stomachs, or they simply ran away. The result of the blast was totally what an impartial observer might call the fates of war: Anselmo was nearly untouched; but only the top half of Ralphie Gambriotti remained. And worse: the crazy American should have been dead, but he wasn't. He was impossibly, horribly alive, the top part of him looking untouched and the rest below his belly button mangled or missing, what remained of his legs just bloody sticks of fresh bones.

"Padre, aiutami!" Father, help me!" he cried out to Anselmo.

"Mai io non soni il padre…" But I am not the priest!

"Dio ti tende padre!" God makes you the priest!

Anselmo in truth was well educated, but he was nothing near a priest. His mother had wanted him to become one, and one time – for six months, instead of the academy in Switzerland – he had actually spent his time at the Vatican college. He had walked away from his ceremony before taking even the beginnings of his priestly vows, but still, he did know the words of the Last Sacrament. He was certain using that knowledge would be a mortally damning wrong – he would be committing a sacrilegious mortal sin, a person who wasn't a padre performing a sacred rite only reserved for the priesthood! *Why, that person would be sent straight to the deepest layers of eternal damnation in hell!*

114

Still, Anselmo knew how to do it, and so he gave the dying man his Last Rites. But his American friend Ralphie was not finished damning him. He had one final wish.

"Uccidimi. Uccidimi ora!" Kill me. Kill me now!

The mortally wounded man locked his gaze on Anselmo with a look of hopeless doom. His legs were gone, his genitals blown away, his entrails dangling from an open abdomen. He should be dead, already. He was a shattered being, what remained of him a bloody mess from the waist down. He asked Anselmo – no, demanded – that Anselmo release him, take him away from the horror he had become. And Anselmo, numb with his own shock and pain, wept as he reached with both hands for maimed Ralphie's throat.

And then Anselmo woke, confused and grateful and shaken, to another place and time. He shook his head, tried to clear his thinking. He looked around the hotel room, saw the Currier & Ives print on the wall, a hunter shooting a deer in the woods, and he understood it was five years later. He was a half a world away, sitting up in a stiff and narrow bed in a rented room in the pretentious Victoria Hotel in a town in the land of the free and the home of the brave. There was angry fist-pounding on the wall, the fellow from the next room was yelling, telling him to shut his mouth and stop his screaming nonsense.

CHAPTER FOURTEEN

This happened in February of 1922, nearly two months before Anselmo left Italy for Illinois to fulfill his promise to his grandfather: Anselmo's dad, Giacomo II, invited his grandfather, Giacomo I, down from Northern Italy to Rome to present him with yet another of his grand plans to transform their family financial affairs, a plan that was sure to cost the old man a big chunk of the family fortune his son rightfully suspected he had hidden from him. They were meeting in Gio II's showy business office, a stack of papers on the large and ornate antique marble conference table between them, Gio II's beautiful secretary (too beautiful to be just a business subordinate) to one side taking notes.

"This coming year I am signing big contracts. I intend to make ten times over what you make," Gio II said to his father. "My company, Futura Industries, is the future of Italian business, the future of European business, the future of the world."

The old man listened with a sinking heart, seeing his son was saying 'my' company and not 'their' company, though Futura had been entirely funded with loans from the north, loans that had never been paid back to the original family business. The old man found his mind was wandering; he was wondering if his son had always been thoughtless and rude; perhaps, as a busy father, he hadn't noticed, or if his son's success (and perhaps the son's loss of his wife) had seduced him into an uncaring middle-aged brashness.

"That may be true," the old man said, being careful and doing his best not to spark his son's unstable personality, his quickness to anger. Giacomo I loved his home in Turin, his orchards, his vineyards in Northern Italy, but he would – no matter how reluctantly – give them all up for this new venture, if only he could believe what his son was saying. But the family's business empire had been burned by their losses in the Great War, and although his son (at least on the paperwork he had provided) seemed to have found new business success, Gio I did not like the mood of the country. "This man, our new prime minister – you seem to believe he is our future as well."

"Papa, have you heard Benito speak?! The fellow is a marvel! A genius! A new Cicero!"

"He is a forceful speech maker, I'll grant you that. But I do wish he would keep his shirt on. He is not in very good physical shape."

"A little overweight, perhaps, but what does that matter? What a patriot he is! Benito Mussolini wants for Italy to take back everything the Roman Empire gave to us – our true heritage!"

"So you are advising I sell everything we have, the lands, the fields, vineyards and orchards and the wine company – everything –   and invest it in…what?"

"In the return of our great heritage! The plan is right there in front of your face! You just have to read it! Modernization. Factories. Machines. The future!"

Giacomo I nodded slowly, not a commitment to action but a gesture that said he understood. Then he unexpectedly turned and addressed Gio II's secretary by her first name. "Sarafini, it is my understanding that you are sleeping with my son. Has he asked you to marry him?"

The girl dropped her notepad and pencil, startled by this unexpected change of subject. Her face reddened and she bit her lower lip, a characteristic gesture. She turned to Giacomo II, her voice rising in sudden rage, "So you tell him of our private affairs?!"

"No, Sarafina, I did not!"

Giacomo I raised a hand to interrupt, hoping to cool down the moment. "That is true. He did not. He did not have to. The two of you are the talk of Rome."

She stood, hiked her short flapper skirt and stormed out of the conference room.

Giacomo II slammed an angry fist on the table. "Now see what you have done! You create a big mess and all for nothing! I am a grown man! My private life is none of your affair."

The old man smiled sadly, "That would be true if you were not looking to be a partner – the major, the senior partner – in this new firm you are proposing, the firm in which you wish me to invest the proceeds of my entire life of work."

"Then your answer is no?"

"No, not true. My answer is, I will consider and ponder and weigh alternatives and get back to you."

"But old man, I am advising you, the time to act is now! This is it, the golden time for the new Italy!"

"And I advise you, middle-aged man: There is merit to your proposal. But I will not be rushed. I would love for our beloved country to be a real power in the world again, but it is a risk. I agree with much of your thinking – at least, in your desire to make Italy great again – and I promise you, I will take action. Soon." He gathered the papers and carefully placed them in a leather briefcase. "My driver is waiting. I must be off."

"What? To where?"

"Turin. I do still have a home, you know."

Giacomo II rose to his feet, unsure what to do next. "But – I had planned dinner! So we could talk; you could get to know Sarafina better. And I thought we'd go to the prime minister's speech tomorrow. He is such a wonder, a true motivator! You'll be impressed, I guarantee it!"

"Thank you, Gio, but Benito can stir up his black shirts without me. However, I agree with you, my boy, and more than you know – something must be done. The homeland is changing and we've got to take action on our own behalf or we'll be on the short end of things. Just be a little patient with me."

A few hours later, the old man sat on an old stone seat in an ancient sports stadium that was nearly two thousand years older than he was. He wasn't moody, or sad, or depressed. He was a realist, and he cut his losses and moved on. He didn't think twice about lying to Gio II about leaving Rome that evening. As his son had told him: *None of his business.* That sword cut both ways. Giacomo II had lied to him for many years as a way of life; that was how he survived, how he had weaseled the money from the family fortunes to start his Futura Enterprises, how he had conveniently forgotten to pay back the loans he now assumed were gifts. In spite of his disappointment in his son, Giacomo I still hoped, dreamed, planned that there would be future generations of Anselmos, his heirs. *Giacomo III was lost to them, but what of Antonio? What of the generations beyond, what of Giacomo IV, V, and VI?* He always thought as far ahead as he could imagine: *What was the best move he could make for them?* The problem was, with Giacomo III slain in the war, and Giacomo II insisting he wasn't about to have any more children, there was only one more Anselmo left to carry on, and he did not get along well with his father. The moon came up, a brilliant yellow-white crescent shadowing the far round edge of the ruined Colosseum wall. The man stood and stretched his old bones. He realized he was thinking like a much younger man, like he was in his son's shoes. That was foolish, of course, and yet it was necessary. His son was a pigheaded fool. He was a gambler, and he'd never figured out he had a responsibility to play forward the hand he'd been dealt. Giacomo I still had the same motto that had motivated him his entire life: *Dream big, go forward.* But that wasn't *gambling*, it was *investing in the future.* Well then, yes – even though he was old, it was time for him to go it alone, to leapfrog his son and make his move as best he could. A couple of big moves, actually.

"*Gesu*, give me strength," he muttered to himself. "I'm just an ancient fellow. *Gesu*, please, a little help here."

CHAPTER FIFTEEN

Brother Paulo finished serving as altar boy for the six o'clock Mass. He tidied up the altar, put out the candles with the iron snuffer and rushed from of the dark and newly deserted church for a jolt of fresh morning air. He took a deep breath and, seeing nobody was looking, he tried a few arm twirls and jumping jacks to get his blood going. His bike had a flat tire so he started walking toward Rosa's place to trade his bag of tomatoes for a breakfast sandwich. He had walked a half a block when he spotted a little dark green wooden soap box racer with the number one painted on its side. He wondered why he hadn't seen it before; he came this way all the time. It was tucked away, in between the sidewalk and one of the brick tenement houses with some other throw-away stuff nobody wanted. A used mattress with what looked like blood stains on it. A wash scrubber pan with a squeeze roller, probably of no use now that somebody had bought a new electric wash machine. A dented tea pot with the bottom burned out. Maybe somebody was throwing that racer out with that other junk. That would be a real shame, Paulo thought. He went over for a closer look. It was a rough but sturdy little beauty, one of those racers the kids pushed down the street, when there was still light enough after working hours on those long summer days before the sun went down.

Although this whole area was called Hungry Hill, there wasn't a big hill, just a slight tilt to the road here or there, but the kids didn't care – even though the winner was usually the soap box car that had the fastest pusher. Two or three of them would line up, block off the automobiles and horse wagons from each end, and some adult passing by might give them a cheerful warning and a go-ahead and sometimes even wave a red workman's bandanna to start the race.

It was no secret Paulo was a racing fanatic. He didn't care what anybody thought, it was none of their business. He found himself wondering for maybe the hundredth time what it would be like, not in a kid's race, but the real thing, driving in the Indy 500, engines muttering and growling all around him as he waited for the start, or maybe it was one of those running starts where the drivers stood in a line and had to run to their cars! Indianapolis was only a half a state away, automobile racing was all the modern rage, and lots of the Italians were enthusiastic racing fans. Heck, they even had their own official entry, *The Spirit of Chicago Heights*. Paulo turned his sporty English leather racing cap backwards and pulled it down a little tighter on his head. He was thinking he was maybe somebody like Barney Oldfield, about to climb on board his famous Green Dragon racing machine.

"Hey, what's up?" A familiar voice behind him said. It was Rosa, on her way back to her cafe from the Mass. He hadn't noticed her in the back of the church, but he should have known, she often was there, praying for the departed soul of her poor Ralphie.

"Rosa, hi…nothing."

"Come on, Pauli, everything is something."

123

For a moment her attention was taken away by the pile of junk. "Somebody got a new clothes washing machine," She was looking at the old wash scrubber, saw that one of the water squeezer rollers was broken. For no reason at all, that reminded her she'd left her mama a lump of dough and hoped it would be rolled flat and cut and ready for the spaghetti and *Italiano* meat balls Rosa's Café was serving that evening. She gave Paulo a playful poke in the ribs, "You really like the old soap box derby racer, huh?"

"Ahh, you know, kiddo. I guess I'm just dreaming about the life of a racing driver."

"So you do two things good – you grow the tomatoes and you think maybe you drive like a demon."

"I do a lot more than two things good!"

She gave him a conspiratorial grin. "So why don't you get in, racer-boy?"

"Well, it's not mine."

"Gino Lambini owns it. Or at least he did. He's got a job pushing cows around at the stockyards in Chicago. He hasn't driven it in years. I think his mom's throwing it out."

"I don't think I'd fit."

"Come on, Pauli" she said, pulling the wooden car away from the protection of the building. "It's not like you're a fatso or anything. Don't be a scaredy-cat."

"Well, *Rosie Rosa*, I'm not afraid, if that's what you're saying."

"Come on. We'll just borrow it for a little bit, to see what it feels like. Get in, *Pauli chicken-liver*."

It didn't take any more convincing than that. Paulo handed her the little sack of tomatoes he'd brought for her, tucked his black frock in his pants and settled himself down in the little wooden car. "By the way," he said, looking up at her and grinning as he gripped the oversized rusty iron steering wheel that had come from some farmer's old tractor, "I really like your hair cut short like that." But then his enthusiasm shifted into high gear and it was all about his dreams to be a racing driver. "Rosa, look at me – I'm in the front lane at Indianapolis!"

"Yes, you are," she said. There was a little slope and the soap box racer was pointing in the right direction. She gave it a running start and a little one handed shove and that was all it took, in Paulo's imagination Barney's mighty Green Dragon was on its way.

True, there wasn't any more than a little slope downhill at this point, but still, it surprised him how fast the green gem of a soapbox racer picked up a bit of speed on its own. Lucky it was early; the street was nearly deserted. His imagination took over and this was *Woow!* This was all right!

And then – too late – he saw Fuches grocery wagon directly in front of him, the ramp down as Old Man Fuches himself was rolling a pickle keg off the wagon while his big brown draft horse patiently looked on.

Paulo tried to steer hard left but nothing happened – he saw too late the steering wasn't connected to the wheels anymore! In fact, it came off in his hands! Paulo and the green racer caught the grocery wagon ramp with just enough of an angle to lift it sideways into the air. It thumped against the huge horse's side. The horse made a Whoosh! Sound, letting out a breath of air. The unfortunate creature staggered a bit but stayed on his feet, and then gave Paulo a sad look as if to say, *What else could go wrong with my life?* The soap box racer with Brother Paulo still in it settled to the ground, the axles shattered and the front set of wheels spinning off in different directions by themselves.

Rosa came running after him; she showed up next to the horse laughing and at the same time gasping her alarm for his safety. But Paulo was laughing too, delighted with his little adventure. She hadn't seen him so happy since before she'd gotten married, happy and carefree like when they'd been swinging back and forth in those good times when they were kids on the playground swings behind San Rocco grade school.

She made sure the horse was okay – she gave him a pet on his nose and she gave an 'I'm sorry' to Old Man Fuches (who seemed a little confused, but said everything was okay) – and then she ran to collect the wheels before they could roll out of sight and, once things calmed down, she helped her friend drag the ruined racer back where they'd found it, Paulo saying he would fix it good as new.

"I don't think that's necessary, Pauli," she said. "They were gonna throw it away. Think of it this way: You gave it a good last run!"

They left it next to the pile of junk, against the same wall where they'd found it, and with light hearts went off together to Rosa's Café to trade a breakfast-in-a-bag for the tomatoes and his promise

of some fresh red peppers from the priest's glass hot
house when they got ripe in a day or two.

CHAPTER SIXTEEN

Grumpy old Doc Whitber was supposed to be back in his office on a Monday, but when he didn't show up by Wednesday, Lina called a phone number he'd left on his desk 'To be used only in case of extreme emergencies'. In other words, *Don't call me, I'm too far away to help you anyway.* The voice that answered from the other end of the line was hoarse and unfriendly; Lina thought for a moment it was the grumpy old doctor himself, but it was his older sister.

"My stupid, stubborn brother Frank, that's Doctor Frank Whitber to you," the old lady said, "was kicked in the head by the only creature more obdurate than he was – a big grey mule he was trying to shoe – and he died right there in our barnyard. I am Cynthia Whitber-Yonders. And who, pray tell, are you?"

"Ohh…oh, no…I'm sorry about your loss. This is Doctor Lina Bright from his office. We became worried about him because he was supposed to be back here two days ago."

"Yes. I know of you. You are his young want-to-be doctor assistant. My son and I are taking the train to the Chicago area tomorrow. We will be there, at his office, to take charge of his affairs. You are forbidden to touch any of his things and I will expect a complete accounting."

"I can't be much help with his accounting. I will show you where his financial books are shelved, but Doctor Whitber handled his own finances."

"And you are not his junior partner?"

"He made me sign some papers, but I think that was mostly to protect himself legally. He kept his own books of expenses and income. I am a certified doctor, but when he is here I function as his assistant, mostly. Receptionist, schedule of appointments, note-taker and chief bottle scrubber."

"But you are an M.D., you are the amateur doctor he told me about. You work there."

"I am not an amateur medical person – I am a 100% real doctor. I have a valid Doctor of Medicine diploma from a major eastern institution. And yes, I do work here. As a fully certified doctor."

"Then I will expect a full accounting."

"And I will expect the two weeks wages he owes me."

"We will have to see about that."

True to her word, Cynthia Whitber-Yonders and her son Roy Yonders showed up two days later at Doctor Whitber's office. There had been a light shower and as they were not expecting rain; the pair showed up frowning and unhappy. Lina, not in a kindly mood because of the sister's attitude, thought to herself it was as if Chicago Heights had given them some sort of personal kick in their pants.

Roy Yonders shook a few rain drops from his brand new, too-large Stetson travel hat and made a frowning display of brushing dampness from his wool suit. "Please give us the keys to my uncle's apartment," he said. "He lived upstairs, is that not correct?"

"Yes, it is true, but I don't have his keys." Lina shook her head. "He only had a single set, and he carried them with him. I have no reason to use his apartment and I have never been up there. I rent a room next door at Rosa's. I think you must have his keys. He would have had them with him."

Roy looked to his mother, who clamped her thin lips in a grim expression and nodded her head just once.

Lina saw the gesture that passed between them, and figured their request for the keys had been an opening ploy to check if the assistant been going through Old Doc's things. "I've never been up there," she repeated. "My own room is on the second floor in the house next door. As I said, I rent a room above Rosa's Café."

"That *Italian* place." Dr. Whitber's sister frowned. "And how do you find the Italians?"

"They are good people, for the most part. This is the Italian section of town. Practically everybody who lives here is from the boot."

"The *boot*?

"Old Italy. Some from Sicily, maybe. Most of Old Doc's patients were Italians. I find them energetic and resourceful. And most of them not rich enough to come see a doctor when they should."

"You call him *Old Doc*?" Roy frowned, looking haughty and judgmental, and Lina realized how much she didn't like either of these people.

"Well, he was very old…"

"I am older by ten years," the sister said.

130

"Well, I didn't mean anything…they say with age comes wisdom…"

"Mother, put this aside for now," Roy said. He gazed around the room with a look of sour appraisal, and then snapped his fingers. "The books. Where are the financial books? We must have the accounting of which my mother spoke to you by phone."

"The last month's ledger is in his desk." Lina pointed behind her. "In the operating room."

Roy went to have a look at them, staring suspiciously at the broken lock where a few days before Louie had made his way in with the injured Parowski. "That door is broken," he said.

"Patient emergency," Lina said. "He really should have left us that key."

Old Cynthia eyed her critically. "So my brother kept his own books. Just what *did* you do?"

"As I said: Doctoring. Everything doctors do." Lina shrugged. "And I picked up the slack: I would perform the procedures he used to do, when he was unable because of his…tremors."

"My brother did not have tremors."

"Quaky hands, then. However you want to diagnose him. Or when he was at the track."

"The track? What track?"

"Doctor Whitber liked the horses."

"I never knew that, but I shouldn't be surprised. My brother was a wicked, wicked man!"

"I don't know… Grumpy, for sure. And near-sighted, a little, maybe…" Lina saw plenty of irony; here she was sticking up for the old doctor who had given her so much trouble with his weakening condition, and with the concern she had

131

for his failing surgical skills and for the disaster that any mistakes he made could bring to his patients. He might once have been a capable medical practitioner or even a marvel in the operating room, but the old man she knew was far past his prime, a fumbling fool of a medical man – still, except for his womanizing and his drinking and gambling – ordinary vices like that – she couldn't imagine much *wickedness* in him.

Roy returned from the operating room and threw a worn ledger book with Doctor Whitber's accounting on the reception desk. He gave Lina an accusing look, "This isn't all of it! You're hiding the full accounting from us. Why, this shows his practice is losing money! And look – he did three stitches for a bag of green beans?"

"Yes, he did. I believe I did already mention to you that the people of Hungry Hill do not have a lot of money. Sometimes he would take produce from their gardens, or a chicken or two, or they would clean his apartment in return for his services."

"That is plain nonsense! We know he ran a profitable business! He bragged of it many times!"

"What are you talking about?" Lina said.

"Doctor Whitber's Marvelous Medical Remedy!" Roy opened a wrinkled newspaper he'd been carrying in his suit pocket and slapped it on the desk in front of her. He pointed to a small ad featuring a picture of a medicine bottle. "This is a popular product! It has to be worth a fortune!"

Cynthia spotted several brown glass bottles on a shelf near the door. "A-hah!" she said. "*That* is what we are talking about!" She snatched one of the bottles and held it up like a trophy.

132

Lina nodded in agreement. "Doctor Whitber handles – handled – his medicinal business from a back room behind his operating room. And from his apartment." She pointed to the ceiling. "You will have to go up there and fish around for yourselves."

Cynthia glared at her. "You know nothing about this side of his practice? That is very unlikely."

Lina shrugged, trying for non-confrontational. "Well, I know his miracle formulation was shipped here about four times a year. It was delivered in a big wooden barrel from a firm that had Chinese writing in its address. And I know he ordered glass bottles and had labels printed in downtown Chicago Heights. He used a couple of teenagers to fill his bottles with a funnel and had them stick on labels…that is, until they got all goofy drinking the stuff and their parents wouldn't let them work for him anymore. After that, he did the bottle filling all by himself, not too easy with his shaky hands and all."

"He had a valuable patent," Roy said. He took the bottle from his mother and held it up uncomfortably close to Lina's face. "It says so right there on the label!"

"Yes, it does say so, but you cannot get a patent on opium. Nobody in the United States can," Lina said. "I do think you better go rummage around in his apartment; if the answers to your concerns are anywhere, they will be up there.

Roy and his mother stared at her for a long moment, but then they took her advice and took the steep wooden stairway up to Doctor Whitber's apartment. They produced a set of keys and opened the door and Lina heard them moving furniture around. They were up there for several hours. When they came back down, each of them was carrying a big suitcase in one hand and a carpet bag in the other.

"Find what you were looking for?" Lina said.

"No, we did not!"

Lina was thinking the old woman looked guilty as hell. She pointed to a paper dollar bill that was half way sticking out of one of the suitcases. "Kept his money under his mattress, did he?"

Roy started to open the suitcase, thought better of it and ripped off the part of the bill that showed, stuffing it in his pocket.

"Come, let's leave this place, Mother!"

Lina stood in his way. "Hey, not so fast! Doc owes me two week's wages!"

Roy pushed her aside and his mother scuttled past them, moving out the front door. "We'll have to get back to you on that!" Roy said. And they were moving away, walking at a fast clip down the street. Lina watched them head for the trolley stop, hoping – but not at all certain – that she'd never set eyes on them again. But she had to admit she couldn't be sure about that; bad pennies had a way of turning up, and she'd been wrong about plenty of things before.

CHAPTER SEVENTEEN

On his last day, the morning before Oliver Pickins's soul was transported to heaven by an army of triumphant angels, he had stopped off at Charley Pilato's table and placed a five dollar bet on a horse he favored that was running later that day at Lincolnshire Downs. This of-track betting transaction took place at the Burgel House, the restaurant and bar that used to be known as Brown's Corner back in pre-Civil War days, seventy years before, when it was a safe house for the underground railroad.

Charley Pilato didn't have an office of his own. He didn't really need one. He rented a tiny room upstairs and hung out at a small space in one corner of the restaurant in the big front room at the Burgel House, and the people who ran the establishment said it was okay so long as a little gratuity changed hands every now and then, and that was good for business all around.

Charley had been taking the electric down south from Chicago and hanging around the South Suburbs for a decade or so, and he was an observant guy who knew the players and most of the angles, and he didn't care if your skin was white or black or purple or green, if you had good money, it was all A-okay with him. *The thing was*, Charley was thinking to himself, *that was maybe a week's wages – a huge bet for a nigger steel worker to be making right out of the blue. Ollie Pickins must know something.* Charley took Ollie's hard earned cash and made a note in his book, but at the same time he gave his customer the knowing eye. "Brown Butter's twenty-five to one, Ollie. Who you been talking to?"

Ollie hesitated, but he knew he had to come across. "Brown Butter's stall mucker says he's a go. Don't spread it around, *amico*."

"I ain't your *amico*," Charley said, "I ain't the pal of no cotton picking share cropper's kid."

"Okay with me, *dago bastardo*," Ollie grinned back. "Just don't let too many people know about the horse. Could ruin things for all of us."

"Yeah, yeah, I know, Ollie. Everybody gets greedy, nobody wins."

Ollie was pretty sure the bookie would be true to his word, within limits; too many bets on a long-odds nag, the numbers guys out at the track figure something's up and the payout shrinks to where it isn't worth it.

Ollie tried to thumb it from Burgels, but nobody was coming up Dixie Highway going the right way so he walked the several miles to the mill and still managed to get there right on time. He didn't have an extra minute or two to dig in his foot locker for a good pair of coveralls so he shrugged into his only choice left in his locker, his oldest and most frayed pair. And then he and his partner, Tripi Bertolli, hustled their way past the shitter and across the yard to take over from the night guys.

It wasn't like nobody warned him. "*Bastardo* sticking on both ends", Frenchie said over his shoulder as the night team headed for the shitter and the showers.

"Oh yeah," Ollie yelled back. "Same as always."

But Tripi was up first, and Tripi was able to wrestle the white hot bars okay, a few minor shudders from the rollers but no real sticking. And then it was Ollie's turn. Ten minutes went by and still smooth running and maybe that had the huge black man relaxing a bit too much because he'd just grabbed the next steel, whipped it around his body and slammed it in the outgoing set of rollers when the first set jammed on him. In itself, no problem – but with the second set continuing to pull steel, he was caught in a shrinking semi-circle of glowing metal. Still, no problem, but, as he went into his fast duck and roll, the torn flap on his old coverall pocket caught firm on a corner of the roller frame and, as he tried desperately to free the garment, the hot bar squeezed in on his lower abdomen and just that fast he was a dead man standing.

He screamed. And screamed. And screamed.

And the other roller stuck. It would have been better if they both had continued as before, one stuck and the other rolling, had simply cut him in two so his blood ran out and merciful death could take him away. But now with both rollers stopped he was trapped, a piece of living meat, roasting on his own hellfire spit on earth.

Tripi ran to shut down the mill but everything was too late, too late, too late. Inside his shock and pain and horror, Ollie knew he was gone. And so did Tripi.

And then, out of nowhere, *Oh dulce Gesu!* Oh, Sweet Jesus! *Angelo della Morte!* The Angel of Death was here! Tripi and Ollie knew about

137

Anselmo. Everybody at San Rocco had heard the rumors from the priests and from their relatives back in the Old Country – everybody at the mill knew.

"Anselmo," Tripi screamed, "Get over here!"

"Anselmo!" Ollie cried. "*Occidimi!* Kill me!"

Anselmo stared back, here and yet not here, mouth open, silently begging Ollie not to ask this.

"Anselmo – *Dio ti perdona!*" Tripi said.

Ollie's sobbing voice broke in near-panic. "God forgives you! Please, man, *please!*"

And Anselmo, seeing Louie's friend nearly cut in two, reached across the steaming white hot metal bar, put his hands around Ollie's straining neck, and pressed his fingers into the grateful black man's throat.

CHAPTER EIGHTEEN

It was six minutes after straight up noon by the starter's clock and Elmond Ridgeway was in the middle of his backswing when that damn pesky Jew accountant of his ruined his shot, came running right up on the tee and breaking Elmond's concentration with the news there'd been another accident at the mill. It was Saturday and so of course Sumner had come from the synagogue and was wearing that goddamn black beanie and that was bad because Jews weren't supposed to be here, they weren't allowed. This was on the first hole at Flossmoor, the same course where they'd held the PGA two years before, and the usual bunch was standing around watching and Elmond was sure he heard a few snickers when his driver took a big divot, turf flying everywhere as the ball dribbled about ten feet forward, not even making it off the tee to the fairway.

"I get a mulligan," he said, and the other three fellows in his foursome nodded and agreed. He was normally a nice guy, but he had a hair trigger bad temper and nobody much got in Elmond Ridgeway's face about anything. He reached out his hand and Eagle-eye, his caddy, placed a new ball in it. The first hole was a slight dogleg right, a difficult par five. The trick was to play it left, but not so much as to get into the sand trap, just left enough to land on the left edge of the fairway with a clear shot toward the apron in front of the green.

But the damn Jew was still jabbering away at him, and how was he supposed to concentrate?

"...died almost immediately," Sumner Silverman was saying, and that finally got through to Elmond.

"Sumner, what the fuck, you're not supposed to be here...Died? Who died?"

"Ollie Pickens."

"Who the hell is Ollie Pickins? Sounds like a nigger name."

"Oliver Pickens works for us. *Did* work for us. He was stationed at repeater #1, the one been giving us all the trouble lately. The rollers were off and on again. Trapped him. Caught him square in the guts. I told you we should have installed safety bars."

Elmond remembered something about that: Sumner had been pestering him with a crazy plan to install some stout posts, the idea being to wrap the hot metal around a safety post before directing it into the next roller. Yeah, sure, safer for the worker, who might only get burned a little, but that would slow down the entire process. *What, a safety post at every station?* It was stupid and expensive and Elmond had said so. Still, now here he was looking like a cheap industrialist. Thank God it was just a nigger, poor bastard wouldn't be able to find a lawyer to represent himself. Not that a damn know-nothing *Wop* or a dumb witted *Fritz* or a *Polack* could do any better. Still, people were watching, the show must go on. Elmond put on a look of grave concern. "Jesus! Is he going to be okay?"

"No, he is not going to be okay! I told you! Ollie Pickens is dead. Nearly cut in half."

140

"Well, I don't mean to sound unconcerned, Sumner, but there's not anything we can do about that right here and now, is there."

"No, but…"

"Schedule a meeting for when I get back to the office. No, it's Saturday – make it Monday. Get the directors, see who's in town. The Flintcote guy. Hot Point. Desoto Paint."

Elmond shooed Sumner away and did his best to put on a brave front; after all, he was a captain of industry and the starter had hit the gong twice and the next foursome was loosening up, shuffling around a bit, eyeing in his direction and waiting for him to take his shot. So, hard to blame him that he rushed it and his ball ended up too far left.

"Sand trap," Eagle-eye said. Eagle-eye was a squinty-eyed teenage caddy who was blind as a bat. Elmond liked the kid; he knew the course like the back of his hand and could track a ball after seeing only 20 or thirty yards of its trajectory. But this time that wasn't going to do anybody any good as this ball ended up buried in the soft sand right against the steep front lip of the left-hand trap and it took two with the sand wedge to get out and, even with the mulligan free do-over, Elmond triple-bogied the hole and that was the start of one of the worst rounds of golf he'd played in years. And all because some goddamned nigger couldn't hop his black ass out of the way of a hot steel bar, like as if that wasn't his job in the first place.

CHAPTER NINETEEN

"Mama," Rosa Gambriotti said, "What if we squeezed our spaghetti dough through a clothes wringer?"

Mindy Gabriotti looked up from the butcher's block table where she was kneading a lump of dough one final time before she rolled it out. She was used to her daughter's odd questions, coming at her out of nowhere, and she smiled, wondering where this one came from. "Well, Rosa, I guess our linguini would taste like lye soap."

"No, Mom, serious: Let's say everything was clean, like sanitary, the rollers clean like a bread pan or a rolling pin or anything else. If you had something like that, you wouldn't have to use a rolling pin, you could squeeze it through the rollers."

"Sure," the older woman said. "*E allora?*"

"So it would save you time."

"*O, si!* I could make a million pounds of spaghetti in an hour."

"Exactly," Rosa said, but she wasn't laughing like her mother was, her mind was far away on something else. "Maybe not a *million* pounds, but more than doing it by hand."

It was later that same Saturday at the steel mill. To make your way from the mill to the front gate there was a wide sidewalk. The workers had to pass between the dirt caked showers and the foul smell of the shitter on the left side and the executive office, a two story brown brick building, on the right. Looking almost like an afterthought, a small wooden structure no bigger than a one man guard shack was attached to the near side of the brick building. This structure – sticking out so it actually blocked a bit of the sidewalk in a way so that you had to walk around it – was painted dark blue. It had no doors to the exterior, and featured a hinged window that opened to reveal a metal grill with just enough of an opening that the paymaster could recognize who he was paying.

It was payday and the day shift was over and there was no time for remorse or pity or anything but getting out of that hell-hole. Louie was standing in line with Anselmo and shaking his round head. "This is not a good sign for us, Mo," he said, throwing one of his short arms out in a gesture to indicate he was talking about the line people in front of them.

Anselmo was not anywhere near recovered; he was beside himself, badly shaken by what Ollie's accident had forced him to do. He'd been daydreaming, trying to push his mind to think of other things, actually trying to put himself in that long-ago happier time when he was a kid in his grandfather's vineyard, running through rows of dusty vines heavy with dark purple bunches of grapes. Anselmo started, coming back to reality. "What? What's the deal?"

"You'll see, partner. They're gonna shave our money, like it's our fault. Remember, I said so. This is no good at all."

"Poor Ollie getting his black ass caught in the repeater is our fault? No. How could that be?"

"Don't try to make sense out of it, Mo – you'll see."

The line was unusually long, not only Ollie's terrible death fresh on everybody's mind, but many of the workers were taking time to complain to the paymaster about the deductions from their normal weekly pay. When it was Louie's turn, he saw right away what the problem was – the company was actually cheating them. It only amounted to a few cents per person, but it all added up. Louie accepted the money – you always took the money first – but he didn't move on.

"This is really short," he said through the grill, raising his voice a little even though the paymaster's face was right there, not two feet from his own. "Sumner, this is *very much way* too short, my friend."

Sumner Silverman pushed his green brim cashier's visor back on his head. "Not you, too, Caproni. Look, Louie, please, lower your voice. Please. Just listen to me: There were three stoppages, and two of them were major. You know the deal. You don't get paid for stoppages."

"Oh, yeah, I know the deal. The machine break, it's our fault. The Polack gets speared in the leg, it's his fault. Ollie gets killed, it's his fault. What do you tell Ollie's poor wife Anita about that, Sumner? We're sorry he cut himself in half but now we gotta take it out of your money?"

Sumner looked like he'd rather be anywhere else than where he was. "Louie, you know I'm not the guy; I don't make the rules."

Anselmo put his arm on his partner's shoulder. "He's right, Louie. He's not the man to blame. He just keeps score."

Louie's face showed he was struggling to hold back his rage.

Sumner reached under the grill and tapped Louie's hand with one finger. He whispered, "They're trying to figure out how little to pay Ollie's widow. Don't say I said anything."

"How *little!*" Louie roared. "What, just because he's-a the black-a man?!"

Sumner gave a frightened look over his shoulder, was relieved to see no one was in the doorway behind him. "Shhhh! Quiet, Louie! I'll lose my job! Yes. Exactly what you said. They're arguing black people don't need as much money. That they're not as valuable."

"*La merda del toro!* Ollie was as good as me! Better, even! He was the best man on the line!"

"We both know he did a good job," Sumner said. "And they know that, too. It's not about that; it's about what they can get away with."

"Son-a-ma-bitch! Some day! I tell you, Sumner, some-a day the change is gonna come! Damn and shit on their house!"

There was the dim outline of somebody filling the door frame behind the paymaster. "Any trouble here, Sumner?"

"No. No trouble, boss." Sumner gave Louie a furtive wave-off, a quick backhand gesture. "Next in line!" he said.

CHAPTER TWENTY

Anselmo decided he'd had enough of just about everything; his reoccurring nightmares, his assignment to pay tribute to the widow Gambriotti, his new guilt as the once-again appointed Angel of Death.

The only thing in his power, he thought, was he could talk to Rosa Gambriotti and make that part of his life go away. Then maybe he could get on a train and go somewhere else, go back to the boot, or maybe lose himself in the American Wild West, like the hero always did in the flickers. Saturday, after Louie's loud conversation with Sumner Silverman at the paymaster's booth, one of the black men who had worked with Ollie told Anselmo that he and Louie were invited to Ollie's memorial service. He told them it was going to be held the next morning over on the East Side, in the black section of town. Louie said he wanted to go, so they agreed to meet and go together. Anselmo suggested Rosa's Café, and that seemed like a good idea all around.

"How we get across town to the East Side?" Louie said. "It's pretty far. If we're gonna walk we have to leave an hour early."

"I'll get a car."

"You gonna *get a car*. You can't just *get a car*. Two things they hang you for in the U.S. of America – stealing horses and stealing cars."

"I won't steal it. I'll borrow one. Rent one, you know, for the day."

"You gonna *rent a car*. I never heard of such a thing."

"What, you want I should rent a horse-and-buggy? Or maybe two horses? You know how to ride a horse?"

Louie laughed and said he didn't, and they parted for the evening.

Sunday morning Anselmo skipped Mass but did his morning jog and then took a bath and did a careful shave without cutting himself, and then rented an automobile and headed over to Rosa's Place. He'd told Louie ten o'clock; he had planned to be there early, but he had to dicker back and forth with the hotel manager, who was reluctant to loan out his fairly new Hupmobile touring car, even though he was tempted by the huge offer of fifty dollars plus a gasoline fill-up for the day. "How do I even know you have fifty bucks?"

"How about I leave you a note?" Anselmo said.

"What, a shifty fifty on my expensive motor vehicle?"

"How about five hundred?"

"You don't have five hundred dollars."

"Mr. Morton Fox over there says I do."

The hotel manager still looked skeptical so Anselmo went across the lobby to where the manager of the First Citizens Bank was waiting for a client, and Mr. Fox was happy to vouch for his good customer Mr. Anthony Anselmo.

But that took a bite out of Anselmo's plan to get to Rosa's early so he could talk with her alone. He parked in front of the Doctor's office next door to the café and waved to Lina, who was on a ladder painting over the words Doctor Whitber, M.D.

He smiled up at her. "Had breakfast yet?"

147

"Are you saying you are going to buy me breakfast?"

He figured that was the best idea he had heard in a long time…in years, maybe. "Yes, I am."

"I will be there in a few minutes," she said. "Got to finish up."

Rosa's mom and dad were helping with the café; Rosa was taking a break, sitting at the largest of their tables, but she wasn't alone. Louie had already gotten there. And then there was her close friend Brother Paulo. Anselmo sighed and took a seat at the head of the table.

"Nobody said you could sit here," the young brother said.

"*Caffe publico,*" Anselmo said. He did not address Paulo with the respectful *fratello* and Paulo's face flushed red with anger.

Before her friend and protector could say anything to get him in even *deeper soup*, Rosa smiled and threw out a friendly two armed gesture of welcome. "*Signore* Anselmo! The talk of the parish is you wish to speak to me. Well, here I am!"

At that moment Lina came in the room, "Hey, what's for breakfast?

Rosa smiled and waved her over. "Lina, you're in luck! My mother made a big pot of soup. *Pasta e Fagioli.* Come sit by me."

"Sounds high class."

"It's the really good bean soup," Louie said, looking up from a big Dutch china bowl in front of him. "The best!"

Lina settled in next to Rosa. The table was full and Rosa said, "Anselmo here is about to reveal the big secret why he came half way around the world to see me."

Anselmo nodded and crossed his arms. "Well, yes I did, and it is a serious business. I have to start with the history of it, back at the start of the Great War, if you will allow me. My family has our roots in Northern Italy, close to the mountains, in the Piedmont region, near the city of Turin. It is very much too close to the Austro-Hungarian border and the crazy *Mangiapatati*."

Lina looked at Rosa, who whispered *potato eaters*. "He means the Austrians," she added.

Anselmo smiled and nodded, and then continued, "My father was asked by the Italian government to help sponsor a military unit. The idea would be that we would be a cavalry unit, mounted on horses, and we would have more horses and we could use them to transport artillery guns, not a new idea but it seemed like a good one for travel through the mountain passes. My grandfather was against it, but my father agreed."

"How did that work out?" Brother Paulo said.

"I think you can guess the answer to that one. But it was even worse than you may think. We were given a colonel who had never been to war or the mountains, this man was put in the ranks to command us. My older brother joined; he said he had to defend the family honor."

"Why did you not join right away?" Paulo said. "Go off to war with your brother."

"I was away at school, in England. When Giacomo was killed – shot through the heart on his

149

first day in the mountains – I was the only son left. It was my duty to bring back his body and, after that, to take over for him."

"Nice story, but so what?"

"*Sta zitto,* Padre," Louie said.

"Yes, shut up." Lina gave Rosa's friend, the young religious brother, an impatient look. "Let Anselmo tell his story."

Anselmo nodded his thanks and tried to hold his own emotions in check. "The *e allora* is that Rosa, this woman here, her husband was assigned to my brigade. He became my friend. My good friend…Ralphie Gambriotto was young, brave, energetic and very unlucky."

"How so, *sfortunato?*" Rosa's voice had dropped so it was barely a whisper.

"Bad luck followed us. After we lost many of our men and most of our horses, those few of us remaining alive were in a trench together."

"How did you lose your horses?" Paulo couldn't help interrupting, but now his interest seemed genuine.

"It was winter, and the snow was very deep that year. We were scouting out way through a high mountain pass, and the entire unit was waiting for us to signal it was okay to move forward. Our commandante thought he was doing a smart advance, but he was impatient; he told us we had to move ahead with speed, and he gave a loud bugle signal to advance, and that was not a good idea. His wish was for us to go forward at once. I had been telling my company to go slower, to pick their way with care. This commandante, who had never been to war, was furious to have his commands

150

questioned. Not only did he have the bugle boy give a loud signal, he shouted through his megaphone that we were to move on; in fact, he yelled we were to double our speed. His voice, loud as it was magnified through his device, was drowned out by a *rombo enorme,* a huge roar from the wall of the mountain above us. And in a moment the snow was upon us, pushing at us, tearing at us, burying us.

"And what did you do?" Lina said.

"Everybody used to laugh at me because I rode a big draft horse, a *cavallo da tiro Italiano.* They are mostly used to pull the artillery pieces, but it was the only one left and *Principe* – that was his name – had a gentle disposition and I liked him so I didn't mind."

"And what happened?"

"Well, *Principe* rode that wave of snow half way down the slope with me clinging to his neck. He saved my life…Still, the terrible damage had been done. My squad, the men and their horses, all of them had disappeared as if they never existed."

"And my Ralphie was one of them?" Rosa said.

"No. That was yet to come. What happened, our commandante proved to be a very bad leader and, over the next month, my father's battalion – my company included – was reduced to almost nothing. No more horses remained, no more artillery. There was disease, and a gas attack. The few of us left alive became one with the trenchers, the unfortunates huddled in the trenches we dug in the bitter cold ground. We found that we ourselves now had to dig with picks and shovels in the rocky soil, to make shallow ditches so that we had any chance at all to survive."

"And Ralphie was with you?" Rosa said.

Yes, he was. Weeks and months went by and it seemed winter would never leave us. After that early time when we dug our trenches, hunger and frostbite and fleas and disease and desertions – that was our army life. And Ralphie stayed true and loyal to our unit and to the Italian cause.

But then there came that one night I can never forget: it was ice cold, it felt to me like more snow coming and I directed my few men remaining that we should stretch a canvas and stake it over our heads for some shelter from the sleet and the cold rain. But nobody listened to me; they said it wasn't worth the effort, that's how far we were down with our spirits.

Meanwhile, the *Mangiapatati* had one or two mortars firing, just a shot or two every half hour so we would know they were still there. And then that one unfortunate shell exploded – the one that landed precisely in our trench. That does not happen but once in a thousand times. And the result was so very bad! The full force of it came down the trench at us. Your husband – my friend Corporal Ralphie Gambriotti – and four other soldiers were between me and where it blew. Being where they were saved my life, but it was their bad turn and they lost theirs.

"Did – did he say anything?" Rosa's lower lip was trembling and there were tears in her eyes.

Anselmo knew, if there ever was a time for lying, this was it, and he did not hesitate to tell a version of events he had told other widows in other meetings back home in Italy. "Yes. He said he loved you very much and that he wasn't worthy of your love because he'd left you – but he'd had no choice because of his honor and his love of his homeland – and he wanted you to find someone who loved you even more than he did and to go on with your life and he would always be watching out for you from heaven."

There was silence for a while, everyone at the table seeing the scene in their own mind, trying to grasp the shock and horror of that moment, and the redeeming grace of a brave man's last words.

"I am sorry I interrupted you with my own silly doubts," Paulo said. "I did not understand your intentions were honorable."

"E comprensibile." A faint ghost of a smile came to Anselmo's lips and he reached across the table and shook the young brother's hand. "A truce for us." Then he stood and took an envelope from his suit jacket and handed it to Rosa. "A letter to you from my father."

Rosa slowly read the letter. "But...4,000 dollars...this is a huge sum of money!"

"Yes, and no. It cannot compare in any way to your loss. The sum of money is in United States currency and it is in the bank in downtown Chicago Heights. The bank people know of you; you are to contact them to make arrangements, what do you want to do with the money. It is now yours. And also there is a medal of honor from the Italian government. It has to be engraved. They have your address. It will be coming to you from *Roma*, across the ocean, the thanks of our grateful nation."

Rosa's mother and dad had been listening from the kitchen. Now they hugged their daughter and then went to the kitchen and came back with trays of steaming bowls of Italian soup. The group ate in silence, everyone deep in their own thoughts.

And that was when Charley Pilato showed up, "Hey, Louie, I heard you *gumbanos* might be heading over to Ollie's memorial service."

"Charley! Yeah, sure, you want to come with?"

"Not me. I'm not that welcome on the East Side."

"What, nobody will bother us today, Charley. It's Remember Ollie Day. Dago-Nigger Peace Day."

"Yeah, whatever you say, Louie, I ain't going. Hey, what'cha got – bean soup?" Charley's appetite was legendary.

"*Pasta e Fagioli.*" Rosa said. "Want some?" Without waiting for an answer she raised her voice, "Hey, mamma, a big bowl of the bean *soupa* for Charley Pilato!"

"Thank you, Rosa," Charley said. He turned to Louie, "I need a favor."

"Sure, Charley, anything."

"Ollie made a bet, early that morning before he caught the big one. And *mamma mia*, wouldn't 'cha know it, no fooling, his horse came in! So maybe you give his wife this for me?" Charley handed over a fat beige envelope.

Louie weighed it in his hand, "Ollie didn't have this kind of money."

"It was really good odds. And Big Al said toss in a little extra. You know Ollie's widow is gonna need it."

"Yeah, she's gonna, alright. Ollie left Anita a batch of young mouths to feed," Louie said. "Okay, we'll handle it."

"Not in the collection basket, right? Hand it to the widow, personally."

"Got it, Charley." Louie grinned. "Trust everybody, but not too much."

"You got that one right, Louie." And with that the bookie clapped him on his back, gave a big, hearty laugh and headed out of the café.

"Hey, what about your *soupa*?" Rosa's mom said.

Charley came back and took the big bowl with the wooden lid on it from her hands. "I'll bring it back tomorrow," he said.

"Don't forget, we need the spoon, too."

"I won't, *mamma*, I promise."

They heard him talking to someone on the street, saying to be careful and not spill the soup, and then his car started up and drove away. Charley never went anywhere without one or two pals who carried pistols and sometimes a shotgun resting on the floorboards behind the front seat.

155

CHAPTER TWENTY-ONE

The group was set to leave from Rosa's Café when Tripi Bernolli, Ollie's mill partner, showed up needing a ride. Tripi said he didn't think the Dinky ran over to the East Side of Chicago Heights on Sundays – if it ever did at all – and he had no way to get there so they all ended up in the Hupmobile with Anselmo driving. Louie rode in the front seat with Lina, Rosa and Paulo in the back, and Tripi standing on the running board, clinging to the door as they made their way across town. Half the roads were gravel and they hadn't been leveled since winter; the way they took was bumpy, and Tripi had to hang on for dear life.

Old Father Kelly, taking his morning constitutional walk with Monsignor Monafusti, saw the shiny new Hupmobile pulling away from Rosa's restaurant with Anselmo at the wheel. "There is a wolf in the flock, *padre*," Monafusti said.

"What? You mean Brother Paulo? How can that be?"

The Monsignor's frown deepened. "No, *padre*. Paulo is just a stupid half-boy and half-man, a *scambino* of weak half-inventions and silly dreams of being the first racing driver who is also a man of the cloth. I mean the bad one is that Anthony Anselmo. You see who he drives off with? He attempts to make friends with the heart of San Rocco, the true people of the flock. I do not like it one bit."

"Could our friends at the police station arrest him?"

"Now that is a very good idea. All we need is an excuse."

The sounds of a radio came from Rosa's, Al Jolson singing 'April Showers' with that showy bass voice of his.

"I never liked Al Jolson," the Monsignor said. "Half way to ballads, half way to opera, and the man is neither."

"He is very popular, though."

"No one can explain the madness of crowds." The Monsignor looked up at the sky and the frown lines on his face deepened as the first spatter of raindrops hit his forehead and darkened the sidewalk around them. "But he is right about one thing; here come the April showers."

Old Father Kelly didn't say anything more. He kept his guarded expression to himself. He was trying to maintain a casual attitude around this supposed man of the cloth who had come with an unusual set of papers from Rome. The papers said he was temporarily assigned to San Rocco's, but they gave no reason. *Most unusual*, Father Kelly was thinking to himself. He was an old man, too old to be fussing in other people's business, and he certainly wasn't going to poke his nose in the Monsignor's private affairs. But that didn't mean he had to like the fellow.

CHAPTER TWENTY-TWO

Anselmo's rented Hupmobile braked to a jerky stop in front of a small warehouse with a hand lettered sign over the door, "Jesus Christ Savior Pentecostal Church". There were no other automobiles in sight, just one horse drawn peddler's cart, a few bicycles and many black people walking on the gravel at the sides of the unpaved street, pausing to gossip with friends and slowly walking here and there. Anselmo and his companions were the only whites in sight and yet the black people politely ignored them. It was as if they weren't there, as if they didn't exist. Except that, as they got out of the Hupmobile, the locals retreated off the patch of narrow wooden sidewalks and stood in the street, the men taking off their hats and saying, "Mornin', Sir" and "Mornin', Maam".

Louie took off his own battered brown fedora and bowed to an old, white haired black lady. "Pardon us, maam, we have been invited here for Oliver Pickins' service. He was-a the good friend of ours."

A smile lit the old woman's face. "Right in this building, Sirs, right in here." She pointed to the warehouse, "It' be only temp'rary. We gittin ourselves a new church building next year, made entirely of fine bricks."

"Thank you kindly," Louie said. "I'm sure that will be very nice."

"We just leave the car?" Paulo looked uncertain, out of his territory.

158

"You want to stay?" Anselmo gestured toward the Hupmobile.

"Maybe," Paulo said, looking uncomfortable.

"I'll stay with Pauli," Rosa said.

Inside, the large room was packed with Afro-Americans in their Sunday go-to-meeting clothes, many of them standing around a sepia photo of Ollie that was set up on a worn artist's easel. Ollie, in his photo, was smiling and looking ten years younger than Anselmo remembered him. The large choir had just begun singing, and their words struck Anselmo to the core of his being.

He felt weak in the knees and his hands trembled as the choir sang.

Into Your hands we commend our spirit O Lord
Into Your hands we commend our hearts

Lina, standing close at his side, was watching him. "You okay, Tony?" She had heard a rumor, something about an *Angel of Death* at the mill, something vague but connected to Anselmo. He had seemed okay talking to Rosa at the café. Grave and concerned, but okay. But now that they were at Ollie's service, he was looking pale and *out of sorts.*

"Yes...I think so...I know this song," he said. And he began to sing along with the choir.

For we must die in ourselves in loving You,
Into Your hands we commend our love.

As Lina watched him, Anselmo's thoughts left the makeshift warehouse church. He was back in the high mountain places where maimed and broken men screamed and died without hope or mercy, without their mothers and fathers, without their wives or children, without the God who had been

159

with them all their lives – with only the Angel of Death to comfort them and help them on their way.

Oh God, my God, why have You gone from me,
Far from my prayers, far from my cry?

Anselmo sang; he had an exceptional baritone voice and it soared along with the rest, and his words were a cry for mercy. His voice blended with the choir, and lifted them with their own singing.

To You I call and you never answer me,
You send no comfort and I don't know why!

Lina looked up at Anselmo, standing close at her side, and she saw the tears running down his cheeks and something that had long ago been hardened in her now crumbled and began to dissolve. She never thought it would be possible, not after her terrible experiences in the war, but this man needed someone to love; and, deep inside, it felt to her like she was going to be that person.

You've been my guide since I was very young,
You showed the way, you brought relief;
But now I'm lonely, nobody's by my side:
Take heed, my Lord, listen to my prayer.

"I have to get out of here," Anselmo whispered, the expression on his face showing he was looking for understanding.

"Come," Lina said. "Come, dear Tony. I feel what you feel. Come with me. You are not alone. I promise you, it will be alright." She saw his tears and her heart went out to him. She had no real awareness of exactly what she was saying or why she was saying it, but it didn't matter. This tortured man with the wonderful singing voice needed her, and in that moment her world changed and she felt a closeness, an empathy, something she'd never felt before, not even in her own terrible times in the war. She took his hand and led him through the murmuring crowd. The negroes parted for them, patted Anselmo on the back as he passed by, thanking him for joining in their song.

CHAPTER TWENTY-THREE

The two of them, Tony Anselmo and Lina Bright, went to the Hupmobile and sat quietly in the back seat, still holding hands and neither saying a word. Paulo started to say something but Rosa put a finger to her lips and shook her head, *leave them alone*.

After a while, Anselmo sat more erect. "I am not a broken man," he said to Lina in a firm but low voice, talking to herself alone. "I will not be a broken man."

"I understand this, what you say," Lina said. "I was there, too. The Western Front. I was luckier than you – I had medicine to help, opiates to send those hopelessly maimed ones on their way."

That was what Anselmo needed; it took his mind away from his own terrible memories. "How did you ever survive that? How did that happen in the first place? You must have been very young."

"My father was a doctor – and a teacher. You know, I told you, I was a child prodigy. I knew how to take a temperature before I could read a book."

"Still, you aren't that old now."

She gave him a sincere smile, "Thank you. I'm glad to hear you think so."

"Well, I do think that…So how did that happen for you?"

"In 1916 I had passed all the tests at the college where my father was a professor of medicine, and they were forced to give me my medical license. This was on the East Coast, New York City. That was when my dad jiggled his way into one of those cushy and pretentious teaching stints he was so fond of accepting. He had to get to England. There was talk of German subs lurking in the Atlantic, but my father could not imagine a boat disaster in his life – he figured the Germans *wouldn't dare* – so he caught an ocean liner and dragged me along with him. By this time I was thinking on my own so I made sure to pack that M.D. diploma from Columbia. After all, maybe I was just a teenage brat, but I'd earned it fair and square."

"And you did get to England…"

"Yep, no torpedoes. Papa was right: They wouldn't dare try to sink the great and indestructible Doctor Bright! Well, in all honesty, we were just lucky, I mean, the Germans couldn't torpedo all the boats, they didn't have enough subs.."

"By then the war was going…"

"Yes, it was. Full blast. As you know, it was one big, bloody mess! Everywhere, all over Europe, there were men hiding in trenches, men shouting orders and men jumping out in the open and grappling and tearing at each other. Shooting, knifing, sword slashing. I don't think there had ever been anything like it before, I mean, death and dying on such a grand scale! Of course, at first, I didn't see that from behind the lines, but it was easy to visualize what happened, I could see it because there I was at a hospital in London, patching up the wounds. You know: that's a bullet that's got to be taken out, that's a piece of flak metal, that's a knife slash, that's a man with a shattered leg run over by a tank." Anselmo was staring off into space, saying nothing. Lina saw she'd gotten too far into her own experiences.

"I'm sorry."

"No, it's alright. Tell me more about your war. I want to know."

"You sure?"

"Yes. I want to hear your experiences…so much like mine, and yet so different."

Lina searched for something she might say that wouldn't bring back too many bad memories. "I guess, in one way, Rosa's Ralphie was lucky; he wasn't there too long, so he missed a lot of really terrible things. There was the poison gas boiling out of canisters into uncertain winds – I was there once for that, I saw it, smelled it, choked on it – deadly poison gas and even the soldiers who released it from its canisters never knew where it was going. You could end up gassing and killing your own troopers – it actually happened! I lived because I found a gas mask on a dead German soldier…at least, I think he was dead."

"Yes," he nodded. "I remember moments like that. Our insane cavalry charge right into rows of cannons that were shooting at us at point blank range."

"Did you ever see the tanks? Those metal monster things?"

"Yes, we had some of them even in the Alps. Metal tin cans with soldiers inside, tin cans clanking around, machines that looked like odd cardboard cut-out toys, but they had cannons and they could run you over without even stopping. You know we were a cavalry division. Our horses were very frightened of the tanks, it was hard to keep them from running away."

"What a bad mess! A war run by big, dumb, stupid generals with rows of metal badges and ribbons on their puffed out chests, generals who were watching men get killed from far away. Generals with big moustaches looking stern from the pages of the London Times.

He nodded, remembering how it was, "Didn't you want to get away from it? I mean, once you saw the awfulness of it?"

"No. For me, just the opposite. Doctors are trained to save people. I, myself, I knew how to save people! I had been trained to do these things!"

"I think I get it. For you it was as if Almighty *Dio* had put you there to do that, to save people."

She nodded, seeing he really understood, the first man she'd ever met who actually did get it. "That's the way I saw it, Tony. But when I talked to my father, he did not agree. He said we were already helping enough, we were already doing our part, by him teaching other people."

"Why did he say that?"

"Well, I think at least a part of him honestly believed it. We argued about it, but he would talk in his cold way, tell me that, if I wasn't going to give him a grandson, my part was to help him teach at Oxford. That meant mostly grading papers."

"Well, I don't know about the grandson thing, but maybe he had a point – teaching others to save lives."

"I don't think so. I think my father was a big phony. He loved the tea parties and the bike rides through the rolling green hills of England. He wasn't going to give that up for bandaging bloody wounds with the smell of rotting flesh and mustard gas in the air. I was not able to change his mind, and he certainly was not going to change mine, so I left him and tried to go off on my own to fight the war."

"That was a very brave thing to do."

"If you'd been trained like I was, you'd have gone to the front lines, just like I did. One look at all that suffering; I know you would have."

"How did you actually get to the battle places? I know women were forbidden to go there."

"It wasn't easy. First, I tried to sign up as an army doctor with the British army, but they wouldn't have me. They actually accused me of forging my diploma! After that, I got rejected by the Frogs, and then the Wooden Shoes, and the Waffle Makers from Brussels. And finally I got turned down by the American army! My own countrymen, and they needed me most of all, and I could not sign up to help them!"

"*Dio* almighty, that must have been frustrating."

"*No place for a woman*, the bastards said. *War is a man's business.* Like a batch of stupid old pigs, they huffed and puffed and did their best to blow my house down…yeah, I know, it was the wolves that did the puffing, but you get what I mean: I could work as a nurse, they told me. But I did not want that, because it meant staying behind at a hospital. Sure, I would be out of danger, but I would not be doing the things I knew best! It meant making beds and tossing out chamber pots while incompetent old men doctors made mistake after mistake that cost badly wounded soldiers' arms and legs and actually killed them. Mistakes that I would not make! Or, at least, I'd make less of them."

"And yet you did get to the front."

"Oh, yes I did! By that time I was crazy-mad from so many idiots turning me down, I am sure I was not even right in my own head. I saw a golden opportunity; I had to tell a little lie and say I knew how to drive an automobile – but it was easy to learn and I think God forgave me for that one. That got me a job with the Red Cross, working as an ambulance driver."

Anselmo nodded in agreement. "Almighty *Dio* forgives the little lie when it is for a just cause. That is why they say *it is only a fib*…at least I hope He does forgive us."

Lina smiled, remembering her moment of triumph. "When I climbed out of that van with the big red sign on the side, there was nobody – no major or colonel or general – nobody at all fussing about who would question whether I could cauterize a bleeding leg or pull metal shrapnel from a screaming man's open stomach."

"*Gesu, Maria e Giuseppe!* Lina, you have done much good in the world!"

"It did work out mostly for the good. I remember all those years in the back of my dad's classrooms. All the long days watching his careful stitching techniques – my poor father was brilliant, you know, in his own way – and I took advantage of it all. I knew the right way to amputate an arm or a leg without killing the poor shattered patient, how and where to saw a bone – all the knowledge I'd snatched from that unwilling genius – and it was worth it! It gave me the skills I needed to do the job."

"And you did get to save those many lives like you wanted."

"Yes, I did. To this day, I have no idea how many. There was a need and everything was an emergency and I actually did operate on hundreds of men, some of them dying and nothing I could do." Her voice trailed off, remembering moments too sad to talk about. "Sometimes I worked days so long they had to drag me away from the operating tents and push me to sleep in a cot somewhere."

"An open heart and a kind and giving spirit in the time of war is not an easy road."

She smiled and squeezed his hand. "You and I, Tony… we have been knocked around by the war, but we must stay open to life. And as you say – we will not let any of that break us."

"Yes," he said. Yes, yes, yes." He gently kissed her on the lips. And that simply – and it happened that fast – in that moment, everything was decided between them.

CHAPTER TWENTY-FOUR

Monday morning at the steel mill, Anselmo and Louie were walking toward their station at the hot beds when Anselmo noticed a difference in the sound of the rollers. "Louie, are they making this thing go even faster? Can they actually do that? I thought they were at their limit."

"Oh yeah. The *bastardos* are making up for lost time."

"But you said it was already too fast…this feels dangerous."

"Tell me about it. *Non gliene frega niente.* The *bastardos* don't give a shit."

They passed Ollie's station. Tripi was up there, cursing a blue streak. He had to jump back as the steel came slapping through his repeater. Louie yelled at Jersey Mike, the line boss. "It's running too fast, Mikey-Boy! You better slow it down!"

"Talk to management, Louie. They say it's you guy's fault for last week. Three line shutdowns."

"OUR fault?!"

"Naw, not you personally. Come on, Louie, you know what I mean: All us guy's fault."

Louie looked around and didn't see anybody he recognized. "Who's taking the place of Ollie?"

The line boss pointed to a young black kid. "That young guy – You know him? That's Ollie's kid."

Louie's face turned purple and he raised his fists, shaking them in the air. "No! Not the very spot where his papa is killed! That's-a not going to happen!" Louie grabbed an extra set of the heavy grabbers, the tongs they needed on repeater stations one and two. "Tripi, we send Ollie's kid down to the hot beds! Do it now! He will take my place down there with Mo!"

Anselmo shook his head. "No! I'm with you, Louie! Send them both down there!"

"But Mo..."

"No, Louie. We're partners."

Louie gave Anselmo a serious look. "You know the danger."

"Yes, I do know it."

Louie nodded. He tapped Tripi's shoulder and as the man moved off the metal grates the shorter man gathered his cannonball shaped body, hopped up on the iron grate grillwork floor plates and positioned himself in Tripi's place.

"You heard the man, Tripi," Anselmo said. "Take Ollie's son and go down there."

The next glowing white hot bar had already started on through. Louie grabbed it, swung it around his big body and wrestled it into the next set of rollers. He looked across the metal floor at Anselmo. "What? Why are you decide to do this? Are you the nut case or something?"

"We're partners, Louie," Anselmo said. *"Compagno."*

The next bar was already on its way. Louie snagged it with his tongs and wrestled it in a semi-circle and jammed it in the rollers. "You have to do it just like that," he said. "You gonna know how to do it?"

"Yeah," Anselmo said. *"Proprio cosi."*

"Okay. Come on over here. You try it."

170

Anselmo snatched the tongs from Louie and moved into his place. The next bar was already extruding from the repeaters. He snagged it and tried to bend it but he didn't have the rhythm yet – he had great reflexes and his motion was actually too quick – but the bar brushed his upper arm, leaving his heavy outer jacket smoking.

"You okay?" Louie screamed at him, his voice pitched high with concern for his partner's safety.

"Yeah, no problem, *mio compagno.* Just like that." Anselmo ignored the fiery pain in his arm, no time for that as he wrestled the next thick bar and jammed it into the roller the way he'd seen Louie do it. The routine was brutal, with no room for mistakes. He knew he had to concentrate because he could see another bar already pushing out of the first roller. He was going to have to visit Doctor Lina, maybe get some ointment to ease the fiery pain burning away at his arm. Nothing was all bad, he was thinking to himself; now he had a really good excuse to see her again. Not that he needed an excuse.

After work, Louie and Anselmo washed up and were heading out the main gate when Louie saw the burn mark on Anselmo's upper arm. "You are a crazy man, Mo. You could have got yourself killed."

"Yeah, I know, but what else could we do, Louie? – were we gonna let Ollie's kid up there?"

"No, I guess not."

"You know we cannot let that happen. And it really is okay, I have the move down now, I can handle it from here."

"Yeah, but look at your arm."

Anselmo pulled up his shirt to show a huge old scar running horizontally across his chest. "You think that's something? Maybe I told you that once I got in a knife fight with an officer."

Louie's eyes widened and he crossed himself, "*Gesu, Maria e Giuseppe*...that was some big knife, Mo."

"Truth is, Louie, it was my fault. I miscalculated. He was on a horse and he was a slasher, not really trained, you know."

"And you were?"

"Oh, yeah. *Sie, otto!* Six, eight! *Parata, spinta!* Parry, thrust!"

"You had some adventures in life, Mo!"

"Yeah, like in the movies. And more to come, I'm sure."

As they showed their badges to the gate guard and made their way out the half open gates, three workmen were walking back and forth, the men carrying hand lettered signs on wooden sticks. Louie told Anselmo to hold up for a moment. He stopped and looked back at the guard. "Hey Marchio – what's going on?"

"Ahh, just some *teste de merda* from the night shift. Nobody's happy about the pay cuts. That nigger gets hisself killed on the line and we all get our pay docked? That ain't fair."

"That's what happens," Louie said, but as he started forward, the guard held him back.

"Wait, just for a minute, *amico*. Here come the bullheads. You don't want to get caught up in it." They heard the blat of an air horn, and then they saw a square police van turn a corner a block away and race toward the main gate. There it was, like a

172

scene on the big screen at the Lincoln Theater movie house – a model T Ford police truck with a driver and four policemen waving night sticks and yelling at the top of their lungs.

Louie turned to Anselmo. "We got the movies here, too, Mo. Right here, in real life. You think about what happens here – The Big Bosses are too afraid to talk direct to the men who work for them. So they call in the police. We want to hang back for a moment so they don't confuse us with those guys."

"I thought we were for those guys," Anselmo said.

"Yes, we are, Mo, but Marchio is right – the timing is important. It does no good to spend the night in jail when we don't have to. The time has to be right or it is just *la mossa del motto*, you know, *the fool's move.*"

By now the police van had stopped. The protesters didn't think to scatter and run, and the police gave them a few hits with their billy clubs and hustled them inside the back end of the truck.

"What will happen to them?" Anselmo watched as the police truck gave a warning blat and drove away.

Louie and Marchio looked at each other and shrugged. "Whatever the boss asks for," Marchio said. "Maybe a week or two pounding rocks in Joliet State Prison. Or maybe they just drive them ten or twenty miles out of town, let them make their way back walking on foot, lots of time to be thinking about their problems."

As they walked along together, Louie was mulling over everything that had happened recently at the mill, and the more he thought about it, the more he became excited and angry. He pounded his left fist in his right hand, "I am telling you, Mo – this is why we say Workers Unite!"

CHAPTER TWENTY-FIVE

Elmond Ridgeway, his courage enforced by the shiny brass Inland Steel logo on the wall behind him, stood in front of the four seated directors and three members of his executive staff who showed up for the meeting he'd called. He shifted his weight from foot to foot, wishing he was anywhere but here. The only meetings he enjoyed were those where he announced corporate profits, but there hadn't been one of those for going on three years, actually since the headquarters in Chicago had bought their mill and merged their local operations into the general corporate scheme of things.

Sumner Silverman sat behind him, bent over at a small school desk, his job to take notes as the meeting progressed. Elmond was fairly certain his operation was still in the black – it had been ever since he'd taken over a decade ago – but Sumner said he was *flummoxed* by the corporate recording system, and he had the paperwork Chicago sent him to prove his case. There were entire pages missing from the report, and other pages had lines blacked out or even physically snipped from the page.

The sweet young thing, Patty (not Elmond's sweet young thing, just his secretary, though God knows he'd tried), also sat next to Sumner, taking notes in shorthand, but Elmond didn't trust her smarts that much as she was just a fresh young girl newly minted from secretary school. The four directors, who had their regular jobs at other local businesses, were restless, impatient to be on their way home or to the gentlemen's club in Olympia Fields. There was Heinie Lufitz who ran Hot Point, George Arthur from Flintcote, Al Raymond from DeSoto Paint Factory and Morton Fox who was a biggie at the Chicago Heights bank.

Elmond started in right away before the directors had time to start jabbering like they always seemed to about their stupid golf scores or the expensive stuff their wives had bought on their latest excursion to Marshall Field's department store in Chicago's downtown Loop. "We have a real *dilemma* here," he said. He liked the idea of a 'dilemma', that word caught their attention right away. "It's a money thing, and it doesn't just affect us here at Inland Steel. It affects you guys, too, at your operations. We're all *confronted* with the same *dilemma*. All of us." He liked the sound of 'confronted'. He had them now. Nobody was going to stray off into golf scores or senseless arguments about who had the best cigar with a *dilemma confronting* them, right there on their note pads in front of their noses. Elmond went on to explain for those who didn't yet *get it*: "I specifically want each of us to examine our souls and to say to ourselves, *Just how much is a worker worth?* More specific, I'm thinking *How much is a nigger on the mill line at Inland Steel worth?*"

"We don't have any black employees at the bank," Morton Fox said. "I couldn't even begin to tell you how to calculate that."

"Well, black or white shouldn't matter that much," Al Raymond said. "Hell, it probably shouldn't matter at all. Is he a good worker? Does he carry his load?"

176

"What do you mean, 'worth', Elmond?" Heinie said

Elmond could see he was losing control. He upped the pitch of his voice a notch. "Look, fellows, let me give it to you straight up: we lost this big black man, Ollie Pickins, a few days ago. I want to be fair, particularly now, because we have lots of worker unrest going on. Ollie had a wife and a ton of kids. I'm not sure how many; seems they all have lots of kids. And yes, he was a good worker. He was 45, he had maybe ten good years on the line ahead of him. Worse luck, he was popular; everybody liked him. Hear me out now: My problem, the company has to give the family something. Some compensation. It's only fair. But what's the right amount? I don't want to be a sucker, here."

A general murmur of assent went around the table.

"Yeah, there's an unhappy mood in the air, for sure," Al Raymond from the paint factory said. "It's all over town. "Labor's getting agitated by the unions, the dirty commies, and God only knows who else. You gotta give him something or there's gonna be a riot."

Heinie Lufitz spoke up. "Few weeks ago we had a maintenance guy got hit on the head by a falling pipe. Said he had headaches, said couldn't work. He even got a note from old Doc Whitber."

"Huh. So, what did you do?"

"Well, he didn't die or anything like that. This was maybe worse – he got a smart ass lawyer, came after us for wages he said he should have been paid."

177

"He's not working because he has a headache because he got careless at work and he wants money for that?"

"Yeah. His lawyer called it 'compensation for lost wages'.

"What'd you do?"

"Gave him a hundred bucks and told him to go away or we'd find a way to give him a real headache. Scared off his lawyer, too. Got the police chief to pay a little visit to his office."

"Score one for the good guys," Elmond said. "But that doesn't solve my problem. I can't just run a black family out of town. We got lots of niggers up on that line, work right alongside the dagos and the fritzs and the spicks."

"Well, we had a clumsy young guy; got careless and lost a few fingers in a stamping machine," the director from Flintcote said.

"What the heck is a stamping machine?" Morton Fox said.

"We make roofing shingles, you know. That's how you make 'em, you stamp them out of big sheets. Look, Elmond, I know it isn't the same thing, this guy I'm talking about being a Fritz and all, but maybe you can gauge it, like a point of reference."

"You paid him for lost fingers?"

"Had to. That's what you do these days."

"How much you give him?"

"Well, he got two hundred dollars for each of three fingers. The stamper missed his little finger so we got lucky there. However, it did nip off the top digit on his thumb but arbitration ruled he still had use of his thumb even the way it was so he didn't get nothing for that."

"Arbitration," Elmond said.

"Yeah, you do not want that. Get a worker's union involved, things get out of hand. We took the kid aside, paid him off fast, gave him the old boot out the door."

"Goddamn socialists," Heinie muttered. " Bolshevik-loving commie bastards. Don't they know this is fucking America!?"

"If it was six hundred dollars for three fingers…" Elmond said, doing his thinking out loud.

"Yeah, but he was a *white* kid…"

"Yeah, but he was a *Fritz*…"

The discussion started to dissolve into a discussion of the value and relative cultural faults of German immigrants with good attitudes and negroes with bad attitudes and poor educations up from the Deep South.

"But from what I'm hearing, this Ollie Pickens had a great attitude. And you said he was one of your best workers."

"Well, yes, he did…and he was."

"Wait, wait, wait – how old was this Ollie?" Heinie looked up from a cigar he was intent on removing from a thick paper wrapping. "How many earning years you say he had left? You have to factor that in."

"Yeah, you do," the man from Flintcote agreed. "The kid who lost his fingers had his whole life ahead of him. Naturally we weren't going to keep him on; he was useless as hell to us. On the other hand – no joke intended – he didn't have a family to support. So that's another thing to calculate."

The meeting dragged on like that until Elmond's headache got the best of him and he called it a day. He wished he hadn't set up the damn thing in the first place. He'd mull it over with Sumner and figure out what Inland Steel could afford without being taken obvious advantage of – or going broke – and Ollie's family was going to have to be satisfied with that. In a way, Elmond figured having Ollie's young son working at the mill was actually a good thing – the family wouldn't want to see their only source of income booted out the door just because they were too greedy to settle on a decent number.

CHAPTER TWENTY-SIX

It was a Saturday night after eight o'clock, a mild evening in May, still twilight with a sliver of a moon hanging low in a clear sky. Anselmo picked up his rented Hupmobile from the side of the Victoria Hotel. He drove over to the side street behind the big orange brick San Rocco church where Louie was waiting in front of his own lunch pail house.. Louie introduced Arturo, a friend of his who worked at Hot Point. Arturo was a skinny little string bean of a guy, taller than Louie by six inches, but still only five or six inches over five feet tall. He had skin pocked with old scars and a deep scar on his neck and he sounded like a frog when he spoke, his voice so deep it was more of a croaking animal sound. "So, you from the Old Country, huh?"

"Yes. Piedmont. Way north," Anselmo said, "And west toward Frogland."

"You speak French?"

"Sure."

"Me, my family was from way south. Other end of the boot. We been here two generations now. We don't speak no frog at all. Never did."

"How about Louie?"

"He's from the middle."

"From Tivoli," Louie said. One hour east of Rome, by motor car, if you have one. Otherwise, you take the bus."

"One hour from *Roma*?"

"Yeah, the family still got a small vineyard there. My cousin takes care of that."

Louie got in the Hupmobile on the passenger side and Arturo sat in back. Anselmo was about to drive away when he noticed a fruit tree to one side of Louie's house. "Hey, something is not right about that tree."

"You can see that even in the dark," Louie said.

"It's not that dark yet."

"Well, you're right about that one. It is special to me. Ten years ago, the peddler comes by in the Spring and he sells me this apple tree. But he leaves and I plant it and it gives only the pears."

"Okay, the pears, but I see somebody did plenty work on that tree."

"You noticed that too, huh, Mo? I learned how to graft branches on fruit trees from *mio papa*. Now my special pear tree gives me five kinds of pear: There's the Bartlett, the red pear, the brown skin pear and two others, I don't know the names."

"Interesting. What else you got back there?"

"Two apple trees. One red grape vine, one of the green grape. Prune every winter, they come back strong, plenty of grapes in the fall."

"You make wine?"

Louie's grin lit up his round face, "*Shooza,* does the Pope wear the tall hat? Last year, I ferment in the keg, but I bottle it too soon, you know? So one night I hear from the basement, Pop! Pop! Pop! That was really something, woke up the wife and kids!"

"The corks came out?"

182

"I wish. No, the bottle – all twenty one of those *diavoli* – they explode, one by one! Lucky nobody was down there."

"*Oddio,* that's sad."

"I can laugh now, but last winter I cried."

Louie directed Anselmo to drive south on Dixie Highway past the big piano factory in Steger, turn right on 34th Street, and on a few more blocks, and then left to the church hall that was in the basement under St. Liborius grade school.

"Saint Liborius, you know him?" Arturo said in his deep voice.

Anselmo had to admit he didn't.

"Patron saint of gall stones," Arturo said.

Anselmo must have looked like he didn't believe it, because Louie tapped his arm. "No, Artie here is not pulling your leg, Mo. You go in the church, you see the statue, the saint has little rocks on the holy book in his hand. He's got gall stones sitting right there on the bible."

"I hear if you get gall stones, they hurt like a stab wound."

"Catholics got a saint for everything," the scratchy voice said.

"You're a Catholic, right Louie?" Anselmo said.

"Naw, Mo. My wife, Anna, is the good Catholic. And the kids. I used to be a good church-boy, too. But now I'm-a the evil Commie Red *bastardo.* Like Arturo here. We're both gonna go to hell."

"You could be both, right? Be both Catholic and Commie red devil?"

Arturo's laugh sounded harsh and bitter. "*Shooza!* Why not? Mix like the oil and the vinegar!"

Louie raised one hand to make a point. "Wait, though: there's a serious part to what he say, Mo. Arturo means it like this: The priest and the revolutionary, they both say they want to help the working man. But I tell you, my friend, they are both the devil, *il diavolo*, you know? They only work for themselves. They do not work for us, not really. And they do not work together and they each want a part of the working man's soul. Me, I prefer the Communist devil. At least they are honest about it. You pay the dues for today, not the money in the Sunday collection basket for a place that only maybe you get in heaven after you die."

"If there is such a place, this heaven," Arturo said.

"You hear the mill gave Ollie's family six hundred and fifty dollars?" Louie spat the words out like he'd been chewing on a bad plug of tobacco. "Stinking, lousy six hundred and fifty dollars for the life of their best worker!"

"How did they figure that one out?"

"Sumner told me they decided it had to be more than if he was just made a cripple, but less than if he was a white guy."

"That doesn't make any sense at all," Anselmo said.

"Now you start to get the idea," Arturo said, the deep growl of his voice sounding as much like a threat as a casual comment.

CHAPTER TWENTY-SEVEN

Anselmo let his two passengers out in front of the Saint Liborius grade school. They went on ahead as he parked the Hupmobile on the nearest side street. He could hear the people at the meeting shouting and cheering and cat-calling as he walked down the steps to the basement hall under the school. He entered through wide open double doors and was surprised by the energy in the room.

A loud shouting match between rival factions was in full force, grown men yelling at each other, yelling all at once and their anger bursting out here and there in the room like spot-fires in high dry prairie grass. Groups of tradesmen and laborers, many still in their work clothes, were gathered at their own tables or simply milling around. Anselmo didn't see Louie or Arturo, even though he knew they had to be somewhere in the hall. As he walked around looking for them he passed a square table with the sign CPUSA taped to the front of it. A bearded fellow in a black suit was wearing a white wife-beater undershirt but no regular shirt. He yelled in Anselmo's direction, "Get one! Get one! Get one!" He had a bead necklace made of dark brown chestnuts around his neck and was wearing a strange cotton stovepipe hat embroidered with multi-colored flowers. The *one that he wanted people to get* was apparently a flyer he was waving in the air. He shoved one in Anselmo's hands, and the headline read, "CITIZENS OF THE WORLD – THE TIME IS NOW!" Anselmo shook his head and handed the flyer back and the man muttered something Slavic and unpronounceable.

"I don't understand what you are saying," Anselmo said.

"Revolt now!" the man shouted in his face. "Revolt! Revolt! Revolt!"

Anselmo nodded and moved on. The Workers Union occupied the next table in the front row below a raised stage. A thin little man with a pencil moustache, a near-sighted fellow with thick glasses who might have been a grade school teacher or a meek garment salesman, gave him a brochure with the headline "INLAND STEEL STRIKE!" printed in red letters. The brochure announced the strike was ongoing and listed the worker's demands: A pay raise of almost double to 30 cents an hour. Lunch break increased from fifteen minutes to a half hour. A morning and an afternoon rest break of ten minutes. Safety posts installed on all the repeaters. As Anselmo watched, another man took one of the brochures, gave out a scornful laugh, crumpled it into a ball and tossed it on the floor. "Never happen," he said. "Not in a million years."

"Why not?" the timid little man who'd handed him the brochure said.

"You are a crazy fellow! Nobody ain't going to raise wages almost double!"

A third man agreed. "Here's the sad truth. They have already offered the scabs they are trying to hire to replace us 3 cents less, down to 15 cents an hour!"

"Scabs? They got dirty, rotten scabs comin'?

"Well, that don't matter – we have to ask for more money or we'll never get anything."

"Don't be stupid. You're just another wobbly bobbly. You talk a big game, but you got nothing to lose. You don't even work at the mill. You're a namby-pamby school teacher!"

"So what? I care about this! And you need all the help you can get!"

"Phony fake!"

"Fool!"

Anselmo moved on to the next table. Socialist Party of America, their sign read in big hand-done block letters. Their table was manned by two chubby men who looked like twins – and like they'd never put in a day of hard labor in their lives.

Above and behind these three tables, a set of partly drawn curtains revealed an amateur stage play setting where several priests were sitting in chairs around a card table and talking with each other. They looked like they were ignoring the rest of the angry boil and stir of the gathering.. That got Anselmo thinking how that stage setting was a miniature representation of what Louie and Arturo were saying: If Louie's vision of reality was right, the priests were there behind the scenes, aloof and above it all, and yet quietly manipulating the puppet strings connected to all their parishioners. Anselmo felt the old sting he'd gotten in his early days before the war, admonitions and warnings to be good from the headmasters of the church in the Vatican. And then, after the war they had reached out to his grandfather, convinced him to send his grandson all over Italy on his mission of repentance, payment for *sins against honor* that they said he'd committed.

Turning his gaze in a half-circle away from the three recruiting tables with the priests elevated on the stage behind them, Anselmo looked out on the rows of bingo tables, already set up for the Steger Bingo Night, a local festivity held once a month with players coming from surrounding towns, from Chicago Heights, from Crete, Beecher and Monee, and even Kankakee, traveling to Steger for a shot at the game winnings and the Big Prize that was sometimes over a hundred dollars. It was a mixed crowd of working men. Only a few of the workers were dressed up for the meeting; the rest looked like they'd just gotten off work, still in carpenter or painter overhauls, farmer boy jeans or conveyor belt whites.

Anselmo was startled by the energy in the room and the general uproar, disorganized as it was.. He was starting to believe this was something at least half way serious. Everyone was talking at once and nobody listened to any of the speakers at each of the three tables as they tried to give their recruitment speeches, button-holing the nearest person within earshot. But, still, disorganized or not, Aselmo was impressed, he felt the energy was marvelous. Adding to the confusion, some of the women members of the parish were moving between the tables with carts, selling coffee and a variety of home-made cookies for a few pennies or a nickel. What Anselmo was feeling was an *intent* here, a mood, a feeling that in some way united them all. *Something good could come out of this.*

Anselmo spotted Louie sitting at a Bingo table in the front row. "Louie, this is a madhouse!"

Louie waved his short arms and grinned. "You see the way it is here, Mo. We are everybody gathered together, all the workers. We have a common enemy, the owners. But nobody *works together.* That is what we need, we have to work together. We have plenty of the desire, but we no gotta the spark!"

Anselmo pointed to the priests, who were standing and now looked like they were thinking of leaving. "I thought the priests hate the communists."

"Yes, in everything else they are enemies. But in this you see they both have the common goal – they both want the heart and the soul and the cash money of the working man. I think we will soon figure out if we all can work together." Louie nodded to Arturo and left him with Anselmo at their bingo table while he climbed alone the few steps onto the stage.

Louie raised his stubby arms as if he was reaching for the sky and his voice was a bellow that demanded attention. "Workers of the Inland Steel – we are here to speak our minds. You know how much I make? Eighteen cents an hour! It is the same as you make! Eighteen cents an hour! I got a wife, I got a family! You too! You got the *moglie*! You got the *bambino*! *Eighteen cents an hour is not enough!*"

Anselmo pointed to the empty stage where the priests had quietly left their chairs and vanished from view. "Arturo, where did the priests go?"

"Who knows? Nobody trust these men of God," Arturo said. "*Uomini di dio! Phaa!*" He made a spitting gesture. "They betray their own!"

Anselmo didn't say anything more. He knew that, back in Italy, the communists did not trust the Catholic priests, and the *uomini di dio,* the so-called

189

men of God, treated the Revolution-loving Italian Communist party with venomous reproach, excommunicating their members on the slightest pretense. He wondered what part the priests of San Rocco and Saint Liborius and all the other local parishes were playing in this movement – how much of their allegiance went to the bosses and how much to the ordinary workers who made up most of their flock? Could they really be counted on to join forces against the rich and the powerful for the good of their working class parishioners?"

That was when Anselmo and Arturo both had to duck because the man with the stovepipe hat at the CPUSA table threw something – it looked like a handful of radishes – at the socialists table and they started to pelt each other with pencils, paper balls, even coffee cups – whatever they could find.

Louie's voice rose above the growing chaos, "Hey. Hey! HEY!! Whats-a matter, you!? We fight each other here? No! We work together, right?"

"Right," a few voices said.

"We work together! Come on – I wanna hear it!"

"Right!" More voices joining in.

"I wanna hear it," Louie shouted. "I wanna hear it *right now*!"

"RIGHT!" they yelled back, starting to get into it.

"And what are we gonna do? We gonna Strike!"

"RIGHT!" They yelled back, now as one voice. "WE GONNA STRIKE!"

And, true to their word, when the night shift was over, the only men who showed up at the mill the next morning were not dressed for work. Instead, they wore casual clothes like they were on vacation. And they brandished rough hand lettered signs that were tacked to sticks and said 18 CENTS IS NOT ENOUGH! Since there was nobody to man the stations, the mill couldn't run any rails, and so they had to shut it down. When the furnaces were going, you could hear it from over a mile away, and so, as far away as Chicago Heights to the north and Steger to the south, the silence was deafening.

That morning Rosa showed up at Lina's office pushing a small four wheeled trundle cart with canvas sides and carrying a washing board wringer and some clothes line.

"Mamma Mia!" Lina said. "What, you movin' in?"

"No, I just need your operating room for a few hours."

"What if I need it?"

"Then I'll be out of there in five minutes."

"But that room has to be sanitary."

"Fresh pasta has to be sanitary, too. When's the last time you used your operating room?"

"Well, yes, you have a point there..." Lina held the door open and Rosa gave her a triumphant grin as she trundled her cart into the operating room. She covered the rectangular operating table with butcher's block paper and set up her wringer. Lina saw it had been converted into some sort of a strange machine.

"What's that odd thing?" Lina said.

"My pasta squeezer. Pauli made it for me. My idea, but he's the mechanical wizard. Don't worry, I soaked it in lye solution, rinsed it a half dozen times. Here, string up this line for me. I see old Whitber had the right hooks in the right places, used to do his own wash, I bet."

Lina watched as her friend attached another device to the front of the pasta squeezing machine. "This is the cutter," Rosa said. Have to be careful, it's sharp and you could cut yourself. But, see, we got ourselves a factory here." She took some lumps of pasta, thick as wooden platters, from her cart and stacked them on the table.. She stuck one in the modified wringer with one hand and cranked the handle. The dough obediently ran through the rollers and then, as its thinner self came out the other end, the cutter sliced it into long ribbons. Rosa took the strips of spaghetti and hung them on the line to dry. "Presto! It's Rosa's Spaghetti!"

"Oh, Lord," Lina said. "We can be thankful Doc Whitber's not here to see this. It would give him a heart attack for sure." Rosa was already positioning another lump of pasta in front of her machine. "But, dear girlfriend, you're gonna make enough pasta to feed an army. What are you doing this for?"

"You heard the workers went out on strike at Inland Steel?"

"Yeah, it's all over town, everybody saying its tough times ahead."

"Well, nothing's cheaper than spaghetti. Good for you, too. And those workers are gonna need all the help they can get."

"How much you going to charge?" Lina asked, but she already knew the answer.

"Oh, I think they get it free. And maybe a Ball Jar of tomato sauce from our basement. Mamma puts up the preserves every August and September. She's unstoppable that way. We've still got preserves from before the war. We keep the Ball Jar people in business."

"Why's she do that?"

"It's right there in Genesis. This Egyptian king tells Joseph his dream that there's seven fat years followed by seven lean ones. He does it with cows, but it's a dream, he means years. So, long story short, you gotta get ready for those bad years. Mamma will tell anyone who asks that it says so right there in the bible."

"Praise *Dio* for women who believe in the word of the Lord."

"Amen to that."

CHAPTER TWENTY-EIGHT

Sitting in his offices in the executive building, the unaccustomed quiet made Elmond uneasy. He knew this was intolerable; he could lose his job. He was going to have to do something to fix this. *And fast!*

A few hours later, Freddy Warberton showed up outside Elmond's office, looking all smug and unconcerned as only ignorant youth can look, as if he had the world on a string when he really didn't have anything. At least, that was how Patty Bergstrand, Elmond's secretary, saw him. She flipped a hand to dismiss him, but Freddy marched right on past her into Elmond's office. That wasn't right by her so she shook her head of meticulously curled chestnut brown hair and got up and went after him, "Hey, you Mister, you can't go in there!" But her boss held up one hand, told her it was okay.

Patty huffed back to her desk, straightened her nylon stockings under her flapper skirt – she could tell, when the decorative line of embroidered palm trees running up her leg was crooked, that one of her garters had come undone – she straightened it out as best she could, and then she sat there in a glowering funk. *What good was it having a gatekeeper if the boss let just anybody in?*

But it wasn't long before things started to perk up; just after the noon lunch break, Sumner arrived with two fellows in business suits from the Inland Steel building headquarters in downtown Chicago, and Patty saw it was going to be one of those meetings where everybody talked in important tones about things they wouldn't be able to do in real life. But at least it would be something to make the time go by. She picked up her shorthand notepad and took a chair behind Elmond. Might as well pretend like she was working, and the thing was, well, she'd heard rumors that the company president's son Albert had been jilted by his fiancée. And, *praise be!*, Albert did show up right after the other two executives from headquarters had made their entrance.

"Sorry I'm late, fellows," the clean-cut young man explained in the breezy way Patty imagined a president's son might have. "I drove down in my new Ford roadster, you probably heard, I got the snappy one with the rumble seat."

"Does it ride okay?" Elmore said. He knew his role, be interested in the stupid kid's car.

"Oh, yeah! Bully good! Quite the ride!"

After everybody was seated, Patty made the rounds, offering coffee or tea, and once she had accomplished that chore – extra cream for the president's son's tea – she took a different seat, this one so Albert couldn't miss seeing her in the background. She hiked her skirt *just a skinch* and crossed her legs so the straight line of fancy palm tree designs was showing. She had great legs. She knew they were one of her best assets.

As she started scribbling in her notepad, Freddy was giving his spy-report on how the workers were reacting to the mill shutdown. "I think the ones who were not in on it from the meeting at St. Liborius were surprised," he said.

"That's pretty obvious," the president's son gave him a skeptical look. "And once they saw what was happening, they had to know we'd be forced to shut it down."

"Well, yeah," Freddy said. "But not so soon."

"Come on, they had to know we'd have no choice. We had nobody to run the steel."

"I guess…" Freddy said, looking to Elmond for support.

"Freddy is our contact with the workers. He's got his finger on their pulse," Elmond said.

"They're gonna fold," Freddy said. "Sooner rather than later."

"Couldn't we have avoided the strike?" The elder of the two men from headquarters was frowning at Elmond as if the strike might have been his fault.

"It was rotten luck," Elmond shook his head in disgust. "There's been lots of talk about a raise in pay. You see the signs out front, *Eighteen Cents Is Not Enough!* We've talked about this every time when we come up to headquarters. We don't have the authority, and you guys won't even budge! Not a penny. You won't even toss us a scrap or two we can dole out to them."

"Money doesn't grow on trees." That comment from Sumner, trying to pacify everybody and avoid a conflict.

"So now it's our fault," young Albert said. "Dad isn't going to like hearing that."

"I didn't say it was his fault."

"Then what did you say?"

Elmond chose his words carefully, "I said that low wages was a big factor in why these men chose to strike right now."

"No, you didn't say that. You said it was rotten luck."

"Well, it's that too. Having one of our best workers killed on the line right now when there's all this unrest…well, that doesn't help anything."

Albert pounced like a young lion, "But that could have been avoided. You could have put in safety posts. I've seen the proposal."

Patty saw her boss was trying to be aloof, concentrating on maintaining a professional look of serious leadership, the one he sometimes practiced in a mirror in the back of his office. Actually, she was thinking, the effort made him look silly, like he was working at a difficult bowel movement.

Elmond couldn't resist shooting Sumner a dirty look, but his bookkeeper was looking down at an open page in his accounting book, his gaze hidden by the green visor pulled low over his brow. Elmond had a temper so bad it was legendary, but he was facing off against the president's son and two other biggies from downtown, and so – easy for anyone who knew him to see – he was trying to hold back the thunder and the fury. "However, you must recognize every move we make goes to the bottom line, Albert. You want expensive safety posts put in everywhere somebody thinks there's a little danger, there goes your profit for 1922 – and maybe next year, too."

"*Our* profit," Albert said. "And now it's going, anyway."

Patty saw the president's son was looking in her direction. She nodded encouragingly and gave him her quiet but respectful smile, the one that recognized he was something of a young business genius. She was sure he caught it; he actually smiled back before he turned his attention back to her boss. "So your brilliant response was, you tried to hire scabs, you want to start up the mill again even though you know you will have to shut it down again if they don't work out – and they probably won't," he continued.

"What else are we going to do?"

"Oh, now you're asking me. Well, I'll tell you this much: Whatever we do, it has to be firm and it has to stick – otherwise the union is going to claim a victory over us. They'll claim they were the ones who shut us down."

"It's not a complete victory for them," Sumner was saying, another effort on his part to cool the dialogue down.

"How so is that?"

"We've got enough rebar and fence posts to keep on shipping for quite a while, and they know it."

"Darn right," Freddy Warberton chimed in.

Patty was thinking Freddy was such a banana-brain! Too bad. He was kind-of cute, but any girl could see he wasn't going anywhere in the business world. *Scrub him off the list!*

Elmond pointed a finger across the conference table, "Well, Albert, you're the guy with all the answers here; what's your suggestion?"

"I think I've got an idea," the president's son said.

CHAPTER TWENTY-NINE

It was two A.M. on a Sunday morning, dark as the inside of a coal mine about three hundred feet down, and chilly – late Spring south of Lake Michigan – and the group of over a dozen drivers were restless, thinking this wasn't exactly what they'd signed on for. They hugged their chests and stamped their feet, ready to climb in their trucks and get on with it. There were eighteen trucks and vans, each with the big tires and extra suspension that could haul dead weight like rebar and posts. Plus, four of them were pulling stout trailers that could handle an extra load, if all went well and if they'd have the time and the energy for it.

Hal Singlebury nodded his approval. Hal had found this deserted dead end street courtesy of a stool pigeon, one of the steel workers who owed his loyalty to the bosses. Thirtieth Street was a few miles south of the mill in South Chicago Heights, just East off Dixie Highway and tucked behind a spur of the C&EI tracks that serviced the famous old piano factory in Steger.

Hal was over six feet tall, and scuffed up and burly as a tree trunk, courtesy of the violence, the brutal moments, that went along with his trade. He didn't care about the politics of the game; he played both sides of the fence – strike-breaker or union organizer – his loyalty went to whoever was paying the tab. He had dark, unfriendly eyes that peered suspiciously out of a face full of pink-white skin, and his jet black hair and a two inch thick black beard gave plenty of warning there was no fooling around with Hal Singlebury, it was his way or the highway. He liked to think of himself as a mercenary, somebody like a Japanese Samurai or a sheriff in the Old West, one of those good guys who were out to protect the down-trodden and the little man. The truth was, he had generally persuaded himself to his convictions depending on who was paying the tab, and in this case it was the Inland Steel corporate bosses sitting snug up there in their high office building in the Chicago Loop.

Hal walked the line of his trucks, kerosene lamp in one hand, alerting his men it was time to move out. One by one they started their engines and lit their front head beams as he passed. It was the dead of night; the angry picketers with their EIGHTEEN CENTS IS NOT ENOUGH! signs should all be at home tucked in their warm beds. There were probably a hundred ways to break a strike, everything from police raids to outright murder; and a dead-of-night attack was one of Hal's favorites.

It didn't take but twenty minutes for his convoy to arrive at the front gates of the mill, and as the Inland people had promised, the gates were wide open. There was a little moment of what seemed like bad luck – the lead truck had to halt as there were three or four strikers unexpectedly standing in their way, waving their silly signs and shouting, "Scabs! Go home!" There was that one short little round guy who seemed to be a ringleader. Hal, riding passenger in the lead truck, wanted to get out and smash him in the face, but the guy tapped a warning on his window with a wooden baseball bat and Hal decided to stay inside.

That was when the strikers began pelting the trucks with eggs. Hal saw his convoy was losing momentum. "Come on, run the silly bastards over!" he said. It was nearly impossible to see out of the front wind screens with the messy egg goo smearing them, but nobody questioned a command from Hal Singlebury. The first three trucks jerked forward and their tires thumped over wooden ten-by-two planks before the drivers realized the planks were imbedded with steel spikes.

It took the rest of the day to fix the tires and get the convoy moving on in back to the stockpiles of fence posts and rebar, and then it took all that time to load up the trucks and get back out on their way. Hal figured the operation was sort of a success, though he was feeling sour and angry at the delay and the extra expense for the time and the tires. He managed to pass on some of the cost over-runs to the steel company, but still he was mad at himself for underestimating the enemy, he should have figured the strikers might pull some stunt like that. He'd heard of the spikes trick; it was just that nobody had ever tried that one on him.

CHAPTER THIRTY

Later that same morning, a few hours after the truck convoy ran over the spikes at the main gate, Monsignor Monafusti showed up at Lina Bright's office.

"Dear young lady," he said with a sniff that was meant to say he had problems but nothing he couldn't handle, should she not be up to the task at hand, "My dear young person, I'm suffering from pain in my shoulders and my hips, and I'm afraid I need your professional assistance."

He limped around the reception desk where she had been pretending to be busy, and without her invitation entered the room in back and sat on the operating table. He leaned his cane next to him. It was longer than a normal walking cane, more like a staff with an ornate silver handle. Lina was annoyed by his presumptive way, thinking, *So that's why Old Whitber kept his operating room door locked.*

Lina followed him into the room and gave him a once-over inspection; he was stooped over and frowning, and yet something didn't look right to her. "How old are you?"

The sour look on his face said he didn't like the question. "Ahh, I am well near to sixty. Why should that make any difference?"

"You know, I can guess your age within a year, either way."

"Nobody can do that."

"I can. A French mystic taught me. She made a living doing it, a person writes it down, bets a franc, and she guesses his age. I'd say you're 43."

"*Ridicola!*"

"Okay, 42, then. And you look like a man pretending to hunch over like a much older man, though I can't imagine why anyone would want to do that. You can straighten up, can't you."

"What does it matter?"

"It doesn't, actually. Not much anybody can do for arthritis, anyway – if that is actually what you have." She took a rubber mallet and tapped his knees and elbows. "Still a pretty good reaction," she said.

"It's the pain. I am always in pain. *Dio Gentile* did not mean for his people to live like this."

"*Dio Gentile?*"

"A caring God. You don't speak Italian?"

"No, but I'm learning fast."

"There are no operations to cure bursitis. I know these things."

"So you self-diagnose and you think you have bursitis. Why did you come to see me?"

"What else could it be?"

"Well, if that's your illness, no, there is no remedy we know of for bursitis."

"What can you give me? Doctor Whitber had marvelous medications." The youngish old man spotted a display of bottles lined up in front of her medical books on a shelf behind her. "Those. Those medicines. Let us talk of them."

"Well, yes...but they are very strong. You have to be strict with yourself, careful to take the right dose."

"I know, of course, I know. Opiates. Relief comes to us from the yellow devils in the Orient."

"I can't really prescribe them. Doctor Whitber wrote the prescriptions."

"I know all about that," the old priest said. He sounded irritated. "The fact is, *Medico* Whitber and I had a deal, but I hear he has gone to Jesus now. *Andato a Gesu.*"

"A deal…?"

"Opium is not on the United States government approval list. You yourself could get in big trouble for prescribing me to use opium drugs. Very big trouble."

"I didn't write you a prescription."

"But you could have. And you would have. However, let us not argue about this. I know the right people, through my connections with the Vatican. I can protect you. You will never have any problems, trust me."

"What would I have to do?"

"My dear young *innocente*, I thought you would never ask." The Monsignor took a butcher's pencil from the recesses of his robe and wrote *55 Dollars* on her prescription pad. "That is per week," he said. "Due every Monday. You can drop by the rectory."

The blood drained from Lina's face. "And if I refuse?"

"Trouble comes in many forms," he said. "Always unexpected."

She nodded once, but she didn't say yes or no. His face took on a strange look, as if he'd become a stranger. She had the impression he might lunge at her. She was glad he was on the far side of the operating table. She backed up, and that's when her left hand unexpectedly rested on the barrel of Billy Franconi's BB gun, leaning forgotten near a clothes tree where she hung her coats and sweaters. Weapons had been a part of everyday life in the war, and the gun came quickly to her hands.

"Don't be silly!" he shouted. "Put that down! You don't know how to use that thing!"

But by then she had pulled the trigger and the small BB missed him by inches and buried itself in the far wall. She pumped the rifle, ready to fire again. "Get out of here," she said.

"I should kill you."

"Out," she repeated, pointing the BB gun at his head. "I wonder if I could hit your eye?"

"But you will be more valuable to me alive."

She motioned impatiently toward the door. "I don't think so," she said.

On his way out, in his hurry to be gone, the Monsignor bumped past Anselmo, who was coming to see the doctor. *"Buon giorno, straniero,"* the Monsignor muttered.

From the brushing contact, Anselmo suspected, as did Lina, the man wasn't as old as he was pretending; early forties, maybe, trying to look like he was sixty. And more; Anselmo was certain now, he had seen him before, actually had met him in Rome.

"Good morning, Monsignor, but I'm no stranger. My name is Anthony Anselmo. And I am quite certain I have seen you once or twice in my father's office." Monafusti blanched, the blood draining from his face. Anselmo noted he held his

205

staff in an *in guardia* position. It was almost casual, the way he handled that long cane, but Anselmo had been fencing since he was a young boy, and he knew the signs. That wasn't a regular staff, it was a *gentleman's protector*, a hollowed out length of hard hickory wood with a sword hidden inside. And the Monsignor was a swordsman.

"*Ridicolo!* Of course I don't know your father!" Monafusti said.

"I think you do – or did, once upon a time. I actually believe you were under the employ of his mistress, a beautiful lady perhaps twenty five or thirty years of age." Anselmo was sure now; he was thinking how impossible it was that this was a coincidence. He thought he'd push a little, "How can you be so certain you don't know my father? I've not mentioned his name."

"*Stupido!* I have enough of this!" And with that, the man in the Monsignor's robe waved his cane in the air and made his way out the door.

"Another non-paying customer," Lina said. "I'm getting used to it."

"Oddly enough, I know him. He is not a nice person."

"I believe it – he tried to extort money from me! He said I was selling illegal drugs!"

Anselmo saw the BB gun at her side. "Did you threaten to shoot him?"

"He's lucky I didn't." She paused, thinking of something else, and then gave him a curious glance, "Your father had a mistress?"

"Still does. Her name is Sarafina Janika. She'd love to change the Janika to Anselmo."

"And what does your mother think of that?"

"My mother died years ago."

"Oh. I'm sorry, Tony. I shouldn't be prying about in your life."

"No, it's okay. I told you I had a brother, too, the one who died in the war. I still have a grandfather. He is a wonderful old man, still very active. Actually the head of our family. He lives on an old vineyard near Turin. I think you'd like him, and I know he would like you."

"Where's Turin?"

"In the upper northwest corner of Italy. Near the Alps. Near the Mediterranean. Near France." He didn't tell her the vineyard was one of the largest in Europe, or that he suspected strongly that the valuable land, and the family fortune – not his father's love – was the true object of Sarafina's desire.

"That man came in here and started talking about pains in his shoulders and knees, and he ended up trying to blackmail me. He claimed I was trying to sell him opium medications.

"How could he possibly blackmail you?"

"There's a law against selling drugs containing the fruit of the poppy. But...how do you know anything at all about him? Tell me about your father's mistress."

"Sarafina Janika is a bit of a street witch. And that man was close to her, something of her personal body guard...or maybe more. Just now you saw he wasn't happy that I recognized him."

"How strange a coincidence he should show up here, half way around the world."

"I don't believe in coincidences, and I don't think you do, either. But make no mistake, that is a man who has to be watched."

"Well, I'm not paying him any money. I'll go to the local police."

"I'll see if my father in Rome has any information…if his brain's not too fogged by his lusty notions. Hey, let's go next door. I'll buy you breakfast."

"Getting late for breakfast."

"Well, lunch then."

CHAPTER THIRTY-ONE

Lina hung a "The Doctor is Next Door" sign in her front window with an arrow pointing toward Rosa's Café and she and Anselmo held hands as they walked next door.

"You two seem to be getting on," Rosa said.

Anselmo pointed to a big sign Rosa had tacked to one wall. STRIKE SPECIAL! It spelled out in big block letters. "What's that about?" he said.

"We give a break to the steel workers and their families."

"What sort of a break?"

"Percent off," she grinned.

"How much percent?"

"Like 100," she said.

"You're going to go broke."

"No, I don't think so. I talked to Ralphie after Mass, and he liked the idea."

Anselmo nodded slowly. "I like it. You do that in his honor."

"Exactly," Rosa said.

"I like it, too," Lina said. "Hey, you got any soup?"

"Does a cow have tits?"

"Hey, girl, that's really gross."

"You know us earthy Italians."

Rosa sat with them as they were sipping hot spoonfuls of the soup of the day. "You like it?" she asked.

"Great!" Anselmo said. "The greatest Italian sausage soup in the world. Who would have known I would find it here?"

"*Mamma mia* knows *zuppa*."

"You just make the soup from whatever you have around?"

"Never. My mother will call you on that, she would tell you that would be a major crime against food *Italiano!* This is *Zuppa Toscana.* You got to fry up the Italian sausage. Then we dice the onions – must be the white ones only – and the crushed red peppers, very important. The salt bacon, we use that only. And the garlic crushed up fine, the liquid, that we will drain from boiled chicken for just this, and then the cream and the diced potato, everything just right."

"So how do you know this recipe?"

"Mamma collects them from all the families on the Hill. If they are from Bologna or Tuscany or wherever, we try to tell everybody when we make their own hometown soup, and it's good for business.

"You should call your place Rosa's Soup Café," Lina said.

"Rosa's *Mamma's* Soup Café! Maybe we say, 'Featuring the Greatest Soups of Italy'."

"*Con le zuppe d'Italia!*" Anselmo said.

Old Frinner, the mail carrier came in looking for Lina. "Doctor Bright? You gotta sign for a letter, so's to prove I gave it to you."

While Lina signed for the legal-looking tan envelope, Mailman Frinner decided he had to have his own bowl of soup. Rosa grinned, "See, Lina, you are good for the soup business."

Lina frowned, puzzling over her letter. "It's from a lawyer. Something about 'a disposition of assets'. If I'm reading this correctly, it looks like old Doc Whitber had assets." She showed the letter to Rosa, "Tomorrow morning. Could you come with me?"

"No, I gotta keep the café going. How about Anselmo here?"

"Sure," Anselmo said. "The strike's still on, and my morning is free. I'll be glad to come. What are you worried about?"

"This letter says that the meeting is for the reading of Doctor Whitber's will. I'' bet you his ancient sister and her son will be there. They don't like me at all and they are not nice people and I'm thinking there will be yelling about something or other – though I'm not sure what."

"Sure. I'll drive us," he said. "I can rent the Hupmobile. I'll meet you here, pick you up a half hour early."

Grinsby and Meyer's legal office was only a few blocks from the Victoria Hotel, but on the way from Rosa's to the meeting, the Hupmobile had a flat tire, and so by the time Anselmo got the spare on, he and Lina were five minutes late and the lawyer, a Mr. Len Meyers, was standing over his desk as he addressed the other two people in the room – as Lina had thought, it was Cynthia Whitber-Yonders and her son Roy – who, from the frowning expressions on their faces, were not pleased to see the newcomers.

"Sorry we started without you," Len Meyers said, peering at them over his steel rimmed reading glasses, "But you are late. And Mrs. Whitber-Yonders here said you had chosen not to attend."

"Well, that is not true," Lina said. "But would that have mattered?"

"Well, yes it does matter…you are the other party mentioned in Doctor Whitber's will."

"You've come too late. We are nearly finished with the reading," Roy Yonders said.

Lina glanced over at Anselmo, her look asking him what to do.

"No problem," Anselmo said. "*Nearly* finished isn't *entirely* finished." He ignored Roy and taking Lina's arm, settled her into one of the comfortable chairs around the lawyer's desk, and then sat next to her. "Perhaps you can give Doctor Bright here a brief summary," he said to the lawyer. "Just to bring her up to speed.

Len Meyers nodded. "Yes. Of course. Basically, Doctor Whitber's surviving family members – that is, Mrs. Whitber-Yonders and, in the event of her death, Roy Yonders here – are deeded all physical properties – the doctor's office building itself and the doctor's instruments and office furniture. We were just getting to the final clause. Here, I will read it officially for all attending parties: 'Doctor Lina Bright, M.D., as the sole surviving member of the prescription corporation known as Doctor Whitber's Magical Medicinal Formulas, Incorporated, is granted all patents and physical properties attached to that corporation.' "

"What?!" Both Roy and his mother spoke as one and then were up and out of their chairs, glaring across the table at Lina.

Len Meyers frowned. "People. Please! A little dignity here. This is a man's last will and testament. And Doctor Bright here looks as surprised as do you."

"I'll bet! She probably got in bed with the old goat – " Roy caught himself, realizing he'd said too much. But it was too late for him. Anselmo stood and put a hand around his necktie and with steady pressure caused him to rise from his chair.

"I – I – I'm sorry, I didn't mean that."

"What did you mean?"

"I meant no offense to the lady. It is just that my uncle was a notorious philanderer."

Anselmo nodded, let go of the necktie and sat back down.

"Thank you, gentlemen. Now, if I may continue," the lawyer said. "It is a simple will. If any of you care to contest it, my recommendation is that we set a court date and resolve any issues."

CHAPTER THIRTY-TWO

Lina glanced around the lawyer's office and saw the dead man's sister was going to have plenty of issues, so she spoke up first. "Here's what I think. Doctor Whitber's medical practice loses money. He owns his building but it is shabby and old and not located in the best part of Chicago Heights. His only profit comes from the sales of his medical formulas, his medicine business. You have seen the books: He loses money on his doctoring. To my surprise, he has willed this corporation to me – but I am a doctor, not a salesperson. I don't want it. But I do think that, over time, I may be able to make his practice work for the people of Hungry Hill. These people need a doctor and I am the only one practicing on this side of St. James Hospital. So I'll trade my inheritance for yours, straight trade. You take the patented formula and all the bottles and the customer contacts and the big barrel of Magical Medicine – everything we can find – and get it out of the office and we've got a deal. But my only condition is that you have got to decide now. If you do not want it and do not agree to my terms, my offer goes away. I'll sell the corporation assets to somebody else. Anyone can see it is profitable and it should be easy for me to sell. I'm sure I could get rid of it in a heartbeat, and for real money."

Lina didn't mention the bundles of cash that had already left the building in the suitcases the mother and son had taken. She knew that money had probably represented Doctor Whitber, Inc.'s corporate profits since he came back from the war (not counting what he'd lost at the race track), but she figured all that was gone money; there were no witnesses other than herself, and no way to prove how much, or even that they had taken it. "What do you want to do?" she said, "Deal or no deal?"

Cynthia and Roy put their heads together, and after thirty seconds enthusiastically nodded their heads. "Deal," they said as one voice.

Len Meyers, esq., was happy to earn a small additional fee for drafting up their agreement. Doctor Lina Bright resigned from her position as manager of the medicinal corporation and ceded all patent rights and all corporate property in return for ownership of the two story brick building next to Rosa's Café in the Hungry Hill section of Chicago Heights. Lina asked the lawyer to add a codicil that all the corporate property that they could find – including patents and actual stock of the "Magical Medical Formulations" had to be out of her building in three days.

"Heck, we can do it this afternoon!" Roy said.

The papers signed, witnessed and recorded, all parties left the lawyer's office on a happy note. As they were leaving, Cynthia even gave Lina a stiff little hug. She could hardly contain her enthusiasm. "I'm sure it is exactly what my dear departed brother would have wanted, dearie, if only he'd been in his right mind."

"If you could use a ride, I'll drive the both of you back to the Hill with us," Anselmo said. "That way you won't have to wait around for the Dinky."

CHAPTER THIRTY-THREE

As Anselmo drove them along in the Hupmobile, Lina found herself thinking of the next step as a cleansing, her mind going over exactly what had to be removed to clean out the old corporation and make way for her medical practice. "There's one desk drawer of paperwork," she said in a voice loud enough to carry to the people in the back seat. "Client addresses, supplier's names and numbers, that sort of thing. And a big wooden barrel of medicine, we can probably roll that one once we are sure it isn't going to leak. And there are bottles and labels and cartons Doctor Whitber used to ship out individual orders by mail around the country."

"Really sporty of you to help us out like this," Roy said. He seemed earnest about it, as earnest as a man can be who is trying to hide that he believes he has stumbled into the deal of the century.

Lina gave Anselmo whimsical smile followed by a faint warning look, *Don't rock the boat.* "There's not that much actual product that is ready to go," she said. "Maybe three and a half boxes, 12 bottles each box of product ready to ship. Maybe ten boxes of empty bottles. The big barrel of bulk product. That should be enough to keep you going until you mix up your own product. Strainers, mixers, measuring cups, it's all yours. And I promise I will forward all his mail to you – new orders, that sort of thing, until you get the post office to do a change to your new address."

"Thank you," Roy said. "I wouldn't have thought of that."

As he drove them back toward Hungry Hill, Anselmo was musing to himself that Lina was one very smart young woman. She wanted this deal done and over – and fast. He'd pretty much figured out why on his own, and he was going to do what he could to help her move things along. "Exactly where are you planning to set up your pharmaceutical business?" he said.

Roy looked at his mother for approval, "Ahh...I thought maybe out of our barn, back on the farm."

"And where is that?"

"Umm...Outside Saint Louis..."

"Okay, that could be easy. We can help you pack."

"There are plenty of empty boxes," Lina said.

"We'll help you get it to the train depot, too. Ship by railroad, that's sure to be lots cheaper than trucking it down."

"Ahh...You think so?"

Anselmo smiled, almost feeling sympathetic: Roy was off the deep end, unexpectedly the owner of a profitable company. All he had to do was figure out who to trust and what to do next. So Anselmo gave him a friendly clap on the back. He was going to do his best to be the good natured expert who just happened to be nearby when he was needed. "No problem, *mio amico*. You can rent a local truck from the manager at my hotel, get everything to the train. We probably won't need muscle power, but if we do, we can get some day labor men to help box your medicines so you can truck them to the railroad depot.

"Maybe if you arrange to ship them from the Steger depot that might be best," Lina said.

"Yep," Anselmo agreed. "With the steel mill on strike, there's plenty manpower available, fellows just hanging around looking for work."

Lina smiled in Anselmo's direction. "I think I'm going to move into his old apartment."

"Huh. Good idea," he said, smiling back at her.

Helping Lina get rid of Dr. Whitber's relatives was easy. The matter of Monsignor Monafusti was more complex, and dangerous. Once she told Anselmo how the man had threatened him in her office, his concern for her safety deepened.

His father hadn't answered his telegrams, and so he didn't know exactly why the Monsignor was in Chicago Heights. But he did find out plenty about Monafusti through the efforts of his grandfather. The strange man with the too-big mustachios and the sword-cane was crooked through and through. He was suspected of murder back in Rome, and Milan, as well. Here in Illinois, passing himself off as a priest, no telling how many sins had been revealed to him in the confessional. Members of the congregation who were cheating on taxes. Cheating on wives. Cheating on business partners. Anselmo's grandfather referred to it as *the old confessional racket – la vecchia truffa confessionale –* and Monafusti probably already had his fingers in a dozen schemes around Hungry Hill. This matter of his squeezing old Doc Whitber – and then trying to squeeze Lina – was probably

218

just one of them. The deeper question for Anselmo – what was Monafusti doing here in the first place? Anselmo suspected it had everything to do with his family, and with the greedy Sarafina Janika, and probably with the hundreds of acres of plump red and green grapes growing on the sun drenched hillsides of Northern Italy, to say nothing of the fortune his grandfather had hidden away in Switzerland.

CHAPTER THIRTY-FOUR

Old Man Weiss gazed to the south across Sauk Trail, looking out across his land from his rocking chair on the porch of the farmhouse he'd built with his own two hands. He studied the corn they'd planted that was now sprouting six inches or so in neat rows on his 107 good acres (he also owned a quicksand swamp and a pond on the same property, and that rounded things out to 160 acres total). He found himself once again, without really thinking about it, automatically cussing out his own granddaddy, who had divided their original homestead acreage, that had been many times bigger, among his six kids. That was what he thought of as *the bad American way* instead of passing the entire plot of land on to his eldest son *the good European way*. It was total *bullroar*, it made no dang sense, and then, when Old Man Weiss's own daddy had followed the same way of doing it, what was left had been divided four more ways and the only little bit what he and his offspring was had been left that was worth anything at all was the 107 acres and that wasn't hardly enough to grow a decent crop to feed a titmouse.

That was why Old Man Weiss agreed when his slow-witted son Willie Weiss declared that, with the planting done and not much to do until fall harvest, he was going into Chicago Heights to see if he could fetch up some part time work to bring in a little bacon. Willie's own son Peetie was on the mend with his hand healing up fine (and Peetie even getting back most use of his fingers, even the feeling in the fingertips coming back), and Old Man Weiss allowed Peetie could hitch on the weeder and drive the tractor well enough to handle the farm work by himself. So the old man gave dim Willie a clap on the back and sent him on his way with his blessings.

Willie came back that evening all excited to tell his dad of his good outcome, that he'd found there was a job at the steel mill even though the strike had shut it down, and, *By Gum!, he'd landed it!*

"I thought I heard the mill was not running," Old Man Weiss said, giving him that skeptical look he reserved for his son Willie and other idiots.

"Well now, it is, but ya' see, Old Man, they make rebar and fence posts by meltin' old railroad rails, and, strike or no strike, them rails keep coming in from all over the country, and there's a big pile in the yard that the railroaders just dumped there, and the mill owners need some workers to straighten things out."

Old Man Weiss didn't appreciate being talked down to like he was a know-nothing kid, but he bit his tongue and tried to ask his questions in an even tone of voice so as to get the information he wanted without pissing his son off. "What do you mean, Willie-boy?"

"It was something I didn't know, Daddy: them there rails are just dumped in there from the railroad cars like pick up sticks. They need workmen like me; somebody has got to go in there with a tool and straighten them out.

"A tool?"

"Yeah, they call it a key. It's like a post hole digger, but with a slot on the action end. Fits right in the end of a rail, you can twist 'em, get them tumbling down."

"That sounds a mite dangerous, Willie-boy."

"Oh yeah," Willie said. "You got to be nimble."

CHAPTER THIRTY-FIVE

It was an ordinary mid-week strike day, already the third week, starting to enter that phase where nothing was happening and it looked like the strike might drag on forever. The Monsignor had taken Brother Paulo away from his gardening chores to walk with him through the streets of Hungry Hill on his daily constitutional.

As they passed Rosa's Café, they couldn't help but see the line of people waiting outside, a line of over a dozen people.

"This is a very bad practice," the Monsignor said. "*Jesu e Maria* do not approve."

"I don't see how Rosa is doing anything wrong," Paulo said.

"Ahh, you are so quick to defend your good friend," The Monsignor eyed him with an unfriendly glance. "Jesus did not approve of strikers, he preached people worked in the vineyards for their money. And his mother Mary hated lazybones slackers."

"But their families have no money. They will starve."

Monafusti's gaze grew more intense, "You haven't been stealing for them more tomatoes from the San Rocco crop?"

"Well – no – just payment for my breakfast eggs…"

"I don't know that I can trust you, Brother Paulo…"

He turned sharply away from his companion and stalked back toward San Rocco's, waving his cane in the air like he was fighting off an army of invisible enemies.

That same day, Louie and Anselmo were manning the picket line in front of the mill, slowly walking back and forth through the sultry air of a June afternoon with a half dozen men from their regular shift. Their assignment was to make sure nobody went in or out of the main gate, except for the executives and their assistants. A crow scolded them from a nearby tree.

"That is a bad luck sign, Comrade," Louie said, giving himself the sign of the cross, tapping his forehead, his stomach and then his left and right shoulder with his right hand.

"I don't think so, Louie," Anselmo said. Black birds always boss around everybody. They think they own everything."

"Yeah, just like the bosses at the mill. The pet bird of Inland Steel should be the crow."

"That's a good idea. He could fly around with a little sign around his neck, 'Screw the worker!'"

They were laughing at the notion when Sumner Silverman came running out the main gate. He was sweating and looked upset.

Louie was about to yell at him for crossing the strike line, but Anselmo put a hand on his shoulder. "No, Louie, the Jewish accountant is more our friend than you think. Let's see what he wants." He waved Sumner over and the man rushed up to them. "There's been a bad accident!" Sumner said.

"Sumner, calm down, you'll have a heart attack."

"What's up, Sumner?" Louie looked at the other sign carriers.   He didn't want anybody thinking he was chatting with management, even if it was only the Jewish accountant everybody in the front office kicked around and looked down on.

"We got a worker back in the yard, pinned under a stack of rails!" Sumner said.   "Please, Anselmo! We have to help him! He could die under there!"

"You mean you got *a scab* in trouble back there," Louie said. You want us to help a scab? What's-a matter, you?! You think we're out here for fun? You think we're on the same team or something?"

Sumner looked to Anselmio for help. The man's face was chalk white – he looked stricken, a person in crisis who didn't know what to do.

Anselmo took Louie's arm, "Wait a minute, Louie. There are some things here we need to be aware of. We don't want the newspaper reporters from Chicago out here saying we were responsible, that we killed somebody we could have saved…scab or no scab."

Louie looked down at his worn shoes. "Yeah, okay…I guess I see that. Thanks, Mo."

Anselmo waved to the other strikers, "Hey, comrades, we have a situation, here. A guy could die back in there. You guys man the line. Louie and I will go see." He took the accountant by the arm, steering him back through the main gate. "Sumner, what kind of shape is he in?"

"I don't know. We can't see too good in under there. He was working with another guy, but that guy saw what happened and he took off."

Louie set down his Eighteen Cents Is Not Enough sign. "All right, all right. Lead the way." He yelled at the other picketers, "Somebody hurt bad back in the yard. We gonna take a look. You guys keep on going. Maintain the line. The strike is still on! Solid, 100% we still on strike! Nobody gets in. I mean *nobody*!" He trotted after Sumner and Anselmo.

The rail storage area was a tangled mess of rusty rails that were piled higher than usual because of the mill shut down. The engineer had backed the loaded flatbeds in on the rail spur that ran into the center of the yard. The crane operators then lifted the heavy steel rails off the railroad cars in loads of threes and fours, using the mill's old crane to lift them off the railroad car. But, because there was no yard foreman to direct them, instead of neatly stacking them, they had just dumped the rails helter skelter onto the gravel surface where they were now piled twenty to thirty deep.

Anselmo and Louie saw the rails were stacked dangerously high. They tried to stay back from the unstable tangle, looking for the worker Sumner said was trapped in there. But from every angle they peered in, they couldn't see the worker.

Louie shuffled his feet impatiently. He wanted to have as little as possible to do with this impromptu rescue effort. "Okay, Sumner, I don't see anything – where is he?"

"Louie, I – I don't know. The pile must have shifted. It all looks the same to me." He cupped his hands to his mouth and yelled, "Hey, striker-breaker in there! Where are you?"

A weak and muffled voice sounded from deep in the pile. "H-here. I am here."

"You okay?"

"My name is Willie. My legs is pinned. I don't feel my legs, I feel like nothing down there."

Sumner picked up one of the heavy metal turning keys and handed it to Louie. "We have to use this to crank them around."

"No," Anselmo shook his head. "That way, this Willie fellow will be dead by the time we get to him."

"What then?"

"We can use the crane."

Sumner shook his head. "We can't do that. The crane operator left right after the strike started. He's long gone, went home to Kankakee."

"I can do it," Anselmo said. "My unit had a crane to put our horses on the trains. In the war. If I could lift a live horse with a sling around his stomach, I think I can lift these steel bars. We just need enough time."

"What should I do?" Louie asked, looking to Anselmo for some direction, asking how he could help.

"I think you take the Hupmobile, Louie. Go get Lina."

"You gonna trust me with your automobile?"

"Sure, Comrade. Take it. You get Lina. Tell her to bring some of Doctor Whitber's Magic Medicine – if she still has any hidden around."

After Louie left to pick up Lina, Anselmo climbed into the crane booth. He started the crane engine and figured out the controls. "Not much different from our crane in the Alps," he said to Sumner, who had managed to scramble up after him. Anselmo reached for two iron levers and the crane's arm swung its clawed gripper toward the pile of rails. Using a lowering bar and a pincher controller, Anselmo managed to snag a bar from the very top of the pile, but before he had it moved aside, the rail slid from the claw and bounced down the side of the small mountain of rails. Somewhere from deep inside the pile, Willie screamed, and then said in a timid voice, "No, I ain't dead yet..."

"It uses a magnet," Sumner said. "That thing." He pointed to the instrument panel.

"Now you tell me. Come on, Sumner, we don't want to kill this guy."

"S-sorry," Sumner stuttered.

Anselmo was a fast learner, and he soon had his rhythm going. Moving the big pile of rails to one side took an hour; the last rail was hardest because he was trying to keep as much weight as possible off Willie's legs. In spite of everything he did to be careful, at one point the entire pile shifted and settled and Willie's leg went sideways. There was a sharp crack as the bone snapped. Willie screamed and went limp. Anselmo managed to get the last remaining rail off of the injured man. N By then Lina had showed and they all ran to Willie's side.

"Oh, *Gott in Himmel*," Lina said. "Look at that leg! It's turned blue-black."

"What shall we do?"

"While he's unconscious let's try to bend it back."

Willie's broken leg was bent at a 90 degree angle from normal, but there was no resistance as Anselmo and Sumner easily moved it next to his other leg. Lina had them strip some boards from a wooden pallet and she made a rough splint to immobilize the leg.

.   Willie's other leg was a little swollen. "Looks like it might be okay," Lina said. "I don't see there's anything else we can do here. Let's get him to St. James Hospital.". Willie had come around enough to take a big slug of Dr. Whitber's medicine right out of the bottle, but he screamed and went unconscious again as Anselmo and Louie lifted him.

They placed Willie behind the front seat, on the floor of the Hupmobile, the plan being to race him to St. James Hospital. Louie, who had never driven a car before, took to it like it was nothing, and drove through the city streets like a madman.

"You think he might be okay?" Anselmo said as he watched the Chicago Heights streets flashing by.

"Fifty-fifty chance he keeps the leg." Lina said. "At least, that's my best guess."

"Isn't this the farmer who ate your egg breakfast at Rosa's?"

"Yes, I think he is the one.".

:This should be worth at least two arrow heads."

Willie Weiss, who was lying across both their laps, stirred a little. "You gotta deal," he said. "A really good deal – two Sauk Indian arrowheads...I got 'em in a sack I keep under my bed in the barn...very rare."

229

"You sleep in the barn?" Anselmo said.

"Oh yeah. Talk to the cows, to keep 'em calm…that's so's the owls don't hurt 'em."

Lina looked at Anselmo, a whimsical expression on her face. "There's a lot we don't know about farming in Illinois."

Anselmo nodded and they smiled, sharing a moment together, something like a time-out in the middle of their race to get Willie to St. James to see if they could save the farmer's leg.

CHAPTER THIRTY-SIX

Elmond Ridgeway made the directors very unhappy by calling another meeting so soon after the last one. Being a director was easy money, and most of the ones at Inland Steel were also directors at other companies around town. But the job didn't pay all that much (relatively speaking) and this Inland Steel strike was getting to be a pain in the butt.

"First order of business," Elmond said, "How much do we pay the scab who lost his leg?"

"Oh, *Jesu Christi*, that again." It was Morton Fox from the bank looking up from the attention he was giving his Cuban cigar.. .

"Sure, sure – everything is just money to you, Morton…but we've got the company image to consider. And with the strikers marching out front, you can see we've got to try extra hard to be fair."

"Come on, Elmond, it's just a leg," Heinie Lufitz of Hot Point said, "And they sawed it off below the knee. Give him the same as the last guy."

"The one who got killed?"

"Yeah. If I remember right, he was a black guy and we factored that in. Just give Peg Leg Willie five hundred smackeroos or so, and let's get out of here."

"Maybe six fifty," Al Raymond of Desoto Paint said.

But that didn't satisfy Heinie, who now wanted to argue the value of a white man's leg compared to a black man's life and come to some sort of a

231

sliding scale that maybe the rest of them could use in their own settlements, and that started a heated discussion about workers having at least some responsibility for taking care of themselves. "Call it the personal responsibility clause, something like that," Heinie said.

Elmond was feeling betrayed by his fellows. He found himself thinking he should have taken Heinie's earlier advice and folded the meeting and gone off to Flossmoor to see if he could get in nine holes before sunset – because in the next minute young Albert, the president's son, stormed in, the young pesterer wondering why he hadn't been alerted there was going to be a *meeting and didn't they know how hard it was to interrupt his schedule and get here from downtown Chicago?*

Elmond frowned and looked over at Patty, but she was scribbling in the shorthand notebook on her lap, looking busy as hell, and since Elmond was pretty sure there was nothing going on there – *his low-life secretary* (daughter, after all, of a garbage man) *couldn't possibly have connected with the son of the president of Inland Steel!* Elmond figured it had to be Freddy Warberton ratting out on him, Freddy out for himself and playing everybody off against everybody else. Freddy's dad had been a good pal in the old days, but keeping his kid around was getting mighty thin.

CHAPTER THIRTY-SEVEN

Paulo showed up at Rosa's Café without any tomatoes. "What?" she kidded him, "Pauli, sweetie-pie, you going back on our deal?"

"N-no. We just can't do it no more. Monsignor Monafusti found out!"

"Pauli Genoa, I cannot believe you! That man is a big crook! People say he's not even a priest! And he's certainly not the boss of you!"

"Well, Rosa, I don't know how you could know he's a priest or not! All I do know is that somebody went into the hot house and chopped down all my tomato plants! And I think it was him. One moment he was cussing at me and – "

"A holy priest was cussing at you?!"

"He is a really good cusser! He knows lots of words I never even heard of! Anyway, there he was shouting at me that I was stealing from the priesthood and stealing was a sin and there was no way to save my soul from eternal damnation! And the next day when I went out to the glass house, the tomato plants were all cut clean off right at the ground. "

"You didn't tell him in the confessional about our tomato deal, did you?"

"N-no, not really…"

"You DID tell him, didn't you!"

"Well, maybe just a little part of it, but that was because I was running out of sins to confess and I couldn't think of anything else – and I didn't say anything about you."

"Oh, Pauli. You are too trusting! Anselmo knew about him from the Old Country. He doesn't even think he's a priest. Or if he is, he was excommunicated. That fake priest man actually tried to get Lina to pay him money or he would tell government agents she was selling opium drugs!"

"I'm sorry, I didn't know, and no, you didn't tell me."

"Or maybe I did and you were thinking about your stupid racing cars or something and you weren't listening!"

"It's my fault. I'm really sorry."

Pauli hung his head and looked so abashed she had to forgive him on the spot. But then she had another thought. "What about the rest of the garden? The priests give the carrots and beans and everything to the poor people, and now with the strike on, our people need all the help they can get!"

"It's all gone. It's like a tornado went through both the hot house and the garden square and ripped out everything. The string beans were almost ready and now they're gone! The first crop of green peppers, too! "

"Pauli, that's too much! There's something else going on here…I don't think this is your fault."

"I don't understand."

"The people this hurts the most are the strikers. With the mill shut down, they need every scrap of food they can get."

"But the Monsignor is a man of God."

"Pauli, stop defending him! He is a man of *il diavolo*!"

234

"No, I cannot believe that. When a man puts on the black robe, he dedicates himself to *Dio Onnipotente*."

Rosa didn't know what came over her, but suddenly everything was too much for her. Her temper flared and she shouted at him, "That's rubbish! You stubborn boy! Come on, I'm too busy to talk nonsense! You take your breakfast and get out of here!"

"But Rosa, I – "

"Fuori, fuori, fuori!"

She had been sweeping the floor, and now she made a gesture at him with the broom. In that moment he had the terrible thought that his lifelong best friend was sweeping him out of her café, and probably out of her life forever. He was thunderstruck at the thought of it. *That would be worse than death, itself!* He was so upset he left in a rush, leaving behind the sack with his egg breakfast, made just the way he liked it by his closest person in the world. And then an even more important revelation swept over him: *She was his closest person in the world!* That meant he truly loved her. Yes, he loved her! Nobody else, just her. He'd always loved her, and he still loved her with all his heart and soul. *But now she had chased him away and there was nothing he could do about it!*

CHAPTER THIRTY-EIGHT

A few days later Ollie's widow Anita came to Anna, Louie's wife, with a proposal that, with the strike going on and all, they should try to find a better way to pick up a few pennies here and there to make ends meet. "You do the washing," Anita said. "I do the stitching and embroidering. We both do the mending. I say we go into business together."

"But…we're already doing that."

"Not officially."

"You mean like have a company?"

"Just a little one. We could rent a small space on the Hill. I can see our name in the window: Anita & Anna. *Everything in clothes.*"

"I think it should be Anna & Anita."

A smile brightened Anita's dark round face, and she took a liberty nickel from a pocket on her apron. "I'll flip you for it."

Louie and Anselmo were walking the strike line under a steady June shower, one of those warm and muggy summer storms, the clouds off Lake Michigan bringing a light rain thirty miles to the south.

"Getting pretty wet here, Louie," Anselmo said.

"You are used to bad weather, Comrade. You told me about your war deeds." Louie shook his EIGHTEEN CENTS IS NOT ENOUGH sign and a passer-by honked and raised his fist out the window as he rolled on past in his dusty, battered old Ford.

"I never said I liked it."

"You also never said yet if you're coming to Fight Night with me."

"Fight Night? Louie, I never heard of it."

"I told you but you weren't listening. I think you got the love bug bite you bad, Mo."

"Well, maybe I do," Anselmo said.

"You gotta come with me. It's boxing for regular guys like us, a chance to pick up a little extra scratch. You don't have to wear shorts and a fancy shirt with no sleeves like in the magazines. Anybody can do it, me even. Get in the ring, last a couple rounds, make a couple dollars."

"What? That's illegal."

"Oh yeah, *amico* – and like we care about that. Brown's corner, the patio behind the building where they hold the *also* illegal beer parties. Friday night, 8 o'clock. I say we gotta be there."

"That's tomorrow night."

"What, you gotta the date or something?"

"No, but…are you going to be there?"

"Hey, I'm-a the one inviting you!"

"Tell me you're not going to get in that ring?"

Louie nodded and grinned. "Was-a the Mother Mary a virgin?"

"Well, I guess I better come along. Keep you out of trouble."

CHAPTER THIRTY-NINE

Anselmo had changed into dry clothes and was sitting behind the reception desk in Lina's office while she was in the operating room, working to bandage a cut on the palm of an old woman's hand, when Anna and Anita walked in. "We're looking for the Doc," Anna said.

Anselmo tossed a thumb at the examining room in back. "She'll be right out. Louie get home okay?"

"Wetter than a *cane bagnato*," she said.

"Yeah," Anita repeated "That's a wet dog, case you don't know."

"Anita, I am from Italy."

"You don't talk like it. You talk like an Englishman. Anyway, you and him were two soaked dogs, more like."

Anna shook her head and gave him a frowning look, even though she couldn't control her mirth. "Don't you dogs know enough to get out of the rain?"

"Louie said you were going to say something like that. We have to do it. Somebody has to walk the strike line to keep it official, he says." Anselmo wondered what Anna thought of her cannonball-shaped husband getting in a boxing ring. Or if she even knew about it. He thought he'd ask. "Louie tell you about Fight Night?"

"He's not going to do that stupid thing, is he?! He'll just get hurt. I told him no!" When Anselmo didn't say anything, she looked worried. "He's going to do it anyway, isn't he?   Tell me, Anselmo!"

"Well, he said he might..."

"That crazy, foolish, stupid man!   *Stupido pazzo!*   He'll get himself killed! Please, Anselmo, you go there with him?   Make sure he's alright?"

"I'll go, I promise.   But you know your husband.   He makes up his own mind about things."

"I know.   He is a *stupido pazzo...*"

Anselmo tried to change the subject.   "How come you're here?   You two don't look sick. What's up?"

Anita held up a neatly hand lettered sign that read *Anna & Anita – Sewing and Fine Tailoring and Cleaning.*   "We're going into business.   We're going to ask Doctor Lina to rent half of her office." She pointed to the reception area.

"But that's where her patients sit," Anselmo said.

"There's nobody sitting there right now."

"Sometimes there is."

"Well, maybe we can rent half of the half of it."

And Anselmo was impressed to see that's what they did.   When Lina was finished with her patient (who paid her with a bunch of fresh carrots, first of the season), she listened patiently and said she thought it was a great idea.   She even agreed to let them tape their hand lettered sign in a corner of the front window facing the street so customers would know they were in business.

Anselmo didn't think much of the idea at first, but he had to change his mind when he saw, over the next few days, Anna & Anita were getting more customers than Doctor Lina Bright.   Maybe that was

239

because, like the good doctor, they knew their customers and they didn't complain about being paid in eggs, radishes and fresh green beans.

But there was something else, a new development that led Anselmo to see the real benefits of Lina's decision. Because Anna Caproni vouched for this strange young lady doctor who came from *Back East*, Anna's cousin Franny DeAngelo came in with a prickly sore throat, and then Franny's brother Andy showed up with a nasty rash on his butt and their neighbor lady limped in with the chronic sprained ankle she'd gotten chasing a stray dog who had stolen a pie she'd left to cool on the ledge outside her open window, and as the word spread around the Hill, the doctor's appointment book started to fill in a bit as if by some sort of magic.

CHAPTER FORTY

Charley Piloto had a couple of the waiters move his favorite table and chair with the soft cushion on it outside in back under the awnings, close but not too close to the makeshift ring that had been roped off in the beer garden. He'd been trying all morning to get a call through to Big Al in Chicago, but it was nearly three in the afternoon before they finally got through, but at least it was the big guy himself, informal and chummy as ever. "Hey der, *paisano*, what's up, Charley?" Big Al said.

"Just calling to remind you and any of the guys who want to, tonight's Fight Night at Brown's Corner."

"Hey, tonight already?" Al's voice was relaxed and friendly, but tinny sounding coming over the phone.

"I told you a week ago. Just calling for a reminder."

"Yeah, yeah, I know. Everything hunky-dory here, nobody greedy, just send us our cut, like usual."

"You not coming, then?" Charley would like to know in advance, to rent a room and maybe line up a girl if Al was staying the night.

"Well, I don' know, I got meetings tomorrow and you know it's a pain in the ass, driving out and the fights are great but then it's the middle of the night and maybe everybody's had a few and we have to get back to the big time, and like that, you know, Charley?"

"Yeah, Al. I know. I don't mind."

"Don't take it wrong, Charley. I think it's fun, and I like the invite. These amateur *stugatzes* pile into the ring and pound each other around wit' their fists, I get a kick out of that. But it's your show, Charley. I know you got it by the balls."

Al hung up from Chicago and Charley went about setting things up. And, truth be told, he didn't mind. He was happy with the way things were; he liked to run his own show. Like Al said, these local numb-nuts hopped in the ring, a buck a round and all they had to do was pound each other silly. The two of them split the silver if they were both standing at the bell; but first guy goes down for the count, the other guy gets the whole dollar for that round. If they stand around, not actually swinging, they get nothing for that round, Referee's call. And the ref always looked at Charley to make sure. Kind of a sweet deal…if you were Charley.

It was early and things were a little slow when Louie showed up with his tall friend, that new guy from the boot. Charley was happy to take the silver dollar that Louie bet on himself. "I get that back if there's no fight," Louie said, just making sure.

"Yeah, yeah, yeah, Louie. You know where to find me. Hey, does Anna know you're getting in that ring?"

"Better me than her," Louie grinned. "That woman is a fighter. She'd take any of these so-called tough guys out."

"No doubt," Charley said. "But you didn't answer my question." He looked at Anselmo. "How about you? You gonna get in the ring?"

"Probably not," Anselmo said.

"Need your teeth for eating, huh?" When Anselmo didn't answer, Charley gave him a serious look. "Hey, just kidding, you know?"

"He knows, Charley." Louie hustled Anselmo away. "Hey, Mo, that's the guy runs things. It don't hurt to be friendly."

"I didn't mean anything, Louie. It's just that he's right. If you win a dollar but lose a tooth, that's not a very good deal."

"Jeez, man, okay, but just don't offend the local mafia." Louie was looking over the crowd gathered around the ring. "Oh, oh. It's that strike-breaking *bastardo*." He pointed across the garden. On the other side of the ring, Hal Singlebury was standing apart from the gathered spectators. He was talking with a lean, narrow-chested man. The fellow didn't look like much, medium height, kind of scrawny. "I bet that's my foe tonight. Easy money, Mo."

"I don't know, Louie. The guy looks like he can punch."

"Yeah, Mo. But can he *take* a punch."

Anselmo, who had learned boxing at the academy in Geneva, had the feeling the guy was a fighter. And that burly strike-breaker fellow – Hal Singlebury - was pointing in their direction.

Charley Piloto had his own take on the match: He figured Louie wouldn't last to the bell on the first round. He knew Louie was tough – hell, all the steel workers were tough, tough as, well, steel – but

Jerry Davis , this guy Hal Singlebury had brought in, was a ringer. He was a semi-pro, and maybe shouldn't be allowed in the ring to pound the local meat. On the other hand, Fight Night wasn't a charity organization and people who got in the ring were grownups, they had to take care of themselves. Charley had heard this Jerry Davis character had recently come up from Tennessee, which was why he wasn't well known. He'd done a little fighting south around Kankakee and in the Monee-Peotone area, and he hadn't lost a match yet. He had quick hands and – my God! – he had nearly a foot reach on Louie! All the guy had to do was dodge a little bit, Louie wouldn't be able to hit him at all. Charley chalked numbers on a little green board he stuck in a slot holder on his table. 6-1. That meant,. if you bet a dollar on Louie and he won, you'd make six dollars. Sounded like easy money, but Charley had heard plenty of rumors about the way this Jerry Davis handled affairs in the ring. If he had to kick a guy in the balls or bite off an ear, he never lost. Actually, Charley was thinking that it didn't matter, it could be 100 to one for Jerry Davis – Louie Caproni, no way.

In their corner of the ring, Anselmo gave Louie a hesitant look. "You're not wearing boxing gloves?"

"For sissies," Louie said.

"You better fill me in on the rest of the rules."

"*Facile, compagno.* Three minute rounds. Ten rounds. He goes down, ref counts to ten, I win, we go see Charley Pilato over there, he pays us."

The bell sounded; it was one of those little hand-held bells farmers used to call in the cows.

244

Louie moved in and missed by a mile with a round house swing. Jerry laughed, darted to one side, he reached down and pushed the shorter man by the head. The crowd laughed. Louie tried to move in again, this time darting forward like a lineman on a football team; Jerry quickly sidestepped and pushed Louie from behind, nearly knocking him over. The spectators laughed again. Somebody threw a crumpled up ball of paper. Somebody else yelled, "Hey, get serious, get that little fat boy out of there, this ain't no grade school!"

Jerry got in the first punch, and this seemed to daze his shorter opponent. Louie just stood there, trying to cover up, but he looked nearly helpless as Jerry followed with a series of sharp lefts and rights from long range. By the time the bell rang, Louie was still standing but his face was bloody and his left eye was bruised and nearly closed shut.

"Louie, we should stop this," Anselmo said. "You'll be in St. James before you know it."

"Naw, Mo," Louie gasped, trying to catch his breath. "I gotta plan."

"What is your plan? He beats you to death?"

"You'll see. Trust me."

The bell rang and Louie shuffled to the center of the ring. Jerry reached out and bloodied his nose. And punched him in his bad eye, closing it entirely. Jerry stood back, then turned and held his arms out wide to the crowd, gesturing as if to say, *What should I do? This is too easy!*"

And that's when Louie dove at him, tackling him at the knees. Before he could get up, Louie was on him, quick like a cat, pommeling him left, right, left, right with fierce powerful roundhouse blows.

Hal Singlebury, who'd been following the action carefully, was pacing outside the ropes as close as he could get. *This was a disaster!* He waited until he calculated everybody was watching the action and that's when he pulled a blackjack from his pocket. Hal had laid down ten big ones on Jerry, and he wasn't about to lose a ten spot. The fighters were on the ground in one corner, Louie straddling Jerry and whaling away at him. Jerry was looking bad, semi-conscious and pinned down while Louie punched him mercilessly.

That was when Hal thought he saw his best shot to change the odds. He reached in to tap Louie a good one with his sapper, but somebody bumped him and he went sprawling to the ground outside the ring and the opportunity was gone and a few seconds later the ref called it a knockout and held up Louie's bloodied hand. Hal looked up from where he'd fallen and realized the guy who'd bumped him was Louie's second, that tall, aristocratic looking *goombah* who'd been with Louie when they'd spiked his truck tires.

CHAPTER FORTY-ONE

Hal couldn't help it; he found himself in a purple rage, yelling at the asshole. "You! You and me! In there, in the ring, to the death!"

Anselmo didn't seem to understand the trouble he was in. He nodded in quiet agreement and walked calmly along with Hal over to Charley's desk. He didn't say anything. Hal was hoping to get in a sneak punch along the way, but his quarry seemed quietly, strangely, oddly alert for an elitist geek like he was. No chance for a stray hit to the guy's kidneys.. *Well, okay, no problem.* Hal had started his career as a brawler and a bar peace-keeper. He could handle this situation. Charley finished paying Louie, and sat watching as Hal and Anselmo moved up in line. When they got to the head of the line, Hal stepped forward and took charge.

"No holds barred," Hal said. "No bells, no rounds. We go until you don't get up."

Anselmo nodded his agreement, not saying anything more.

"I'm saying – to the death," Hal said, making sure everybody understood.

Again, Anselmo nodded.

"You know what that means, right?" Charley eyed Anselmo. The fellow seemed like a decent guy and Charley didn't want to see anybody maimed for life, but on the other hand, it was just business.

"I know what death is," Anselmo said.

That was when Rosa and Paulo, Anna and Lina showed up. Anna rushed over to the table where Louie was sitting alone, a wet towel over his swollen eye. "Oh, Louie, you *stupido*, look at you!"

"Anna, I'm alright. And look!" He opened his hands, and pushed seven silver dollars across the table to her.

Lina moved slowly to stand next to the ring. Anselmo nodded briefly; telling her he knew she was there.

"Hey," she said. "Put these on." She handed him a pair of thin leather gloves. He smiled and accepted them, pulled them on while Charley took in lots of money, offering even odds on a *Duel to the Death*.

And then in the next moment Anselmo stood facing his opponent in the center of the ring, Anselmo looking like he'd stepped off a poster of a boxing match at Madison Square Gardens, and big shouldered Hal slumped forward like the street thug he was.

"Oh, Marques of Queensbury, are we?" Hal sneered and grinned as the bell rang. And he was rewarded with a hard right between his open guard and straight into his face. The punch was picture-perfect, Anselmo's gloved fist catching Hal on the jaw, Anselmo's elbow snapping just right, the full force of his weight multiplied by the carry-through, his hard fist flattening the side of Hal's face with the unexpected hit.

The powerful blow caught Hal off guard. He staggered back but even as he was recovering his stance, Anselmo hit him again. Both hits happened so fast almost nobody at ringside realized what had happened. Spectators, interrupted with a beer in their mouths or a half finished jeer, wondered why Hal the Brawler was just standing there.

For his part, Hal was dazed. He didn't have any notion what to do. His fighting career had been one of grappling, of snapping opponent's arms or legs or squeezing the poor sucker unconscious in his powerful grasp. He'd never taken two such punches straight to the head.

But Lina knew. The man was badly hurt. "Tony – NO!" she shouted.

Anselmo was about to knock his opponent out when he heard her voice. *Tony! NO!* Some iron melted in him then, and instead of delivering the killing blow, he stepped back. As he did so, Hal slowly slumped, went down on his knees, and fell forward to lie silent on the floor. The referee did the ten count and held up Anselmo's hand. Anselmo looked across the ring to see Lina, with Anna and Rosa, at ringside.

"Thank you," he said, his lips mouthing the words, his eyes never leaving Lina for a moment. "Thank you for saving me."

Charley Piloto's sixth sense had been working, and he'd bet on this Anthony Anselmo newcomer and pulled in a small pile for himself. While he paid off Anselmo he kept wondering if there was some way he could make this work for him in a longer range way. "Hey," he said. "You need a manager? We could go places, kid."

"No, thank you," the man from the boot said. "I've already been to those places." He smiled at the girl with the strawberry blond hair who was standing close at his side. "And back again."

"Well, if you change your mind." Charley smiled, trying for friendly as he pushed over the few silver coins the guy had earned in addition to saving his own life. "You'd have got more if you'd carried him a few rounds."

"That one's on him," Anselmo said. "He learned a good life-lesson. The guy has a glass jaw, but you actually never know if you can take a punch until you get hit."

Charley had to agree that was true. That is, if a dumb *stugatz* like Hal Singlebury actually ever could learn anything.

CHAPTER FORTY-TWO

A few days later, when Monsignor Monafusti was called into the head priest's office at the San Rocco rectory, the first thing he thought of was somebody must have spotted him slashing about, cutting down the tomato plants in the glass house. But it wasn't that at all. Ancient Father Morris Murphy muttered and fussed and hemmed about, straightening the vial with holy water from Fatima and the small wooden cross carved from the very grove from where *Gesu's* cross had come.

"You, Monsignor Monafusti, are a fraud," the old priest said. He went into a coughing fit, but not before thrusting a parchment across the desk. He took a long drink of water from a big glass. "A complete and wretched fraud."

Monafusti saw the paper bore the papal seal. *Oh, great, from the Vatican, itself!* "There must be some mistake," he said.

"No mistake, *Mister* Monafusti." Father Murphy saw Monafusti made like he was about to get up. He raised a hand, his gesture saying *Sit down, miserable fraud!* "And no need for haste – everyone has been informed."

"What? Who? How?"

"Everyone in the parish. At Mass this morning. And you know how news spreads. You didn't attend the Mass, so I believe you are one of the last to know."

Monafusti shrugged. No need to pretend; the jig was up. "How did you find out?"

251

"You said you were from the Joliet Diocese. They are apparently very busy saving souls over there, and took a long time to get back to us. But – unfortunate for you – they never heard of you. The same for Chicago, the Chicago Diocese never heard of you, either. The Vatican…well, they do know a great deal about you. They excommunicated you, you may remember."

"I was framed by that woman's husband! I never did any of those things!"

"None of my business, Mister Monafusti, but when it comes to breaking the law in Rome, apparently, the list of complaints against you is long. You have fifteen minutes to gather your things and get out of the rectory. I suggest you leave Hungry Hill entirely. There are some rumors flying about, schemes and tricks you have been up to."

"That is slander! Who said anything bad about me? I'll have it out with them! I'll have their heads!"

"The Chicago Heights chief of police, for one. I don't believe you will be *having it out* with him. There are several complaints against you by respectable parishioners. I don't think you'll be having any of their heads, either."

Father Murphy had another coughing spell. As he drank more water, he pointed to the door. Monafusti was visualizing how he might strangle the old man. He could use the priest's ornate silk robe hanging right there, waiting for his next high Mass. He would stuff the thing in Murphy's mouth and sit on him. That should be enough to make the fellow give up the ghost. Leave no marks, no trace.

Death by old age. Happens to everybody, the human condition, too bad.

But the timing was off. He reached back with one hand and was fingering the gold trim on the green silk robe when there was a knock on the door and that young nuisance Brother Paulo walked in without waiting to be bidden.

"You sent for me, Father Murphy?" he said.

So Monafusti's meeting was ended and he had no alternative but to leave Father Murphy's office. He retreated to his small bedroom where he gathered the brass knuckles and his knives and his civilian clothes into a small carpetbag. He changed to his civilian outfit, dumping his Monsignor robes on the floor. One last look around the room and he picked up his sword-cane and was ready to go.

He left the rectory quickly without saying a word to another soul. But instead of getting out of town as the old priest had suggested, he waved down a fresh bakery goods delivery truck heading the right way. The driver dropped him off in front of a shabby boarding house next to a bar in South Chicago Heights. The man held out his hand like he was expecting a tip, but all he got was Monafusti's look that said *What, are you crazy?* Monafusti was in a sour mood, remembering Father Murphy's notion that he vamoose from Chicago Heights. *No, dear old priestie-boy, I won't be going back to Italy until I finish my business here in your wretched backwoods Illinois. And if you're lucky, that won't include burying you in the woods.* But then he had a lucid moment and shrugged off his anger. After all, Murphy was just a stinky little fish of a common priest, and a righteous man couldn't just go around killing everybody. There wasn't enough time, and, besides, he had real work to do.

CHAPTER FORTY-THREE

"Hey, carefully, Monsignor!" Brother Paulo protested as Monafusti pushed past him, but the man with the red trimmed robe didn't apologize and was out the door before Paulo could say anything more.

"He's not a Monsignor," Father Murphy said. "He's a fake priest. That's why he never said Mass. He doesn't know the words. He did do confessions, but I doubt he knows any more Latin than *Ego te absolvo*"

"Oh…" Paulo went silent, wondering what it meant that he'd confessed his sins to a phony priest. *What sins had he confessed? Were they forgiven? Would he have to confess them all over again? Were any of them mortal sins that would send him to hell?* He thought about it; he was pretty sure he was safe.

"Never mind that," Father Murphy said. "*Dio* will punish him. I am here to talk about you."

"Me?" Paulo's mind went racing. "I swear, I had nothing to do with the loss of our vegetables! Some crazy person must have gotten in the hot house garden. I know some people say it's against God's law to have tomatoes out of season. Maybe it was that."

The old priest held up one hand, "No, Paulo, not that. And I know you had nothing to do with it. We know the destruction of our garden also was thanks to our imposter priest. Mister Monafusti is responsible." He was interrupted by another coughing fit and reached again for his water glass.

"But, father – you wanted to see me."

"Yes. Well, on that, I'm afraid there is good news and bad news."

Paulo's face went white. Seeing his reaction, the old priest reminded himself this was a good boy and he had to be kind. "Paulo, we have discussed your future at great length here among us. Now the diocese is always looking for fresh young blood, no matter what, but that is the bishop's way, not our way. We have no purple ring the people must kiss. We give them communion, forgive their sins, and most of all, we care for them. What I'm saying is, we take a more personal view here on this level. And, I'm afraid, we have decided the priestly life is not for you."

"N-not for me?"

"Perhaps in ten or twenty years things may be different for you, but for the right now, we think *Dio* has other plans for you."

"Ohh…"

"Don't be too upset about our decision. Someday, you will see it is for the best. For now, I understand our garden has been utterly destroyed – not just the tomato plants, but our beans and carrots and even the young lettuce."

"Y-yes," Paulo managed to stutter. "Yes, it has been, and maybe it was in part my fault, for growing things out of season, but –"

Father Murphy held up one hand. "No need to explain, Brother Paulo. We have proof it was that wicked Mister Monafusti. Yes, *Mister!* Listen to me, Paulo: He never was a Monsignor! Or, if he once was, he was defrocked by Rome long before he ever got here."

"But – how do you know he ruined the garden?"

"He bragged about it to one of the nuns. He thought she was under his spell and she'd never tell anybody."

"But why?"

"He said somebody hired by the steel mill paid him to do it. Somebody he met in Svoboda's Bar."

"Why would they do that?"

"We have so much, thanks to your gardening skills and God's grace, and you know we've been giving much of what our garden produces to the poor – and lately that means we have been giving food to the strikers."

"And, what? The mill owners paid him to destroy our garden?"

"Well, he said this fellow did. He didn't even know his name, and he didn't care. He gloated about it, like it was some sort of personal victory for him. He said he met someone at a beer parlor and *they made him an offer he couldn't refuse*. That man has the morals of a starving wolf. Good riddance to him!"

"And you sent for me because…?"

"I have been watching you, Brother Paulo. What I am about to say is no offense to you. But seriously, I do think you are not meant by *Il Santo Padre* for the priesthood."

"But I –"

"Now, now, do not be alarmed. There is good news here, too. I do believe The Holy Father has other plans for you. Paulo, you are a great gardener.

257

We have seen it. We have tasted your skills, you might say. We want to hire you. We will pay you good money. Please, we need you. Be our gardener! Make our garden grow again!"

CHAPTER FORTY-FOUR

It was nine at night and the Café Rosa was nearly deserted. Lina and Anselmo sat at their favorite table, holding hands like teenagers and not saying much, lingering over a last cup of tea before they went their separate ways.

Their quiet moment was disturbed by the sound of someone singing. And that someone had a terrible voice. He sang,

By the light of the silvery moon,

I want to spoon, to my honey I'll croon love's tune...

Rosa came running out of the kitchen. "Oh, *mio Dio*, oh *mio Dio!*" She was out of character, flustered, not knowing what to do. She looked in a small mirror on the wall, patted her hair and then took off her apron.

Lina grinned at her, "Who is it, Rosa?" She said that ,even though she'd guessed what was happening. No, not guessed – she *knew* what was happening, the way women always seemed to know these things.

And the terrible voice continued:

Honeymoon, keep a shining in June

Your silvery beams will bring love dreams, we'll be cuddling soon

By the light of the moon.

Lina's smile broadened and she squeezed Anselmo's hand a little tighter. She knew the answer, but she raised her voice and asked Rosa again, anyway. "Who is it, Rosa? Here, let me help you." Lina went to the front door and opened it, and in walked Paulo, his arms full of early summer flowers – fresh cut daisies and shooting stars and purple lilacs and even some white roses he'd found somewhere.

"Pauli…" Rosa started, then fell silent, the words stuck in her throat.

"Oh, Rosa," he said. "Please forgive me. I've been such a crazy fool to argue with you about anything."

"But Pauli, you cannot do this, you are given to *Gesu…*"

"Not anymore, Rosa. Father Murphy has set me free. He has chosen me as Almighty God's gardener, instead! No more priesthood. No more *Fratello* Paulo. I just grow his plants."

"But…how?"

"It is God's plan for me, dear lovely Rosa. Father Murphy says so. Instead, San Rocco offers me to be their gardener."

"And… the rest?"

"And for the rest, my dear, dear, dear Rosa – I am set free of my vows to *Jesu,* and I am free to love you!"

And then her beloved Pauli tossed the flowers on the nearest table and was holding her in his arms.

As for Anselmo, later that night he had an awakening of a different sort. He thought the spirit of his friend Ralphie Gambriotte came to set him, too, free. Alone in his bed, he dreamed his mission with the widow Gambriotti was complete. It had come full circle. He envisioned somewhere off in a dreamy sort of a heaven, Ralphie Gambriotti looked down and smiled and gave him a wink and a salute before disappearing into the clouds. Anselmo stretched his arms and sat on the edge of the stiff and narrow bed, wondering what was next for him.

CHAPTER FORTY-FIVE

Old Giacomo's small temporary office he'd set up in his bank in Geneva looked like a general's headquarters: There were no windows, but there were maps on every wall and white notepapers pinned to every map. But Old Giacomo didn't need any windows, and the maps were not from Italy or France or any place in Europe; they were from far-away California, and they weren't road maps, they were geologic and topographic maps that indicated rock formations and hill slopes and elevations and streams. And the notepapers detailed water supply, irrigation and soil types and current orchards and vines and even types of grapes. "You'll note the Americans seem to prefer almonds and pecans," the old man said to his banking consultants, "while we like hazelnuts and walnuts."

"So you have resolved to go forward with this?" Nopani Anunzio said, his statement actually less a question than an opening to their meeting.

"Yes, I am," the old man said. "You have the certificate, I am of sound mind and body."

"Oh, be serious, dear friend." Nopani said, his face reddening. "No one here questions your state of mind." He gestured around the room and his three associates nodded their agreement.

"But you do question this decision of mine. And you know my son will try to block this."

"He is not in the employ of your business."

"I know. You had him removed at my request. But he will fight me." He leafed through the papers

262

on the desk in front of him and handed over several documents, one by one. "A certificate as to my sanity, certified, of course. One of the best psychologists in Paris. Studied under Sigmund Freud, if my information is correct. This next document, registered and binding, certifying my grandson Anthony Anselmo is in charge, should something untoward befall me." He paused and then gestured toward the maps. "And now, the grand move! You know the United States of America is in the grip of several factions of religious and social reactionaries. And we see their so-called Great Prohibition is in place now over two years. The doomsayers there believe it will go on forever. Too bad for them. But I am assuming they are wrong, and I am thinking this is a great opportunity for us."

The men around the table leaned forward. They had been forewarned that Giacomo Anselmo was arriving with great news. "I have agreed to a deal," he said. "A straight trade, land for land. Just over five hundred of our acres of orchards and vineyards around Turin for over fifteen hundred similar acres in Sonoma County in the state of California."

Nopani was surprised at the size of the deal. "But…that's over half of your holdings in Northern Italy. "Yes. Actually, over eighty percent. I would have done more, but confess that I was betrayed by my own sentiments. I could not give up the old house, and a few of the beloved vines around it, tried and true over the years with their steady yields. And my favorite hazelnut grove, how could I give that up?"

"A perhaps more difficult question: How will your company survive in America without the wine revenues?"

"Oh, I think they will do fine. There's grape juice, and raisins, and raisin blocks."

"What are raisin blocks?"

"Just what it sounds like. Only many people in America do not yet know that individuals can buy a raisin block, and if they take it down into their own basements and add water – and if they are not careful to prevent it, alcohol will be formed."

The men in the room looked at each other, realizing the foxy old man had done more research than they had imagined.

"And," Old Giacomo added, "don't forget consecrated wine for Mass. Those priests drink a lot. And I hear that, in many Catholic churches in the United States, passing around the golden chalice is becoming as popular as taking the blessed bit of communion bread."

"Very well, then," Nopani said. "Where do we sign?"

CHAPTER FORTY-SIX

Another meeting took place at about the same time, this one half way around the world in a small beer parlor in Matteson, an old German settlement located a few miles west of Chicago Heights. Hal Singlebury nodded to young Albert, who Sumner Silverman had introduced as the president's son, Sumner thinking somehow they might find a way to peacefully settle the worker's strike. "Pleased to meet'cha," Hal nodded. "And this is the labor lawyer I told you about. Amos Farley from Harvey, Illinois. He's got the right connections; his team solves labor problems for us all the time."

Hal didn't bother to introduce the well-knit man with the big mustachios and the silver handled cane who sat next to him. *Better to keep as many of his cards to himself,.* Hal was thinking, *until the time was right to play them.*

Amos Farley was well dressed, wearing an expensive imported suit and tie. And he was the blackest black man either Albert or Sumner had ever seen. He was a true straight-from-Africa black man, blacker than black, blue-black, just off the boat black. But he spoke like a college professor with that precise East Coast clip to his voice, and that had a way of throwing off everybody in the room..

He had showed up late and that put Hal, who had arrived earlier with Monafusti, in an even fouler mood than usual. Hal had the same suspicion he always did, that Amos Farley was looking down his nose at him. Hal would have punched him in the face and walked out to let him pay for the drinks when he got back up off the floor, but he needed the black man if they were going to take down the strikers. And that wouldn't have happened anyway, because Amos showed up in a Stutz driven by a muscular young black guy who looked like a heavyweight boxer.

Hal motioned to the bartender he'd have another boilermaker. Amos said he wasn't drinking hard stuff, but he ordered a Pabst draft beer for himself and one for his bouncer.

Sumner was toying with the moisture stains around his cool beer glass. "I didn't know we were talking about importing southern black workers. Interesting idea. Is it true they work for a dime an hour?"

"Yes, if we do it right," Amos said. "The best we ever negotiated was six cents, an actual nickel and a penny per hour. That was for the Chicago stock yards strike. You may have read about it in the papers. That piece of business was one nasty mess…but it turned out okay."

Young Albert nodded. "I heard about those riots."

"Yes. The police had to get rough. Unfortunate, but two men died."

"Rumors in the newspapers said the two of them were union organizers. The papers thought they might have been targeted," Sumner said.

Amos shrugged, looking off into the distance as if he was trying to remember. "Nobody knows, really. Anything can happen in a riot."

Hal, impatient as ever, slammed a fist on the table, and that startled everybody. "Well, what do we do? Amos, you're telling me you can get us a bunch of these hungry sharecropper niggers from Mississippi."

"Louisiana," Amos corrected him. "As many as you need. And they are *negroes*."

"Right. Louisiana, Mississippi, Alabama. Who gives a crap, no difference. You round 'em up. We'll load 'em on trucks and drive 'em back up here."

Amos gave Hal that superior smile that had him biting his tongue. "No, friend Hal, that costs you way too much; there's gas and food and you have to hotel them at least one night and maybe two or three."

"Hotel? For God's sake! Why?"

"Why, Hal, to keep 'em from changing their minds, from getting in trouble, from running away, running back home, running God only knows where."

What Amos said made sense, and he was the expert, but Hal didn't like to be contradicted, and, the deeper truth was, he could have made a pile contracting for the trucks. The expression on his face said he was thinking maybe this wasn't such a good idea. "Well, I'm not convinced. Are you so sure? Maybe couldn't we do it with my trucks, Amos?"

Amos ignored what he thought of as *typical white man's attitude*. He put on his happy black man's face, "Say now, Hal; if the weather goes bad or you meet with trouble on the road and you're in Tennessee or Southern Illinois down around

Springfield, what are you going to do? I know you use trucks for breaking strike lines – but that's short stuff; we're looking for a long haul here. That's where my company comes in. We have a verbal handshake with our friends at the railroad company. We can and will hire this bunch of hard working sharecroppers we are talking about for you; we can get you however many you need. We will put them on railway cattle cars, you know, the ones with wooden slats. It's all under the table; cash changes hands and nobody knows nothing about nothing."

"You can make that happen?" Sumner said, nodding his approval in young Albert's direction.

"Oh, yeah. Sure as anything, we'll put them in those cattle cars and ship them on up here by rail. They bring their own food, sleep in the cars, piss out between the slats, the train does not have to stop for anything. As you-all well know, there is a big rail yard south of Crete, maybe four or five miles south of Chicago Heights, no further than that. That's where you meet us with the trucks. You load up our splendid crop of workers in your trucks and you get to be the heroes when you dump them off at the mill."

"Sounds like a workable plan," Albert said. "I say let's get going."

"And Amos – you'll be there to make sure everything runs smooth?" Sumner was concerned about the details, as he always was.

Amos frowned and flicked his suit jacket like some cigarette ash might dared to have landed there. "Me? Not personally. I've got our people to handle everything, all the way. Don't worry. Nothing will go wrong."

"I don't know," Sumner's worry lines deepened around the corners of his eyes. "What if the strikers are waiting at the main gate, like last time? They're sure to be there. They're not going away. What if they're there?"

"Sumner, calm yourself," Albert said. "If that happens, then we'll have our friends, the police with their clubs; they'll show up right there and then to keep things quiet and friendly."

"Remember last time – the strikers got out those spiked boards and they flattened Hal's truck tires."

"Oh yeah," Hal said. "I remember that, alright. I think I'm gonna hire a squad or two of my own guys, you know, bring them along to help the cops keep the peace."

Albert shrugged. "It works for me. Hey, they started this. Whatever will be, will be."

Sumner couldn't shake off his worry. "Somebody's going to get hurt," he said.

"Oh, yeah," Hal agreed, anticipation in his voice.

"Sumner, I said let's get going," Albert said.

Amos looked them over, saw the time was right. "Eight thousand," he said. "Half now and half when they show up in Crete."

"Sumner," Albert said, "Do it."

"But Mr. Ridgeway doesn't know anything about this."

"Elmond Ridgeway is – to use your language – a *putz*. I said, *Do it!*"

Sumner sighed as he reached in a shoulder bag and pulled out a fat wad of fifty dollar bills. He started counting them out on the table in front of Amos.

"And I need my two thousand," Hal said.

CHAPTER FORTY-SEVEN

The next day Anselmo drove over to Louie's house to pick him up for their shift on the strike line, only to find Louie wasn't waiting in front of his house. Instead, Anna was sitting on the swing on the front porch, knitting as she rocked back and forth.

"It's a baby blanket. And no, I am not having a *bambino*. It's for a customer," she said, answering his unasked question. "And that crazy husband of mine is out back. You can hear the racket."

Anselmo nodded. "Pretty loud," he said.

"He's a crazy man," she said. She pointed to the left side of the house. "You can use the side gate. See for yourself."

Anselmo didn't know what to expect, but, whatever he was thinking, it wasn't what he found; Louie had a small blacksmith shop, complete with a white hot fire going in a home-made clay-over-brick hearth. He grinned when he saw Anselmo.

"Hey, Comrade Mo! Just in time," he said. He set down a mallet and snapped off a welding torch he'd been using, then reached high as he could in an opening in the hearth and brought out a hot earthenware platter. He set the platter down on a workbench with a proud gesture, "It's my invention! Three kinds of cheese and the marinara sauce and the sausage *Italiano* on the flat bread!" Louie ripped off a piece and handed it to Anselmo.

"Louie, you're full of surprises. Hmm, good! But we have to go. Come on, your commie friends are impatient for their revolution – they wait for nobody. We can eat on the way."

"Anna let me borrow the pan from her kitchen. I gotta take it back in before we go. But wait, Mo. We have a little time. I got-a one more invention for you. Here, try this on."

Louie set aside the hot platter and picked up a strange piece of gear. It looked like two slightly curved sheets of metal, two foot by two foot square, both held together with two one inch wide straps of leather.

"I made this one for you," he said. "Here, put it over your head, try it on."

"It's like armor plate," Anselmo said, getting the idea right away. He slipped his head between the straps and the steel plates hung in front of his chest and also covered most of his back.

"Yep. Stop a bullet sure. Look, how it fits you good, Mo! I got your size right! You put the shirt on over, nobody will ever know! See here, I'm almost finished with mine."

Anselmo tapped the metal plate on his chest, "This thing's going to work?"

"*Shurrra!* We not trust those strike-breaker *bastardos.* Next time they will want to kill us. "

"A suit of steel! I feel like Percival, a knight of King Arthur!"

"We're fooling around now, but I'm-a serious. You did hear about those Chicago strikers, got themselves shot dead!"

"Yeah, I read about that in the papers. You think your invention is going to stop a bullet?"

Louie shrugged and his grin grew even broader until, with the smile lighting his wide round face, he looked like the Cheshire Cat in Alice in Wonderland. "Well, if it doesn't," he said, "we'll never know."

CHAPTER FORTY-EIGHT

Anselmo pulled the Hupmobile to a stop on the empty kid's playground south of the St. Liborius grade school. "Why don't you just buy this automobile?" Louie asked. "You're always renting it, anyway."

"I did," Anselmo said.

Louie was amazed, stared at his friend as if he was some sort of strange animal. "You did? I was just kidding."

"The hotel manager never used it. It was just sitting there. And I pretended I really didn't know if I wanted it, and so when I was walking away he gave me a really cheap price."

Louie started to say something, but Anselmo had gotten out of the driver's seat and was talking to a man wearing a suit who had braked his bicycle to a halt on the sandy ground.

"Are you *sure?*" Anselmo was saying. This got Louie's attention because there was a note in Anselmo's voice Louie hadn't heard before. Something like alarm. *Something bad was happening.* The man who had showed up on the bike checked his pants legs, to make sure they were still in their plastic bands, secure from the bike chain, and then he peddled off at a fast rate before Louie could come around the car to see who it was.

"What, what, what? Who was that?" Louie asked.

"That was our friend Sumner Silverman. He says Inland Steel has hired a trainload of sharecroppers from down south to break the strike. This is going to make it difficult for us! Sumner says they'll work for seven or eight cents an hour."

"No, this cannot be! Black men up from the south? How can we be sure? And what is Sumner Silverman doing talking to us? Maybe it's a trick!"

"No, Louie. They treat him like he's not good as them. He doesn't like Elmore Ridgeway any more than we do."

"So what is this? They think they are gonna break our strike with cotton pickers?"

"I think so. Sumner says the train gets here late tomorrow night. A special run, eight or ten cattle cars. They are bringing dozens of men. Let's figure it: if they have a dozen to a car, they are bringing maybe over a hundred black men from the Deep South up here just to break our strike. He says those southern black men are desperate for work. They will do anything. And he says this time Inland Steel doesn't care about cost. Anything to destroy us. They'll get that mill going no matter how many of those black men get killed trying to do it."

"*Son-a-ma-gun!* Louie said. "What are we gonna do now?"

"Listen to me, Louie: This is no time for panic. I think we can figure this out. Sumner says their plan is to meet up at a rail yard south of Crete. They think they will get their strike-breaker trucks out there, load up these black *bustafasados* and run them right past us at the main gate. It will be night, past midnight. They think there will only be three or four of us on the picket line with our Eighteen Cents Is Not Enough signs. But no, we cannot let

275

that happen – I'm thinking, *How about we do something before that!*"

"So… you think we have to meet them at the train yard?"

"*Si!* That's it! We make sure those black men never climb down out of those cattle cars. We can't let them off the train! We turn them around, we head that choo-choo train going right back the other way!"

"You think we can do that?"

"Louie, we have to. There's no other choice."

"You are right, Mo! Yes! We gotta do this. Come on, let's tell the comrades!"

Louie took his friend by the arm and practically pulled him along into the stale tobacco smoke gathering in the basement of the Saint Liborius grade school.

CHAPTER FORTY-NINE

Driving his Hupmobile back to the Victoria Hotel, Anselmo found himself thinking, as he had many times over the years, how bad or unpleasant things seemed to happen in his life in groups of threes. When he was young, his mother had died, and then his baby sister a few months later, and then his grandfather had nearly died of yellow fever. Then, after a quiet time, there was the period when his brother had been killed in the war, followed by the disaster in the mountains when his company lost their horses in the avalanche, and then – the third thing – when the mortar round had landed in their trench, mortally maiming Ralphie Gambriotta. And now, half way around the world in Chicago Heights, Illinois, the Polish guy had been speared in the leg, followed by Ollie's horrible death, and…what was coming up next?

He didn't have to wait long. Back at the hotel a telegraph was waiting for him. It was from his grandfather and said simply: LA PUTANA E INCINTA. That could only mean one thing – Anselmo's father's mistress, Sarafina Janika, had somehow managed to get herself pregnant and convinced Gio II it was his baby.. She had been trying for years, in spite of Giacomo II's absolute strict warnings that, if she ever got pregnant, he would never marry her and that would be the end of their relationship. Now she was calling his bluff.

The rest wasn't hard to figure out: It was no secret that Sarafina wanted to give Giacomo II a male heir. With the Anselmo family reduced to the one son – himself – and with his grandfather nearing eighty, there was a large inheritance to be had. Anselmo wasn't sure exactly how large it might be, but that didn't matter: to Sarafina, herself crawling away like a cockroach from a poverty stricken youth in the slums of Rome, it had to seem immense. She was going after what she saw as her financial destiny. What troubled Anselmo as much as anything were a few of the conversations he'd had with his grandfather, and the things he'd observed on his own around his father's office. He now knew that Sarafina had known Monafusti from the younger days when he was known as a ruthless thug running around the streets of Rome, reportedly selling his extermination services to the highest bidder when he wasn't occupied with his fencing lessons. Anselmo's father, Giacomo II, no saint himself, had not been above using underhanded tactics as he went about building his empire (that often drifted from the clothing industry to loan sharking). Anselmo suspected Sarafina had introduced her street trash friend to his father to help him out of a nasty situation or two; but now it was looking like, as the old saying went, *i suoi piccioni stavano tornando a cassa a posarsi.* That is, his pigeons were coming home to roost.

CHAPTER FIFTY

The next morning Louie and Anselmo met Louie's squat little pal Arturo and four other comrades at Rosa's Café to firm up what they knew they had to do.

"No mistakes. We are sure without doubts that a train full of strike breakers is to arrive in Crete, Illinois tonight," Louie said. "I give each of you a list of ten of our members – and they must each contact all of their comrade friends. There will be no notes, nothing in writing. Do you understand? Each of the ten comrades you contact will call on as many others as they know. We have to be at the railroad switching yard that is a few miles south of Crete. You all know where that is. Midnight. Bring baseball bats, torches, flares, anything to make a scene."

"Yeah, we'll kill them if we have to!" Arturo growled.

"No, we won't kill them. We don't want anybody going to jail. That defeats the purpose, you know? But we have to frighten the hell out of them. They cannot get off those cattle cars. They gotta go back to their *old cotton fields back home*, like the song says.

Louie's wife and Ollie's widow had come over from Lina's building next door and were sitting in a corner of the café, quietly keeping an eye on Louie, trying to assure themselves the men weren't going to get in real trouble, go off the deep end, get in over their heads and end up dead or in jail. They

279

pretended to be folding a box of new bedsheets they were planning to decorate with embroidery and sell in their clothing enterprise.

Ollie's son had been sitting nearby, working on a high school project with one of his pals. Hearing Louie's speech, he laughed and took one of the sheets and put it over his head. "Boooo!" He said. "Git on back south, you strike-breakin' niggers!"

"Don't you go funnin' around like that, boy!" his mother warned.

"Wait," Louie said. "Wait, wait, wait, Anita! That's a good idea!"

"What are you talking about, *idiota*?" Anna said.

"No, Anna, the boy has a good idea! Black or white – nobody knows who's under the sheet – and these Deep South men, they are very afraid of the Klan!"

Arturo spoke up, his froggy voice full of enthusiasm, "We cut eyeholes, it's the real deal!"

"Hey, don't run away with your craziness," Anita said. "We run a business. You gonna buy our sheets for real money?"

Anselmo reached for his leather wallet. "How much do you want?"

Ollie's boy was really excited, "I want to go with!"

"No," Anita said. "Absolutely not!"

"We'll take care of him," Louie said.

"You see it makes no difference, Mamma," the boy said. "Nobody knows what color skin the man is under the sheet! Papa would want me to do it! I have to do it for Papa."

Their spirits were high, but their mood darkened when Paulo parked his bike outside and came rushing into the café. "I heard the priests talking. They know!" he said.

Louie shook his head. "They are always at the worker meetings. Of course they know. The question for us is, What are they going to do?"

"They cannot be trusted," Arturo growled.

"It's not that they are bad people," Paulo said. "But I heard them talking. They argue that striking is an evil thing to do. They say *Gesu* was all for work. They think striking is about the lazy way. Striking is a sin."

"That's not good," Anselmo said. "They will go to the police and get us arrested before we can do anything."

"What should we do?"

"Well, we could lock them in the wine cellar under the rectory," Paulo said.

"Hey, Paulo, good idea!" Anselmo said.

"That just might work!" Louie seconded him.

"I was kidding..."

"No, no, no, good idea, Paulo," Louie was thinking it through. Finally, he seemed to make up his mind. "Don't worry, Paulo, we won't involve you, I get some young comrades and we take care of it and nobody gets hurt. After we send the train back, we let them out."

"Sure," Anselmo said. "Plenty of wine down there. They'll be okay."

CHAPTER FIFTY-ONE

"Hey, Swen," Monafusti said, "How about another boilermaker?"

"Sure, Francesco. You want the cheap whiskey?"

"No, I do not want the cheap whiskey," Monafusti said. "White lightning makes you go blind. You know that. Should I be insulted? Why would you even say that to me!"

"Don't be so touchy! Don't get your feathers ruffled. I was just joking around, my friend," Sven said, pointing under the bar to where he kept the good stuff. "The cops can't be everywhere all the time."

"Yeah, crooked *bastardos*. They say they confiscate, but then they keep all the good stuff for themselves."

Sven catered to veterans, and he had his patriotic notions at the tip of his tongue, "We like to serve the real men who served in the Great War. Patriots who answered the call and did their duty for God and Country. Men like this, we make boilermakers appear like magic from somewhere under the bar. We like to hear their stories of being brave or loving strange foreign women or whatever – you know, the stuff that happened to them *over there*. This is Sveningers!"

"Hear, hear!" the customers all shouted and raised their glasses

Sven went to a back room and returned with a beer in the unlabeled brown bottle. He reached under the bar and came up with a shot glass and filled it to the brim with Old Forester that had trickled down from Canada, services of Big Al's friendly group of providers from Chicago. He brought his offer to Monafusti and set it triumphantly on the bar in front of him, "What 'cha doing' here after dinner, Fusti? You're usually out of here by now."

"I want to go hunting, Sven," Monafusti said. "I'm looking for a rifle."

"A rifle! What kind of rifle?"

"I am thinking to hunt deer, so maybe an Enfield."

"Naa, the Enfield is crap. Talk to Broomie over there. He was trying to unload a Carcano a week or two ago."

It was that easy. Broomie Slepski was a giant of a man well over six and a half feet tall, but he was wide and soft looking, and he had a friendly way about him. *And, boy, did he know guns!* He had a garage full of weapons he'd shipped back from Europe after the hostilities, and every now and then he was known to let one go if he was in a good mood and if the price was right. Monafusti arranged to meet him in the woods near Sauk Trail at a fairly isolated location west of Steger, the Italian saying he wanted to shoot a tree trunk or two, get the feel of the hunt. They met at dusk near a picnic area. Slepski was waiting for him, sitting at an old table and things looked pretty good; the Carcano was a short barreled bolt action carbine, just right, Monafusti was thinking. Broomie showed him the serial number and said he was pretty sure it was made just after the turn of the century, maybe 1904 or 5. The beechwood stock had a dark stain, a sign maybe the previous owner had met an unhappy ending, but Monafusti couldn't care less about that. He worked the bolt action, jacked a bullet in the chamber and it seemed smooth enough. He'd had a Carcano when he took himself on a brief assignment in the Northern Italian Front early in the war and it had done the job.

"Range supposed to be good up to a thousand meters," Broomie said. He handed Monafusti three extra clips. "Two three's and one six rounder."

"How much you want for it?"

Broomie gave him a sharp eyed look. "I'm thinking I'll take sixty dollars."

"That's too much," Francesco Monafusti said. He raised the barrel of the Carcano in a short arc and shot Broomie Slepski squarely in the chest. Broomie said something that sounded like *Urk!* as the air was forced out of his lungs, and he toppled over like an axed tree trunk and lay there shuddering on the ground behind the picnic table. Monafusti realized he hadn't thought things through; now he was going to have to drag this big heavy guy off somewhere and dig a shallow grave to hide the body if he couldn't find a deep enough ravine to just roll him down.

CHAPTER FIFTY-TWO

Anselmo and Louie and their small gang of comrades enthusiastically herded the priests down a steep wooden steps and into the wine cellar without any real difficulty. They left with the angry threats of excommunication and eternal hellfire ringing in their ears.

"I was going to hell, anyway," Louie said.

"All good Commie Reds go to hell," Anselmo said.

"Only maybe they find salvation if they are members of the CPUSA."

They picked up Paulo from Rosa's Café, and, at the last minute, Lina yelled from next door to wait a minute, she had to get her black bag, she was coming, too. And then Rosa showed up from the kitchen with two wicker baskets stacked with fresh bread rolls and jars of hot soup. It was closer to midnight than eleven when Anselmo pulled the Hupmobile away from the curb. "This is feeling more like a frolic than a military operation," he said.

"Do not kid yourself, Anselmo," Lina said. "Get serious now. I have my doctor's bag, and you see Louie here has his favorite baseball bat."

"Yeah, to hit some home runs," Louie said.

Anselmo drove them south through the sleeping towns of Steger and Crete, but they were not alone. Dozens of automobiles and even a few motorbikes were heading in the same direction. When they got to the railroad yard parking lot, it was filled to overflowing with parked cars, and a large crowd of hundreds of men – all workers on strike or sympathetic to them – were milling about the rail head at the entrance to the roundhouse.

Louie's wife Anna and Ollie's widow Anita were handing out white sheets with neat eyeholes cut in them, and the CPUSA had set up a small table and was handing out unlit torches with instructions not to light the tarred end until the train got there.

"Anna!" Louie called out. "You are not supposed to be here! Who's at home with the kids?"

"*Stupido!* What you think? Angelo's old enough to take care of the younger ones! I'm gonna leave my man out here with nobody to take care of him? I don't think so!"

Louie looked to Anselmo for help, but his friend only shrugged, *Let it go, pal. Too late now, anyway.*

And it really was too late. They heard the distant wail of an approaching locomotive, and saw, about a mile down the tracks, the wavering bright beam of its headlamp cutting toward them through the dark.

Skunk Ralph had been sleeping in the half-empty boxcar that was parked all alone on a spur in the Crete railyard. He woke with a start, wondering what was happening. First there were all these people showing up, something like an angry mob, and that was plenty hard to figure out. He watched from a corner of the boxcar, but then a man with a long gun slung on his back pulled himself up through the open side door. The man was ordinary sized, with a big moustache and a quick, wary way

286

about him. "What you doing here?" he said, pulling his rifle around so it pointed in Skunk Ralph's general direction.

"Wait now with that firearm, Mister Sir...I didn't do nothing. I'm from Tennessee," Ralph said. "Just up here looking for work, construction work, building projects, roads, sidewalks, like that. ."

"What do you know how to do?"

"Cement, mostly."

"I did not know you had to know how to do that."

"Oh, yeah," Ralph said. "It's my specialty."

The man with the rifle wrinkled his nose. "*Gesu*, you smell *terribile!*"

"That's 'cause I ain't had no bath in a week. Gotta find a pond or a creek."

"Why don't you go do that? I mean, right now."

Skunk Ralph had been hobo-ing it for years, and he got the picture right away. *The man with the gun is always right.* "Sure, no problem," he said. He held up both hands and skooched himself to the open side door. And then he dove head first on out of there and was gone.

CHAPTER FIFTY-THREE

The train from the Deep South pulled to a screeching stop in the center of the railroad yard. George, the engineer, hadn't been expecting anything more than a greeting by the captain of the yard, but there was no captain in sight. Instead, there was a milling crowd of angry men waving placards and baseball bats. Sprinkled in the group were – by God and by Jiminy – some Klansmen in white sheets! And men with torches! The next moment some fool blasted off what sounded like a shotgun! Then the crazies were banging on the sides of his cattle cars with their bats! They were next to the steam engine, too, shaking their fists, glaring up at him in the relative safety of his locomotive cab and shouting all kinds of threats!

George couldn't see the cattle cars from where he was, but he could only imagine – the doors of the cars were still locked, no way those blackies were going to get out and make a run for it. On the other hand, he couldn't see anybody risking their life to try for a getaway. He was just the engineer, for Almighty God's sake, and there wasn't any rulebook for something like this. He didn't know what to do. Wait for orders, he guessed. But he wasn't going to wait too long. This crowd was looking ugly, and no telling what they might do. That was when he thought a second time about the torches! Christ Almighty, the cattle cars were stuffed with hay, that's what their passengers slept on at night! All it would take would be one little spit of burning tar from one of those torches and some of those poor black men would be roasted alive!

Anselmo had the same notion as the engineer. Once he saw the danger – the boxcars, one or more or even all of them, could too easily go up in flames – he urged the men with their torches to stay back.

"No, we don't stop!" Louie shouted.

"Don't stop, use the bats!" Anselmo said. He ran a broom stick he was holding like a sword across the nearest cattle car. "Rattle their cages!"

That was when, from three tracks over and fifty yards down the line, Francesco Monafusti drew a bead on Anselmo's chest. "Thank you, Anthony Anselmo," the man said, noting that Anselmo's light colored linen shirt made a fine target as he tightened his finger on the trigger. He was squeezing off the shot perfectly, but at that precise moment, with his finger tightening, there was a slight jostling bump and then Monafusti was flustered by whatever had happened and he couldn't be sure if he'd hit his target or not. He had been preoccupied with getting rid of the smelly hobo-man, and he hadn't noticed a stubby yellow yard engine moving up on his blind spot from the rear to switch the boxcar he was on over to another line. And now the boxcar, with him in it, was being moved away, and his shooting position was lost. The crowd of angry people was swirling around the cattle cars, yelling, screaming, rattling their baseball bats and their two-by-fours with the spikes on them against the wooden slats of the cattle cars while the black people, with no real idea what was going on, looked out on them in wide-eyed terror. Everything was madness and Monafusti had no idea if he'd taken out his easy target or not.

CHAPTER FIFTY-FOUR

Louie became uncomfortably aware of the honking car horn blats announcing the arrival of the police vans when the cops were still a long way away, still bulling their way down the side road from Dixie Highway. He started to say something to Anselmo, then stared at him, "Comrade, how did you cut your arm?"

"Bullet just nipped me." Anselmo was calm, back in his war mode, the realization that no matter what you did, bad things could happen. *So don't worry about it.*

"That's the same arm where you burned yourself in the mill."

"Yeah? You think it's a sign?"

"Oh, *si!* We know for sure somebody takes a shot at you."

"Maybe not shooting at me in particular," Anselmo said. "Plenty of people out here with guns."

But even as he spoke, he was scanning the area, looking at the possibilities. Once you've been in a battle zone, you never lose that sense of uneasy awareness. He tried to shake it off. "Anybody seen Lina around?" he said. "I probably could use a bandage."

"What are we going to do about the cops?" Louie pointed to the small police caravan, halted at the gates by a swarm of men waving their EIGHTEEN CENTS IS NOT ENOUGH signs at them.

"Let's have a little more forceful talk with the engineer, get him to move the train on out of here. I can get a bandage any time, but I've never been on a locomotive before."

They climbed the metal steps and found themselves in the cramped quarters of the engine cabin.

"Hey, you guys can't be here!" the engineer yelled at them, brandishing a coal shovel like a weapon."

"Yes, we can," Anselmo said. "And you have to put that shovel down and get this train out of here! There's a dozen guys with tar torches ready to light your cattle cars on fire. Those cars are piled with hay and those black men are trapped in them! Put this thing in reverse and get the hell out of here! Right now! Or you'll be responsible for their deaths!"

"No, I'm sorry but I can't do that. I have to wait for instructions…"

"Yes, you can! We are giving you the instructions! Do it now!"

Louie glared at the man. "I know how to do it. Want me to move this train, Mister Locomotive Man?"

"Nobody touches my engine!"

"Then get going," Anselmo said. "Or we'll throw you off and do it ourselves."

That was when George the engineer decided he had to cooperate. It was an interesting development. Louie had been bluffing; he had no idea how to get the train moving, but George certainly did, and in thirty seconds while Louie watched (and learned how) the entire line of cars –

the ten cattle cars in the middle and a barn red caboose in back – shuddered and jerked and started moving backwards out of the rail yard. The train slowly moved up to a walking speed and then a somewhat faster pace and then a good trot. The men in the police vans yelled and shook their fists and waved their billy clubs, but they couldn't stop the train as it backed out of the yard.

"How come the cops didn't come in past the gates, Louie?" Anselmo said.

"Our trick with the spikes in the wooden boards works twice times in a row!"

George didn't share their enthusiasm. "Fine. Great. You guys are the geniuses. So, what do we do now?"

"You drive," Louie said. "And we sit on the bench over here and watch you do it until we get to New Orleans. If you drive good, maybe we stop half way down for coffee."

CHAPTER FIFTY-FIVE

A few hours later the train was now several miles down the way, still picking up speed as it headed south. Louie took off his breastplate armor. The metal gave off a hollow ring when he tapped it, and he started tapping it in time with the choof-choof-choof turnover of the engine. "How much you think it would take to make the wheels of your train hop off the tracks?" he said.

The engineer glared at Louie. "You wouldn't dare! That's a federal offense!"

"You bring the strike-breaker here. You take food from the table of the working man. My wife, my *bambino,* they gonna starve. That's an offense against God!" Louie showed his armor plate to Anselmo, who gave it a critical look. "Hey, yours is thicker than mine!"

"Weighs more, too. You're a tall, skinny guy. I didn't think you could carry that much weight."

"Well, a steel plate this thick, it might be able to derail a train."

"Oh, like you're the experts," the engineer said.

I did one once," Anselmo said. "It was an Austrian train. This was a few years ago, back in 1917. In the Alps. All it took was a hunk of limestone about like this big." He indicated the size of a watermelon with his hands. There wasn't much conversation after that, just the choof-choof-choof of the engine, the klik-klik-klik of the wheels on the rails underneath them, and everyone buried in their own thoughts.

"Did they get it back on the tracks?" Louie said. He'd been thinking about what that must have been like.

"No, they never did. Never got the chance. It went into a deep ravine."

"Lots of people die?"

"It was a munitions train, loaded with artillery shells."

"So I'm thinking they probably loaded the shells on one car, the fuses on another one?" George, who had been to the war as well – though mostly railroad supply in France and Belgium – considered himself an expert and so he was interested in spite of himself.

"That would have been better for them," Anselmo said.

CHAPTER FIFTY-SIX

The train slowed down now and again as they headed south, passing through the lights of small town after small town. They stopped the train to give George a chance to telegraph ahead to let the railroad people know they were coming and they had to clear the line. Their little train was still running backwards with the caboose out in front. Louie and Anselmo formed a small peace pact with George and the engineer grudgingly let Louie sound the whistle every once in a while and the engine picked up speed in between towns as they kept it heading back the way it had come.

The way it worked out, Anselmo and Louie didn't have ride the train all the way to Louisiana. The sun was well up by the time they got to near Cairo in Southern Illinois, and that was where Paulo, Rosa and Lina caught up to them. Anselmo spotted the Hupmobile racing along on a road parallel to the tracks, Paulo in his racing glasses, intent on the road ahead, and the two women waving at them like they were having a good time.

They had George stop the train, and they climbed down off the locomotive. Louie waved goodbye to the engineer. "Don't come back or I stick my steel plate under the wheels and then I hit you with the baseball bat for your reward."

"Hey, what happened to our peace pact?"

"Our treaty is only good south of Illinois. Otherwise I smack you with the slugger."

"That won't happen, Louie. I'll be in here and you'll be out there."

"Not good for you to try your luck, Georgie Porgie Pudding and Pie. Better stay south of Illinois. Maybe be safe, stay south of Missouri."

"Yeah, you might be safe south of Missouri," Anselmo said. Being so recently from the Boot, he wasn't sure exactly where Missouri was, but it sounded southern and far away, and he was pretty sure Louie knew what he was talking about.

CHAPTER FIFTY-SEVEN

The pregnant woman and the man with the big mustachios who had tried to bribe Lina sat close together in the chairs on the other side of the reception desk where she was sitting. They were restless and uneasy, looking over their shoulders at the intermittent bunches of customers who came in to the office, almost all of them to do business with Anna and Anita.

"Isn't there somewhere private we can talk?" the woman said, tugging the brim of her large traveler's hat low over her face.

"Well, there's the surgery room," Lina said, "but then I'd have to charge you a consult fee."

Monafusti leaned across the desk and spoke in a low voice that was both urgent and forceful. "Please. This is for your sake, alone. I have very important information for you, Doctor Bright, and I don't want to embarrass Anthony Anselmo's lover in public."

"So this isn't about blackmailing me for selling Doctor Whitber's Magic Medicine?"

The woman looked genuinely puzzled; she frowned at her partner, then leaned forward, "Then you admit you are Anselmo's lover!"

"I didn't say that. Are you nuts in the head?" She eyed the woman's stomach, distended in spite of her heavy traveler's dress. "I see you are very pregnant. Is everything going okay with that?"

The woman's face flushed angry red. "That is none of your business!"

298

"Actually, that is exactly my business. As a doctor, you know." Lina made a gesture to her M.D. diploma from Columbia University on the wall behind her. "Seriously. You are over seven months with your child – that's my guess, it could be lots more – you have put a strain on your baby because you say you have traveled here from Rome, a very difficult voyage by sea, over two weeks in cramped quarters – I read the papers; it was stormy, wasn't it?"

"You don't know me. How do you know anything about me?"

"I've taken that trip myself. And then you had to get here from the East Coast. Not pleasant."

"I'm just fine. And that doesn't answer my question: How do you know me?"

"My opinion – professional opinion, of course – is that you don't look fine. And you do look a little flushed in the cheek – maybe even feverish. Let me take your temperature, perhaps?"

The woman shook her head, sputtered her words. "No, of course you will not take my temperature. I mean, about me – how do you know about me traveling, coming from someplace? That is my question." She looked to her companion, but he was no help, frowning silently at the floor.

Lina sat back in the secretary's chair, enjoying herself in spite of knowing she was facing two very dangerous people. She could see Anna and Anita's customers straining to hear every word. *Stay calm, Lina*, she kept reminding herself. *After all, in a few hours half of the neighborhood will know everything that is said here.* Lina smiled. "Very well: Everybody on Hungry Hill knows this is

Mister Monafusti, lately shamed for many crimes and reduced from the title of Monsignor because he is a fraud. You must know that nearly everyone in this neighborhood has met him. He's probably had half the people at San Rocco's pay for the sins they told him in the confessional. He tried to extort money out of me for selling medicine with opium in it. I reported him to the Chicago Heights police. They checked with the proper authorities in the Old Country, and they found out a lot of really bad stuff about him. They can do that these days, you know."

"But –"

"As for you, your name is Sarafina Janika. There is a police search for you in Italy right now, ever since the unfortunate poisoning of your boss."

"Poisoning?!"

"The inspector in Rome was in contact with the Chicago Heights police chief. He said the blue color on the victim's skin is a clear indication of arsenic. Your boss was eating a cake somebody gave him. Lucky for him, he spit up most of it."

Monafusti got to his feet. He took Sarafina's arm and pulled her up. "Come, my dear. I can see this was a mistake. We'll let Doctor Bright sink in her own *malessere*."

"Yeah, right, you do that," Lina said.

Sarafina swayed on her feet. "Did he die? That – that man that somebody poisoned?"

"You mean your ex-boss? No, he'll be alright. He'll be sick for a while, but it looks like he has a great chance to recover. However, let's go back to you – you don't look at all well."

"I told you, I'm fine!" Sarafina snarled her words, practically shouting her denial.

300

"Well, that is my professional opinion and, since you didn't ask, I'm not going to charge you for it. If you get any worse, Saint James Hospital isn't far from here. Just take Dixie Highway north a few miles until –"

"Let's go, dear," Monafusti said, interrupting as he pulled his companion across Doctor Bright's reception room and hustled her out the door.

CHAPTER FIFTY-EIGHT

The atmosphere in the executive conference room at Inland Steel was one of quiet gloom. The board of directors, to a man, had failed to show up. They had sent Elmond Ridgeway a brief 'cover their asses' memo stating the article in the Chicago Heights Star was the first they'd heard of the failed trainload of black strikebreakers, *and whose bright idea was that, anyway?* Elmond was sitting alone with Albert, with nobody else but Patty there, the pretty young girl positioned close right next to the handsome young man, elbows touching, Patty with her pencil and note pad, ready to take notes should anyone say anything. The two of them seemed to be getting on well, a little joke about one of Louis Armstrong's jazzy songs bubbled up between them and then the lengthening silence again.

Elmond was about to fold the meeting and call it a day when Hal Singlebury showed up. "You got a lot of nerve," Elmond said.

"What? Come on! Don't blame me! We nearly pulled the damn thing off!"

"Yeah, yeah, I know. If it only hadn't been for the boards with the spikes in them, the police would have gotten there on time and yadda-yadda-dipsy-doodle-dandy!"

"Well, that is true…" Hal's usual boisterous manner was subdued by Elmond's scornful attitude.

Elmond pointed to the man with Hal, "Who the hell is this guy?"

"The answer to our prayers. This is Mister Munafusti, a situational manager out of Rome. He can actually work miracles."

"Oh, great. And where did you meet this miracle worker?"

"Not Munafusti", the man with the large mustachios corrected Hal. "*Monafusti.* Francesco Monafusti, at your service."

"And what can you do for us, Francesco Monafusti?"

"In spite of what you have been told, I do not do miracles. Think of me more like a magical act. Make fun, if you will. Even call me Mister Magnifico Monafusti, if you will! But – I – get – things – DONE! You don't know how I work, and you don't want to. But I make your worst, your most terrible, your most impossible problems go away. I make them disappear, one by one. That is my promise – and that is my job!"

Hal opened his arms like he was spreading manna from heaven. "And he works through my company, so you're in no way involved with any of his solutions."

Albert gave the fellow with the too-huge mustachios the once-over, seeing the humor in the situation. He grinned at Patty and said, "I wonder does he charge by the hour or by the miracle?"

CHAPTER FIFTY-NINE

Monafusti's recruitment program was brief but instantly effective while it was in play. He found a small pack of five or six teenage high school dropouts hanging around the alley behind Svoboda's Nickelodeon bar and grill at 24th and Butler. Their leader, a scrawny kid named Mungo Skrazi, didn't really think of his guys as a gang, just a bunch of pals his age who spoke street slang and thought school learning and church talk about *Gesu* and keeping away from nailing loose and willing girls was pure crap.

Monafusti looked over the prospects, who were gathered in a line playing pitch the penny against a fairly smooth wall back of Svoboda's. It took him less than a minute to get the lay of the land. He moved in behind Mungo, caught him in a bear hug and gently pushed an ice pick about a quarter inch in between the two ribs in the kid's back closest to his heart. Naturally, Mungo howled like a stuck pig.

"Shut up," Monafusti said. "I push two more inches, we're into your heart and you die."

"W-what do you want?"

"I want to hire you and your *amici* to do a few jobs. That's all. I'll pay you good."

"O-okay," Mungo said.

Later that same day, they showed up outside Rosa's Café. It was that time in the late afternoon when nobody was around. Hal watched from his battered Ford while Monafusti filled a glass quart milk bottle with gasoline and plugged the top with a strip of cotton cloth. They were standing on the narrow strip of land in front of Rosa's Café, near Lina's office. Monafusti quickly handed his home-made gas bomb to Little Farti, one of Mungo's troopers.

"How come Mungo doesn't get in on this himself?" Hal said.

"The kid is a spaz; got a bad throwing arm," Monafusti said. "Shut up and let me do my job before somebody spots us."

"Yeah. Well, it's true, I got the best arm around," Little Farti said, the pride obvious in his voice. "My dad says I'm gonna pitch for the Cubs some day."

"What's your dad know?" Hal grumbled.

"My dad pitches semi-pro ball for the Steger Roustabouts. He taught me a lot."

"So you can hit a window about the size of a barn? That's all we need to know."

"I can hit a thing like that size easy."

"You do that," Monafusti said, "I'll give you a silver dollar. I have it right here." He took a glittery coin from his pocket, held it up to show Little Farti."

"Okay, man!"

"I light the wet cotton here, you throw it in the window over there." Monafusti pointed to the window fronting Lina's office with the signs Lina Bright M.D. and Anna & Anita showing.

"What if I get caught?"

"You don't get caught. You throw the bottle, grab the silver dollar out of my hand and run away before anybody knows anything about anything."

"Okay," Little Farti said.

CHAPTER SIXTY

Anselmo heard about the fire somebody started on the lawn next door to Lina's office while he was waiting for a telegram from his grandfather. Paulo joined him at the Victoria Café, his original idea to convince Anselmo to let him drive his Hupmobile in an amateur run at a clay oval down in Springfield, but all he could talk about was the news from Hungry Hill. "Some crazy kid tried to throw a gasoline bomb at Doc Lina's front window!"

"*Dio mio!* What happened?"

"I didn't see it, but I heard when he went to throw it, some of the gasoline had leaked on his shirt and it caught fire. He burned himself something bad."

"Come on, let's go over there!" By this time, Anselmo had left his breakfast and was heading for the door.

"But your telegram?"

"It'll be there when I get back, Paulo. Do you know? Is Lina okay?"

"Yeah, she is. The kid panicked and threw a wild toss, the glass bottle landed next door in front of Rosas – it landed in some shrubs, it burned a white rose and a lilac bush. The lilacs were blooming, beautiful purple, a real shame. "

"Anybody else hurt?"

"No, the gas just burned, nothing ever did blow up. Rosa and her mom came out, started a water chain, hand pumping, filling buckets from their rainwater cistern. I think I can save the lilac bush with a load of special blessed chicken poop, but maybe not the roses."

"What about the kid?"

"He's not going to be throwing anything for a while – if ever. He got his arm burned pretty bad."

The Hupmobile was parked in a vacant lot to one side of the hotel. Paulo headed for the driver's side of the car. "I get to drive, right?"

"Wait, Paulo. Yes, sure, you get to drive. But wait. There's something wrong here; my car isn't parked where is should be. It's usually right over there, next to the back door."

"What, the people here drive your car?"

"Well, this is their vacant lot. The hotel lets me park it here free as long as I'm renting my room, and they can push it anywhere they want to get it out of the way."

"You let them do that?"

"Sure. You know, the hotel manager used to own it. Sometimes he still thinks it's his; he takes it on shopping trips. Usually asks me first, though."

Paulo was impatient to get behind the wheel of the big green car. It had been moved close up against the hotel wall, so close Anselmo couldn't squeeze into the seat on the passenger side. This gave him a reason to go a little slower and look things over; there did not seem to be any reason to park the Hupmobile in that particular spot so close against the wall. After all, the lot was almost empty.

Anselmo got down on his hands and knees. And then he crawled under the car.

"Mo, what are you doing?"

"Just looking around, Paulo."

He came back out the way he'd gone in, dusting off his hands and the knees on his pants.

"Well, what did you find?" Paulo asked.

"Looks like four sticks of TNT with pressure triggers set front and back of the right front tire."

"What?"

"Yep. Set to go off when the Hupster here is driven either forward or reverse. I guess we better call the police."

"But…who would do that?"

"My guess would be somebody who doesn't like me."

CHAPTER SIXTY-ONE

Sarafina Janika went into labor the evening after Anselmo discovered someone had tried to blow him up. Sara had been arguing with Monafusti all day.

He had a cold, precise way about him. "Sure, you got him drunk and yourself pregnant, but your plan is stupid! It will never work! I have told you a million times! Gio will dump you like a hot brick!"

"No, he will not. I know my Gio. He is hard outside, but just a soft cream puff inside. He will see our sweet little baby and it will melt him!"

Monafusti handed her a yellow paper. "No, he will not," he said. The telegram said simply, YOUR BASTARD IS NOT MY CHILD. SORRY. GIO

Her pains started in earnest and that was when he eyed her and gave her a cold proclamation, "We are finished, Sara. My decision is made, and it is final. We now go our separate ways."

"What? No! Everything we have done and you now give up?"

"This was my project long before you ever heard of Gio Anselmo or his Futura Industries! I have invested *years* in the Anselmo family, since before the war! I now give up *nothing* except you! You got yourself pregnant. Your plan was stupid. I was against it from the first, and now you see Gio is publicly denying you carry his baby. Goodbye, Sarafina Janika, whatever your real name is, our partnership is over. From now on, we go our separate ways. I take things in my own hands without you."

"Oh no, Monafisti. No! You can't just abandon me. I know too much about you. I can ruin you!"

"You know everything, and you know nothing. What can you do? We are here in America, home of the free and brave. Have your nice *bambino bastardo*. Goodbye."

Arturo was coming out of The Orchard Bar in Steger when a man with oversized mustachios that he didn't recognize came up to him and asked for a light on his cigar.

"Why don't you get your own match?" Arturo grumbled in that froggy voice of his, but even as he spoke, he paused and reached in his pocket, took out a small tin metal container and screwed off the lid. He retrieved a match and scratched the head with his thumb. But as he leaned forward to light the cheap stogie, the man stabbed him once in the stomach with an ice pick.

Arturo screamed and fell to the ground, clutching his stomach. His assailant could have easily killed him as he lay there, but he kicked him in the head, breaking three of his teeth, and then ran away.

The bartender heard the cries for help and came running out the door. At first he couldn't figure out what had happened, but finally he saw the blood from Arturo's stomach beginning to make a red bloom on his white undershirt. He managed to flag down a couple of *Fritz* woodworkers from the Steger Piano Factory who were driving on home in

311

a model T that had seen better days, and they half carried Arturo and dumped him in the back seat.

"Ver do you vont we should take him?"

"I don't know...St James Hospital?" the bartender said.

"No," Arturo grunted. "You take me to the lady doc over on Hungry Hill."

CHAPTER SIXTY-TWO

Anselmo and Louie were walking the strike line in front of the main gate at the mill when Paulo drove up in the Hupmobile to give them the news about Arturo.

"The doc says she could use your help," Paulo said.

"You go, Mo," Louie said. "We just got another half hour here."

"Not a good idea to leave you alone here, Comrade. Strange things are happening. Come on; It's a weekday night. Eight o'clock. Nobody's going to try to bust in here right now."

"Okay," Louie said. "I will come with you."

The man with the ice pick had been standing in the shadow of some overgrown Dutch Elm trees. He frowned when he saw the strikers leaving together.

"Okay, some other time," he muttered to himself.

Paulo dropped off Anselmo and Louie in front of the doctor's office. He parked the Hupmobile and waved as he headed to the café next door. "You guys handle it. I gotta see my sweet love Rosa," he said.

When Anselmo and Louie walked into Lina's reception room, the German immigrants who'd brought in Arturo were sitting in the reception room. The bright overhead lights were on in the operating room. Anselmo went to the small bathroom and washed his hands. He put on a sanitary smock and knocked on the door to the operating room.

Louie sat next to the two Germans who had driven Arturo from Steger. "Is he going to be okay?" Louie asked.

"Ve don't know nothing about that," one of the Germans said. "*Gott* only knows."

"Ve be going now," the other man said, polite and hesitant, as if asking for permission. "Our vives vill be wondering ver vas ve off to."

As they left, Lina opened the door from the operating room, "Tony, glad you're here! I need your help! Wash your hands and arms at the sink! Use plenty of the lye bar soap."

"Done, already," Antonio said. "I'm ready to help."

Louie peeked in the door, and saw Arturo lying on the operating table. "Arturo! Be strong, Comrade!"

Arturo seemed to revive for a moment, "Louie! Some sneaky *bastardo* knifed me in the guts!"

"Do we know him? What did he look like?"

"Big hair," Arturo said, making a gesture with his fingers like he was preening a moustache.

Anselmo nodded to Louie, "I think we know him." He looked at Lina, "I don't see much blood...the bad guy stabbed him with a paring knife or an ice pick, I'm guessing."

"Something's not right, Tony," Lina said. "He's too pale. I think he's bleeding inside."

"How is that possible?"

"Really easy, sometimes if a knife punctures a vein deep inside, nobody knows until too late."

"What do we do?"

314

"You in this with me?"

"Yes, I am," he said. She poured a small portion of Doctor Whitber's Magic Medicine into a cup. She shrugged at his questioning look, "Old Whitber had a secret stash in the attic.".

She cleaned the wound area and isolated it with a sanitary abdominal pad.

"The wound is so small!" Anselmo said "It's really just a puncture."

"Yes, but it goes way in," Lina said. She opened an exploratory cut in Arturo's stomach area. A small two inch incision was all it took and dark blood came welling out. "Oh, no…it's a vein," she said. "There." She opened the incision further and soaked up the blood with sanitary towels until she found the exact spot where the blood was welling from a small hole in a thick vein that was behind the soft bag of Arturo's stomach. She cut a long, thin slice of an inner skin layer from the side of the incision she had made, and tied it around the vein.

"Will that work?" Anselmo said.

"Sometimes."

She damped up the blood as best she could and then sewed up the incision she'd made and bandaged the wound with a large abdominal pad and four inch wide strips of gauze.

"That's all I can do," she said.

They sat together in the reception room, waiting for the ambulance wagon to take Arturo to St. James. Lina looked tired, but Anselmo could see she wasn't relaxed. "What are his chances?"

She shook her head. "Look at this." She handed him Arturo's blood stained undershirt and a

315

magnifying glass. "Look there. Around the puncture hole in the cloth."

"What am I looking at?"

"That light brown stain. And those brownish crumbs of something. That's from animal defecation… something like a cow pie."

"Oh." Anselmo's spirits dropped; he knew the deadly trick. Soldiers in the war learned to dip their bullets and their combat knives in any offal they could find, an almost certain way to infect a wound.

In a half hour the ambulance showed up, and Arturo was still alive when they drove him off to St. James. Lina heard later that the hospital staff managed to find an acceptable blood type and give him a transfusion, one pint of precious O negative blood, the type that worked on almost anybody. Arturo seemed okay for a day and a half but, after that, sepsis set in with a raging fever, and a few hours later he died in his sleep.

CHAPTER SIXTY-THREE

But before Anselmo could leave Lina's office and head back to his hotel room, Sarafina Janika returned. She was now in labor, tired and in a sweat, and looking worn and frail. She struggled and swore and screamed until, some hours after midnight, with Lina and Anselmo's help, she gave birth to a squalling baby girl. Sarafina looked exhausted, gasping as she lay on Lina's operating table.

Anselmo turned off the bright overhead electric lights. Lina held the five pound girl in her arms and then handed her to the new mother. Sarafina accepted the baby and held it close as she drifted in and out of sleep. After a while she started talking in a low monotone.

"Anthony…do you think he will marry me?"

"Yes…" Anselmo said. "My father is a fool. I'm sure he will."

The silence lengthened between them. After minutes she spoke again. "Anthony…you have to know…I'm not really your enemy."

"I believe it," he said, even though he was sure it wasn't true. He didn't believe her, but he was thinking it wasn't the time for any of this, and he couldn't see any reason to contradict her. "I say we make a truce between us."

"Alright," she agreed in a small, muffled voice.

"I'll telegraph my father with the good news."

There was a long pause. She seemed to be sniffling, putting on the appearance of a little girl lost.   "Thank you, Anthony…I'm sorry…for everything."

He sighed, trying to keep his words to a minimum.   "Done is done, Sara, and you have to rest. It's a cold world out there. We will be friends. We have to be friends, for the baby's sake."

"You should know this one thing: Fusti and I are at an end. We are done, finished."

"After so many years?"

"He is a bad man. Too evil even for me."

"He is wanted for murder."

"You did remember him from Rome, didn't you…I told him you would."

Anselmo couldn't help himself; the words just tumbled out, "You poisoned my father."

"No. That was Fusti, not me."

"You had to have agreed to it."

"I had to…or he would have killed me, too. But I didn't bake that cake. He bought it from the finest pastry shop in Rome. He made me pick it up from the shop."

"And added the poison himself?"

"Yes.   But I think he added too much, and that's how Gio knew, by the bad taste."

They were silent for a moment, each deep in their own thoughts.   "Fusti…wants to talk… to you," she said.

"What about?"

"He wouldn't tell me. He has…a plan for you." And she drifted off to sleep.

Lina took the baby from Sarafina's limp arms and placed it gently in a bassinet next to her. "She has an easy answer for everything." she said. "What do you think, Tony?"

"Of course, I don't trust her, but son-of-a-gun, I don't think I can do anything. She's going to be my father's problem." Anselmo was thinking Rome was half a world away, and there was no way to prove Sarafina was responsible for the poisoned birthday cake. Another thought came to pester him, "And, you know, dear girl, we've got to be careful; that crazy man is on the loose out there, stabbing people."

Lina arranged a cot so that she could stay close and watch over Sarafina overnight. After the new mother and her baby were settled in, she sat in the reception room with Anselmo.

"Who ever thought any of this would be possible? What do you make of this?" Lina said.

Anselmo smiled. *"Un mondo strano.* Now I've got a baby sister," he said. "Well…half-sister…"

"So then, in a way, her plan works for her. She's managed to break into your family."

"Yes. And I'd be willing to bet my dad will probably marry her. For appearances, I'm thinking. And, who knows, maybe he loves her."

"Love is strange…What about your grandfather?"

"My *nonno* back in Turin – I know you'd like him – he's a realist. He won't trust Sarafina anymore than we do, but he'll love the baby. A baby granddaughter! She'll want for nothing."

"And your dad?"

"As long as Sarafina doesn't try to poison him again…well, we'll have to see about that one."

The silence lengthened between them. That was the way they were, content to be together. And then his next sentence dropped like an unexpected songbird's call out of a calm and beautiful twilight sky.

"Marry me," he said.

"I thought you'd never ask," she said, the quiet smile he loved so much lighting her face.

CHAPTER SIXTY-FOUR

"Christ, we can't just go on killing people!" Elmond paced back and forth in front of Hal Singlebury and Francesco Monafusti, the two of them seated on the far side of the ornately inlaid walnut-and-oak conference table in the big room next to his office. "Chicago's been on the phone all morning yelling at me – the Chicago Heights police chief had the gall to drive up to the Loop and *interrogate* the president of Inland Steel!"

Hal looked at Monafusti and they both shook their heads. "Well, so what, interrogate? What about? This is all news to me."

"Don't play funny with me, Hal. Businesses frequented by our strikers are getting burned, their families are being terrorized, church gardens getting torn up, we even got some dead bodies some people found out in Sauk Trail Forest Preserve – AND, I had to pay for a trainload of strikebreakers who never even got off the train!"

"Okay, we brought the blackies up from Louisiana, but that's all we know," Hal said. "That other stuff, no."

"Sure. Right. You know nothing. And I been paying you two for exactly what?"

"Advice. Counseling. Nothing else." Hal threw out his arms, a magnanimous gesture. "You don't want to know any more than that."

"No, of course I don't! Look, forget all this! This is the last of it! The end! The strike is over! The Chicago office can't take any more. We're going to the table."

"What, negotiate?! No! You don't want to do that," Hal said. "Hell, Francesco here and me, we haven't even started."

"You've done more than enough! You guys are fired, fired, *fired!* Get out of here! I don't ever want to see either of you again!"

"Well, okay, Elmond, if you're that dead set on stupid – but you still owe us thirty-five hundred bucks," Hal said.

"I can't believe what I'm hearing! You got your nerve!"

"Yes, we do. And you're gonna pay us the money you owe us or we're gonna see that police chief ourselves to talk about things. What did you say his name was?"

Elmond was about to explode, but there was something about the Italian with the big mustachios that stopped him. It wasn't Hal; Hal he could deal with. It was this other guy. There was something alien and unpredictable about *mustachio man*, it was like being too close to some kind of a wild thing that didn't belong there, a wolf or a snake maybe a hungry tiger. *What the hell,* he found himself thinking, *it's only somebody else's money.* He yelled at Patty, who was waiting in his office, told her to alert Sumner that two clients were coming to his office to be paid for services rendered.

"Remind Sumner it's cash, no checks," Hal said to Patty as they headed for the stairs down to the paymaster's office.

"It doesn't feel like it's over," Rosa said to Lina as she set a plate of eggs in front of her.

"Well, the strike is settled…" Lina said. "

322

"But a lot of evil things have happened and I don't see anybody going to jail"

"Maybe they will, in a week or two."

"You should be happy. You're getting married!"

"No," Lina said. "You're getting married. I told Tony I'd think about it."

"Oh, man, girlfriend, he's a gorgeous hunk of manhood and he's crazy about you. What's to think about?"

"Well, like what am I going to do with the rest of my life. Marriage is fine and great and wonderful, but I want more. I can do more. I was meant to do more."

"I don't get it."

"Yes, you do, Rosa. You already have more. You have your wonderful restaurant here. A life with your Paulo is just icing on the cake."

"But you're a doctor…"

"It's not me I'm worried about. It's Tony. I don't think he knows what he's going to do with his life. I guess he has opportunities, but he hasn't been clear about what he'd like to do. Will he stay in this country? Will he go back to Italy? He hasn't told me, and I don't think he knows. And I'm not going to be one of those trail-along wives."

"Well, I think maybe he does know. But we've seen he has problems with his father's mistress, and he thinks that Monsignor who turned out to be not a Monsignor might be somehow involved in all of this.."

"Could they really be after his family money?"

"Tony seems to think so."

"Nobody has that much money," Rosa said.

"At least, not in our world," Lina agreed.

"I think you just have to talk to him."

"I think you're right, Rosa."

"Yes…and until then, there's eggs *a la Gambriotta*."

CHAPTER SIXTY-FIVE

Anselmo had instructed the morning chef at the Victoria Hotel Café to make a northern Italian omelet the way he liked it, the egg thickened with cream and folded over with mushrooms in the center (although the mushrooms were preserved in a Ball Jar, not fresh), and just a touch of Jamaican sweet-hot sauce. He had finished eating and was working his way through a pile of papers from a thick folder that his grandfather had mailed from Turin, nothing he had to sign off on, just copies of the new land deeds and maps of the new orchards and vineyards they now owned in California.

He saw the man with the oversized mustachios and the too-small Van Dyke beard when he came in the door, watched him talk to the head waitress, who pointed in his direction. Monafusti tipped his woolen British hat to the girl and started in Anselmo's direction.

"Ah, Anthony Anselmo," he said. "I think you have been avoiding me."

Anselmo wasn't sure how to answer that. He carefully gathered in the spread of contracts and maps and placed them on top of the folder to his left side. He gestured Monafusti was to sit across the table from him if that was his wish. Monafusti nodded and took a seat. He removed his hat, placing it on the table next to him.

"Care for anything?" Anselmo asked. "Had breakfast? Tea, perhaps?"

"No. Nothing. Just a moment, first, to inquire as to the health of your father."

"Nothing new. Recovering, the last I heard."

"Unfortunate, how these things happen."

"Yes."

"I mean, they lately seem to happen so often, to your family. Sarafina was talking just the other day; she thinks you should buy an insurance policy."

"Very thoughtful of her, but I suspect that might be more than I could afford."

"Well, I do not know, considering *l'alternativa* could be so…grim."

"And what might that be?"

"For one thing, those you love could go missing, one by one."

"The whole *famiglia*? And my friends, too?"

"Well, your family isn't that much, any more. But, yes. It could happen. Them, and everyone you know, and care for. All your *ostaggi alla fortuna*, your *hostages to fortune,* as the great English play-writer said."

"I should never let that happen."

"Them first – and after, you come into focus. You know you can't be watching forever and always. And without your insurance policy, someone might kill you whenever it might be convenient."

"The way you killed my brother."

"You think you know about that? You know nothing! Your brother was a trusting *idioto*."

"So you shot him in the back!"

"No. That is pure nonsense. I will tell you. It was a matter of family honor, a duel. He had a fair chance."

"Shot in the back. I saw it. The army showed me the body."

"You saw the body...No. You come to the wrong conclusions. We did our dozen paces. I just counted a little faster than he did." Monafusti smiled at the memory. Then he shifted his weight, leaning forward. "Enough of this: it is time to get down to business, Mister Anthony Anselmo." Monafusti's suit jacket was open, his tailored vest looking neat and trim, the sleeves of his jacket long and a little loose, the latest fashion in Rome. "Let's get down to business, my *caro amico*. Dear friend, you are a rich young man. You can buy your way out of this. I am offering you a one thousand U.S. dollars insurance policy and you will be safe."

"A thousand a month?"

"A thousand a week. Pay once a year, in January. I will provide details, a contract you will sign, banking instructions."

"I'll bet you will."

Anselmo sat upright in his chair. He seemed the image of a thoughtful man, a man calmly considering his options. He noticed Monafusti twitched his shoulders, uncomfortable as if he was wearing his suspenders a bit too tight. Monafusti's cane was leaning against the wall, within easy reach but not an instant threat. Anselmo watched the man with the big mustachios, curiosity plain on his face. Anselmo was looking like an ordinary man who wanted clarity, simply wanted to be sure about some details – for Dio only knew what reason – details that he found of importance. "Please, indulge me, *Mister* Monafusti, let me understand what you're saying – if I choose to pay this money, then myself and my people are all safe from this…this bad luck and misfortune of which you speak."

"Yes, everyone will be safe."

"And is the rate guaranteed? It's not going to be twelve thousand dollars more next year? And then more the year after that?"

Monafusti shrugged, "Well, I can't guarantee that. There is inflation…things like that. I'd say twelve thousand seems a little high."

"And I'm guessing that you have a backup plan – some alternate course of action if I cannot agree, if we cannot resolve our situation with a satisfactory arrangement."

"Of course."

"Then I'm going to have to go with your back up plan, that alternate action."

Monafusti's pleasant attitude dropped from him like a wet towel. His lips twisted and he said, "Well then, you can have it!" and he pointed his left arm across the table at Anselmo. The move seemed overly dramatic, out of place for a quiet mid-morning business meeting between two well-dressed men in a fairly quiet café, but at the end of the gesture Monafusti's arm jerked as it pulled leather strings tight and triggered a gambler's derringer rig hidden at his wrist, a hide-out weapon that fired a bullet directly into Anselmo's chest.

Anselmo coughed and was pushed back in his chair as the small bullet hit the steel plate his comrade Louie had made for him.

"You wear a metal plate!" Monafusti said.

328

"I work in a steel mill. What did you expect?" Anselmo reached in the folder on the table at his side and came out with the small silvery pistol his mother had given to him as a present on his twelfth birthday. "Now you are a man," she had told him with a proud smile. "You deserve a man's present."

Anselmo cocked the hammer and fired the snub-nosed little gun once, the bullet striking Monafusti in the chest.

"*Assassino!* You have murdered me!" Monafusti said, his voice filled with disbelief.

"No. You shot first. In America, this is self-defense."

Even with a bullet in him, Monafusti had the reflexes of a reptile. Anselmo saw the man reach for his cane. Monafusti grabbed it with one hand and had his hidden sword half out of the hollow case as Anselmo cocked the hammer of his little pistol again, carefully aimed and fired a second shot. This time the bullet caught Monafusti in the center of his throat. His eyes went wide and his arms jerked out and then he slumped sideways and slowly sagged to the floor with one of his legs up and bent across his chair seat. Anselmo cocked the small revolver a third time. He stood and moved around the table to look down at the fallen man. Monafusti's jaw was working but no sounds came from his mouth. After a few moments, his gaze drifted away from the smoking barrel, close and still pointing directly at his face, and then whatever was left of him was gone.

The waitress was staring at Anselmo from the doorway to the kitchen.

"Better call the police," he told her. "I don't think we'll need an ambulance."

There were a lot of witnesses, and most seemed eager to get their name on the front page of the Chicago Heights Star. The fellow with the big mustachios was under suspicion for a half a dozen crimes in his native Rome and at least a half dozen more in Illinois, and he had clearly shot an unarmed man before the victim somehow obtained a weapon and fired back to protect himself.

CHAPTER SIXTY-SIX

It was after the strike settlement was official and both parties agreed the mill was to start up again in two days. Louie and Anna were in the church garden behind the hot house helping Paulo and his new apprentice Ollie Junior re-seed the vegetable garden when Anselmo showed up with two dozen small tomato plants ready to be replanted.

"The farmer who paid Lina with arrowheads came across with some tomato sproutlings," Anselmo said.

"Hey, Mo!" Louie said. "We're back to hell next week!"

Paulo looked up from planting tiny carrot seeds in a long row. "What was the final deal?"

"They offered 20 cents, we demanded 30...we settled at 25!"

"That's a big victory, Comrade," Anselmo said.

"Not so big." The short little man shrugged his broad shoulders and gave Anselmo his wide, Cheshire Cat grin. "Maybe 25 Cents An Hour Is Not Enough, either. Just enough for now."

"I see. So the war goes on."

"La guerra continua, Comrade."

"It's never over, my friend."

"Well, sure it's over," Paulo said. "The workers are going back to work. They got their raise. It's a big victory."

"It's a victory, but it's not the war," Anselmo said. "Did they agree to install the safety posts?"

331

Paulo looked to Louie, who frowned and shook his head. "Not this time. Safety posts is a top demand for next time."

"Yeah. Not this time, but I'm thinking there's no next time for this boy's father." He pointed at Ollie Junior, who had been silently watching Paulo seed the garden..

"What are you saying, Mo?" Louie said.

"We have to take a second look at ourselves, fighting in this endless war against the managers, the owners, the people who control the company. Not quit. Just look in the mirror and review our options. The newspapers say the CPUSA is the bad guys. The unions, the socialists, are evil, they say. But you know we just want a fair wage, money to feed our families and some safety so we don't get hurt along the way.

"Yes, I am the one always telling you that," Louie had set down his trowel and was watching Anselmo. "But what are you saying?"

While they were talking, Lina had showed up with Rosa. "Sorry we're late," Rosa said. "Mamma doesn't know the meaning of the words *fast egg*."

Anselmo nodded, "No, problem. You're just in time." He turned his attention back to Louie, "Comrade, I'm saying we are already the winners here, with this glorious victory in the strike, but we cannot let ourselves be trapped in this one struggle."

"It is a just cause."

"Yes, that is true, Louie. But we must not allow ourselves to be trapped in hell. Just as there are others to continue this fight, there are better battlegrounds more suited to our talents."

"What are you talking about, Mo?"

"I'm talking about your pear tree with the five types of pears, and your grape vines and apple trees in your back yard. I see the pride when you show me these talents you have."

"But – just leave the mill?"

"For a new war – something dearer to your heart. How about a fight against nature, against floods and droughts to raise crops and orchards and vines!"

Louie looked like he was about to cry. "A beautiful dream. I used to dream about such things when I was a boy. But Mo, we don't have this choice."

"No, Comrade, I have come here to offer you a choice!" As he spoke, Anselmo was unrolling a geologic map of California and spreading it on the soil in the hothouse. "All of you." He pointed to Ollie's son. "Your family, too."

"Where is this?" Louie said.

"In the middle of far-away California," Anselmo said. He gestured to Paulo, "You and Rosa can come if you want."

"I don't know…" Paulo said. "I'm *Dio's* gardener here, and Rosa has the restaurant and some other crazy new plan."

"Pauli's right, we can't leave this behind. But I'll come visit you on vacation," Rosa said. "We'll have plenty of money if I can get my spaghetti factory going."

"Wow, a spaghetti factory."

"Spaghetti and macaroni, too."

"You're full of surprises. I'll miss you, dear girlfriend," Lina said. "Don't forget, they like spaghetti in California, too."

Louie was eyeing the map, his plump forefinger tracing one of the slopes. "What if I could bring my pear tree...?"

"Why not?" Anselmo said. "I'll help you dig it up."

"And the grape vines...*Pappa mio* brought them here from the Old Country."

"Deal," Anselmo said.

"The apple trees might be too old to transplant, but I wonder, I could maybe buy a sapling and graft some branches on."

"Works for me," Anselmo said, smiling at Lina as he shook Louie's hand.

A grin showed up on Louie's wide face as he thought of something else. "You know, Comrade, I'm thinking there's gotta be somebody whose gonna fight for the rights of the California grape vine worker, too..."

"Hey, wait a minute – that puts us on opposite sides of the fence."

Louie's smile broadened, "I promise, Mo, I'm gonna be fair."

THE END

A FEW WORDS FROM THE AUTHOR

It was one Saturday evening in the late 1950's, I remember it was in the Spring after my dad died. I was home from college, spading the garden for my mother, and Louie was transplanting young tomato plants over on his side of the alley. Louie was a nice guy, Italian immigrant, short and tough, shaped like a cannonball. I remember it was the last year before Pete, his son-in-law, built a house on that lot. I said hi, and it didn't take much to get Louie talking; I guess he was lonesome for those old arguments with Dad, *Come back to the church, Louie; No, Jack, you get some brain in your head, join The Party.*

Louie stood on the bare earth in his vegetable patch, wiping the sweat from his brows with a red workman's handkerchief. The bald top of his head barely came up to my chest, and he waved his hands as he talked.

"Angelo tell-a me you now work over at the Inland Steel."

Angelo was Louie's son, a kid who'd come back from World War II to ride his Harley through the single stoplight in Steger doing over 110 miles per hour. He'd found a girl who had tamed him down some and was married and working as a tile layer in Park Forest, where the new homes were springing up in rows like carrots and beans. I admitted to Louie that I had been up on the hot beds over at the steel mill, earning money so I could go back to school in the fall.

Louie nodded approvingly, looking at me. "I work-a the hot beds myself, when I was-a the younger man."

"My dad said you started there."

"Thes-a was back in the 1920's. 1922. I was a young-a man then, let me see, I am-a born in 1891, so at the time of the steel mills I am-a 31 years old." He was thinking back, remembering how it was back then. "Mary, she was-a about six, her sister was-a 3. Joe was-a only one, and Angelo, he's-a not born yet. I'm-a working for ten or twelve hours a day, six-a day a week. And I get-a the pay 18 cents an hour."

"Eighteen cents!" Even in the late 1950's when I'd climbed up on the smoking hotbeds at the Inland Steel mill for a summer job, I'd pulled down over two dollars an hour.

"Shuur-a!" Louie nodded. I'd made his point for him. "And I was-a married man, with those-a mouths to feed, shoes for growing feet! Eighteen cents! That's not enough! You cannot live on that!"

I put down my spade and drifted over to the picket fence. It was getting too dark to see what I was doing anyway.

"So, what did you do?"

"We shut-a down that plant!"

"Noooo…you didn't?"

"Oh, yes, yes, yes, Johnny-boy. We tried it before, and we fail. But this time, son-a-ma-gun, we made it stick!"

"How'd you do that?"

A grin split his face from ear to ear; he couldn't be happier. He crossed the alley, waving his arms in the air. I felt the ghost of my father was hanging out somewhere close, pleased at the sight.

"We told-a them we was not a-coming back until we got-a better hours, better working conditions—and 25 cents an hour!"

I thought about it for a moment. In the late 1950's 25 cents didn't seem like much, but that had to be a big raise for back then.

"And did they give it to you?"

He shook his head no. "Shuuuuuuff!" He made a deprecating sound with his lips and looked at me as if I had no sense at all. "No. And at-a first, the bosses over there wasn't worried at all. At least, they never showed it."

"What did they do?"

"They just stood there, grinning. Those fat-a-cat owners, they seen walkouts before. They tell us stuff like, 'You guys be shuffling back in here after a couple days.' Fffffffuttt! Apologizing for what? For something that wasn't our fault? Willing to work overtime at half pay to make up the loss?"

"They would have made you do that?"

"That was the way. Work it off or don't come back."

"That doesn't seem fair at all."

"But not this time!" Louie raised his hands like he was going to call down lightning and thunder from the sky. "This time we got-a organized. We plan and we save for months. We set aside food, and clothing, and coal for the winter. And for this one time, the black-a robes at the Catholic church agree to work together with the socialists."

337

"I never heard of such a thing."

"Oh, yes, yes, yes! We form-a the truce for a little while. You know the church is-a rich as the owners—maybe more rich—but nobody in the priest-house is gonna melt down the gold-a chalice so the worker and his family can eat. But there was-a few young-a priest, they cared. And they got-a the collections from all the peoples to buy food and medicine. They did their part. And my comrades did-a their own part with the organization of the men, and the picket lines, and the raising of the spirit. Comrades march together, as we sing this-a song!"

I must have looked confused. Louie patted me on the shoulder. "You have to try to put yourself in the place. This raising up of the spirit is-a big problem when you got poor people and no money and nobody ever stood up to the boss before. You got your wife looking at you wondering what you are up to, and you yourself have no sureness of where it's-a going to go. You don't know if it can go. So we have bonfire meetings, and sing-a the songs, and we teach the people to be brave."

"I guess that's important," I said.

"You have no idea. It's-a not easy to be brave when your children cry from-a the hunger and your wife look at you, quiet like, with her eye. The days go by, one by one, and our people get more and more nervous. But still we march back and forth in front of the entrance to the mill, and nobody crosses and the picket line holds."

"Why didn't people just run in, or come through in trucks?"

"Nobody was gonna cross that picket. We had ice picks for car and truck tires. We had sticks and rocks. Maybe a gun or two, in-a the pocket or behind the belt. We are protecting our jobs, our wives and children, our lives. 'Inland Steel's gonna freeze over before we let you in there,' we yell at anybody trying to cross our line. We are angry, and we have the ugly look on our faces, We gonna bash you. Somebody is gonna get hurt, here! It sound to you like we are the bad people, maybe—but we know we are in the right! We must win, or we have nothing!"

"So that's how you won."

Louie shook his head, "Oh, it not so easy as-a that, Johnny-boy. Those-a day drag by and become-a many, many weeks. And when the strike don't crumble, the owners start-a to worry real bad. You see, a short-a strike was-a not so bad for them. In a strange way, it was even good, because they wouldn't have-a to pay the men, and they could do business off their big-a stockpile of steel out in the yard. They get some of their bully mick-cop friends to help them clear the entrance for a few minutes, and before we can bring in more men, they get their trucks to come in a bunch and take away that steel. Okay, we have to let them do that. A score for them. But as more days go by and go by, they start to run-a out of this or that, and pretty soon they have to say to their customers, 'Sorry, we got no more in our nice stockpile.' Now they are losing profit. Now, they gotta do something."

"What can they do? Sounds like you closed the place down."

"Well, they do have a sneaky plan. They meet in secret and agreed to send two or three of their foremen down to New Orleans. These little boss-a-men are going to come back on the E, J& E railroad with eight or nine box car loads of husky black-a men. These black-a men are beat into the ground. They are so dirt poor from picking cotton for a few pennies an hour, and they got their own families to feed, you know. They are gonna jump at the chance to ride a box car north and make 18 cents an hour. Only, the owners ain't gonna pay 18 cents, they're going to pay the black man 12 cents an hour to break our backs and teach us a lesson, once and for all. And you know those black-a man are still going to jump at the chance, because it's-a twice what they make picking cotton.

"So you can come back if you'll work for 12 cents an hour?"

"You got it-a now, Johnny-boy! If you are a plant manager or a rich boss, that's certainly a good plan for them. Those black men are so beat down in-a dirt, 12 cents is a sweet wage to them. They are ready to kill for 12 cents an hours."

"What did you do?"

"Oh those were terrible times for us. We been on strike more than a few weeks by then. Lots-a the men don't feel so sure no more. They go home and look at their wife and their little kids looking back at them, and they have-a the fear deep in their gut.

"Sounds like the bosses had you on the run."

"They thought they did. If only they can get these hungry black-a men up from Mississippi and Louisiana. If only they can sneak the black South men into the plant and start those mill ovens roaring

340

hot again, the strike is broke for sure. But, Johnny-boy—that ain't the way it's gonna happen. You see, we gotta secret man listening in on the management meetings. They gotta one man on their insides who they look down. He's an outsider. They no like-a him, they no trust-a him...but they need him because he is the keeper of the books. He knows where the money is hidden, where the dollars are all buried. Behind his back they call-a him miserable Jew-bastard. Still, he know it, what they say about him. He knows the only reason they keep-a him is he does the financial book-a so good to keep their tax low with-a the Uncle Sam. He's like a clerk, their low boy on the pole, but he come to all the meeting to keep-a the notes, because they lazy, and that's-a job too low for them.

"But what they don't-a know, their miserable Jew-bastard is-a special man. He's-a read Marx, he's-a follow Lenin, and he's-a know the Russian Revolution by heart. He's-a love-a the justice and the people. And so he leak-a the word to us about these-a black South strike-breaker men coming up on the railroad train.

"Now, here's-a where the comrades have-a big argument with the church about what to do. The priests all say we go to the authorities and let the police make-a the illegal strike-breaker go back South to their cotton-a field. But we don't trust-a the police. Nobody ever give us a fair shake before. We have to make-a our own luck!

"And, we don't trust the black-a robe priest, either—so we gotta tie them up real tight and leave them in the back of the church. That way, they don't

341

have to see if we commit any sins, it's good for them, you know?

"After that, we get all the men together, and organize a big-a rally by the train yard south of Crete, maybe ten or fifteen miles south of Chicago Heights. See, we know that's where the train has to come in and switch over. We light the huge fire, and we give our men all white-a sheet to wear. We know the Southern black-a man is afraid of the white sheet, that means the death and the hanging and the beating to them.

"We have some black-a men of our own. Our black-a men , they work with us. Black make no difference, white make no difference—we are steel workers! We have-a rights! We need-a justice, a fair wage, a life for our families! So white and black, we all put on the white sheets. You know, Johnny-boy, it make-a no difference if you're inside the sheet.

"Oh, what a night that was! When that loco-a-motive come puffing and steaming in, we're all standing there in our white-a sheets! We wave our flaming sticks, flaming with burning tar. We shout and yell and wave our bats and sticks—and that's a sight to see. We rattle our bats against the slats on the open boxcars. They were using that kind usually for cows and sheep. Those black cotton pickers could see out-a the slats with-a wild look in their eye. They don't want no part of it. We keep up the yelling and some men shoot-a the rifle in the air, and not one black-a man move to get off that train! I tell you how it happened, Johnny-boy! In-a the true fact, they barricade the door from the inside to protect themself!"

Louie paused and sighed, realizing where he was.

"So, it was all good then, right?"

"It's not a safe-a thing, young Johnny. You get-a these men to take the chance of their life to strike for a good-a cause, and at first they are so afraid, but when it get-a going, they finally got something to take out their anger and frustration. We gotta them worked up to a fever, and I could see it's close to going run-away out of control. That was the most dangerous time. I had been so sure we had to do this, but at that moment, anything could happen.

"The railroad yard boss, he sees-a the pistol flashes going off, and that our men are beating on his box cars. We already break some of the slats on the cars—pretty soon our men are gonna get in and somebody is gonna get killed! That boss, he tries to call the police and some of his own yard workers, but we already cut-a the telephone lines. And his own men, well, they are workers too, and are more in favor of us.

"After that, the yard boss gets into a panic. He orders the locomotive, which is still hooked to the cars, to back out of the yard.

"We have a plan for that, and we have ten of our best-a men climb up on the train, armed with the pistola, the shotgun, and knives, too. Son-a-ma-gun, that train is-a gone not five minutes and there is-a thirty or forty policemen show up. Those-a black robe turn-coats gotta free somehow—and, the first thing, they call the cops!"

"So the Catholic priests betrayed you and shut you down?"

"Not-a quite…not-a quite, Johnny-boy. See, the yard manager, he's not give-a the instructions how far south the train is supposed to go, so our men stay with the engineer and make-a sure it goes down to Southern Illinois. When it gets that far, they warn him they'll be waiting if he comes back. Then they hop-a off and watch it still heading back south for New Orleans. Only after that, our men take-a the long walk along the tracks back to Chicago Heights."

Louie hitched up his suspenders. He reached his hand across the fence and rested it on my shoulder, "This-a whole thing happen a long time ago, but if-a you don't think maybe it's-a so important any more, maybe you gotta think again. If-a the men not die in the American Revolution War, you not have-a the freedom you got today. And, if-a we not send those black-a cotton picker men back to New Orleans, you not have-a your good pay at Inland Steel today. We won-a that fight, and after that the owners agreed to sit down and talk for real for the first-a time ever. We got-a the better working conditions and the shorter hours."

I smiled across the fence at him. "Did you get your 25 cents an hour?"

He looked up at me and a big grin lit his round face, "Does the Pope wear-a the tall hat?! And that was the real start, that the unions meant something! And we never look-a back, we march-a forward for the good of the working man!"

HISTORICAL NOTE: The successful Chicago Heights Steel Mill strike of 1922 was one of the first and most important organized labor actions against U.S. business since the start of the industrial revolution. In the years that followed, the unions and the Communist Party of the U.S. managed an on-again, off-again love-hate relationship, each at times making a move to control or disband the other, and each claiming victory for any and all advances that were made in behalf of the working man. As for the Catholic church, to this day it continues (though often in the shadows) to vie with these other two gentlemanly entities for the hearts and minds of the working classes.

A Few More Words From The Author

Strike! Is a fictional novel set against a backdrop of labor unrest that took place in the industrial town of Chicago Heights in the 1920s. It is a work of fiction. The names, characters, organizations, places, events and incidents are either products of the author's imagination or are used fictitiously.

All the characters portrayed in the novel are fictional creations of my own imagination. In the late 1950s, my family's neighbor, upon hearing I was working on the hot beds of the Inland Steel mill, told me about a labor strike he was a part of at that same mill in 1922. I researched what he had told me and found that his strike was successful – indeed, famous – as a prototype protest that resulted in better working conditions and higher wages for the men who worked there. So while this is a fictional novel with fictional characters and a plot built in the dramatic narrative style, it is also a sincere tribute to the working people of this great nation who fought for the right to earn a decent living, for safer, more humane conditions in the workplace and for the dignity of working men and women, no matter the color of their skin, the religion of their choice, or the country and culture of their ancestors.

It has been a great experience for me to personally reach back and breathe the atmosphere of the richly textured social stew that was America a hundred years ago. It feels like the closest I'll ever get to time travel. The research brought to light old and forgotten attitudes and ideas that amaze and even bewilder me – a shocking honesty, glorious passion and greed and bravery and forgiveness, brutal cruelty, an uncensored sense of humor and an overriding love of humanity.

John Michael Klawitter

Questions For Discussion

1. The title STRIKE! refers to a famous labor strike that took place in 1922 at the Inland Steel mill located in Chicago Heights, Illinois. It was one of the first strikes that was successful in that era. This is a fictional novel based on reality. How did the author know the facts about this incident?

2. Italian Immigrants made up over 40% of all people moving to the United States between 1840 and the 1920's. What were the conditions in Italy that led to such a mass migration?

3. What are some of the characteristics of the communists, the socialists and the Catholic church that you may have learned from this book?

4. What aspects of society that were apparent in the 1920's seem similar to the way things are today?

5. What most surprised you about the way people of different ethnic groups interacted over a hundred years ago. What did you find similar? What struck you as most different?

6. If you were living back then, how do you think you would have reacted on hearing of Ollie's violent death at the mill, and the mill owner's calloused reaction?

7. Brown's Corner was a dropping off point for the Underground Railroad, bringing escaped slaves north from the Southern States where

slavery was still in effect until the Civil War. Some of these escaped slaves stayed in Chicago Heights, building a negro community on the East Side. Would you be surprised to learn that they stayed fairly isolated and still were fairly segregated one hundred years later when the author was growing up in that area?

8. As a young teenager, the author once tried to strike up a conversation with two black girls. This was while sitting in the gymnasium seats at Bloom High School. The author sat next to them and said "Hi." One of the black girls pulled a scissors from her knit purse and said, "Get away from us, white boy, or I's gonna stab you in the eye!" Why do you think she reacted the way she did?

9. In Chicago Heights, as in many other urban areas of the United States where the author lived or visited in his younger days (New York City, Chicago, Detroit and Los Angeles) ethnic groups (Polish, Germans, Italians, Blacks, Irish, Hispanics, Jews, Chinese) tended to settle together in the same locations. Why do you think they did this? Do they still do this today?

10. How do you think living in urban areas in the U.S. are the same as they were 100 years ago? How do you think they are different?

11. The title of the novel Strike! is unusual in the sense that it uses an exclamation mark. How does this make it different from the same word without the mark? Do you think this adds to the interest of the title or did the author make a mistake in choosing it?

12. The author has chosen to use several common slang words from our past that today are proclaimed 'forbidden' words by many (some of them actual professional teachers and semi-celebrities) who aim to dictate customs and manners in our society by revising historical details. Do you think the author should go through his manuscript and remove these words?

13. In his younger days, working in factories and on construction gangs to pay his way through college, the author worked with people of many ethnic backgrounds. Rather than ignore their ethnic backgrounds, the people he worked with accepted them, joked about them, poked fun at each other's differences. Does this surprise you? Do you think this is good, or would it be better to ignore the subjects of race, cultural and language differences and religion as 'out of bounds' when talking with each other?